Dare to be

The Daring Daughters Book 3

By Emma V. Leech

Published by Emma V. Leech.

Copyright (c) Emma V. Leech 2021

Editing Services Magpie Literary Services

Cover Art: Victoria Cooper

ISBN No: 978-2-492133-27-5

Other Works by Emma V. Leech

Daring Daughters

Daring Daughters Series

Girls Who Dare

Girls Who Dare Series

Rogues & Gentlemen

Rogues & Gentlemen Series

The Regency Romance Mysteries

The Regency Romance Mysteries Series

The French Vampire Legend

The French Vampire Legend Series

The French Fae Legend

The French Fae Legend Series

Stand Alone

The Book Lover **(a paranormal novella)**

The Girl is Not for Christmas **(Regency Romance)**

Audio Books

Don't have time to read but still need your romance fix? The wait is over…

By popular demand, get many of your favourite Emma V Leech Regency Romance books on audio as performed by the incomparable Philip Battley and Gerard Marzilli. Several titles available and more added each month!

Find them at your favourite audiobook retailer!

Acknowledgements

Thanks, of course, to my wonderful editor Kezia Cole with Magpie Literary Services

To Victoria Cooper for all your hard work, amazing artwork and above all your unending patience!!! Thank you so much. You are amazing!

To my BFF, PA, personal cheerleader and bringer of chocolate, Varsi Appel, for moral support, confidence boosting and for reading my work more times than I have. I love you loads!

A huge thank you to all of Emma's Book Club members! You guys are the best!

I'm always so happy to hear from you so do email or message me
:)

emmavleech@orange.fr

To my husband Pat and my family ... For always being proud of me.

Table of Contents

Family Trees

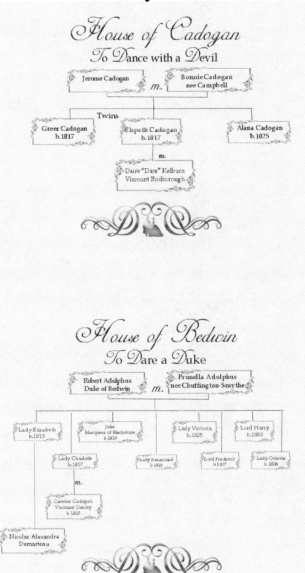

House of Cadogan
To Dance with a Devil

Jerome Cadogan — m. — Bonnie Cadogan nee Campbell

Twins

- Greer Cadogan b.1817
- Elspeth Cadogan b.1817
  - m.
  - Daire "Dare" Kelburn Viscount Roxborough
- Alana Cadogan b.1825

House of Bedwin
To Dare a Duke

Robert Adolphus Duke of Bedwin — m. — Prunella Adolphus nee Chuffington-Smythe

- Lady Elizabeth b.1815
- Jules Marquess of Blackstone b.1819
- Lady Victoria b.1825
- Lord Harry b.1833
- Lady Charlotte b.1817
  - m.
  - Cassius Cadogan Viscount Oakley b.1815
- Lady Rosamund b.1823
- Lord Frederick b.1827
- Lady Octavia b.1838

Nicolas Alexandre Demarteau

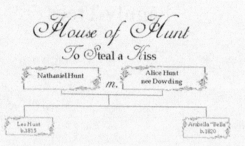

House of Hunt
To Steal a Kiss

| Nathaniel Hunt | m. | Alice Hunt nee Dowding |

| Leo Hunt b.1815 | Arabella "Bella" b.1820 |

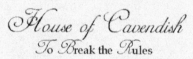

House of Cavendish
To Break the Rules

| Silas Anson Viscount Cavendish | m. | Aashini Anson aka: Lucia de Feria |

Twins

| Ashton Anson b.1816 | Vivien Anson b.1816 |

House of Trevick
To Follow her Heart

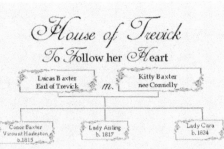

Lucas Baxter
Earl of Trevick

m.

Kitty Baxter
nee Connelly

Cunor Baxter
Viscount Hadeaton
b.1815

Lady Aisling
b. 1817

Lady Cara
b.1824

House of St Clair
To Wager with Love

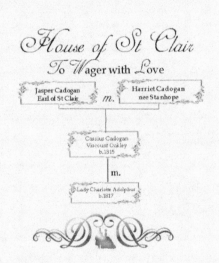

Jasper Cadogan
Earl of St Clair

m.

Harriet Cadogan
nee Stanhope

Cassius Cadogan
Viscount Oakley
b.1815

m.

Lady Charlotte Adolphus
b.1817

House of Morven
To Winter at Wildsyde

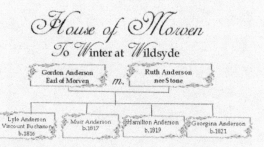

| Gordon Anderson Earl of Morven | m. | Ruth Anderson nee Stone |

| Lyle Anderson Viscount Buchanon b.1816 | Muir Anderson b.1817 | Hamilton Anderson b.1819 | Georgina Anderson b.1821 |

House of de Beauvoir
To Experiment with Desire

| Inigo de Beauvoir | m. | Minerva de Beauvoir nee Butler |

| Hartley de Beauvoir (adopted at Age 6) b.1809 | Kathleen de Beauvoir (adopted at birth) b.1824 |

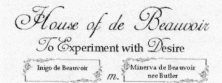

House of Rothborn
To Bed the Baron

Solo Weston Baron of Rothborn	m.	Jemima Weston nee Fernside

Larkin Weston b.1816		Grace Weston b.1821

House of Knight
To Ride with the Knight

Gabriel Knight	m.	Lady Helena Knight nee Adolphus

Florence Knight b.1817	Evie Knight b.1822	Felix Knight b.1824	Emmaline Knight b.1826

5

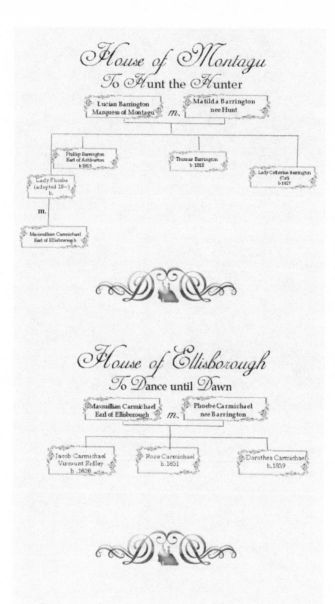

House of Montagu
To Hunt the Hunter

Lucian Barrington
Marquess of Montagu *m.* Matilda Barrington
nee Hunt

Phillip Barrington
Earl of Ashburton
b.1815

Thomas Barrington
b.1818

Lady Catherine Barrington
(Cat)
b.1827

Lady Phoebe
(adopted 18--)
b.

m.

Maximillian Carmichael
Earl of Ellisborough

House of Ellisborough
To Dance until Dawn

Maximillian Carmichael
Earl of Ellisborough *m.* Phoebe Carmichael
nee Barrington

Jacob Carmichael
Viscount Ridley
b.1826

Rose Carmichael
b.1831

Dorothea Carmichael
b.1839

Prologue

Of course it's a waste of money but waste it we must, though the boy is an imbecile. For God's sake, don't let them expel him. Pay anything. At least he excels at sport or he'd be a damned embarrassment. If he didn't look so much like me, I'd think his mother had produced a bastard.

—Excerpt of a letter from Viscount Roxborough to his man of business, regarding his son and yet another threat of expulsion.

5th November 1824, Eton College, Windsor, Berkshire.

"Dead, sir?"

"I am afraid so."

Daire Kelburn stared at the headmaster, uncertain what to do with this information. He had the notion that he ought to make some effort towards a show of emotion on hearing that his parents were dead. Both dead. Drowned. A boating accident somewhere in Italy. He considered his mother and father and tried to find something he felt for them... anything. There was a panicky sensation fluttering in his chest like a trapped bird, not at the thought they were dead, but because he realised it didn't matter, not to him. Surely that was not normal? A fellow ought to feel something, some… sorrow, yet he could not manufacture so much as a sniffle. At the age of thirteen, he had spent so few of those years in his parents' company that he could barely remember what they looked like. If not for the huge portraits at his home in Derbyshire, he'd probably have no memory of their faces at all.

"Of course, with your father gone, you're Roxborough now."

Daire blinked at him. Oh, of course. The title. He was Viscount Roxborough. Oh.

"I must say you're taking this very well," the headmaster said, with the first show of approval Daire had ever seen from him. The man got up and put a reassuring hand on his shoulder. "Very well."

"Am I, sir?" Daire looked up at him doubtfully.

"Indeed, indeed. Stoicism, that's what this country needs. Bravery and determination and endurance. You've been something of a thorn in my side, haven't you, my lad? But I'm glad to see there's some grit there beneath the frivolity. By the by, congratulations on gaining a century at the weekend. That was a good match, well played."

"Thank you, sir. May I go now?"

"Yes, yes, run along back to class."

With a nod, Daire walked to the door and let himself out.

He stood there for a moment, still puzzled by what he ought to do now. He assumed there would be people to take care of the funeral, and his father had staff to run the estate and such. Well, he must have, as he was never there. So… everything would trot along as normal, then.

"Dare? You here again?"

Though his name was Daire—pronounced Darah, to rhyme with Clara—none of the boys had ever called him anything but Dare. It was too apt, as he'd never turn down a dare of any sort. He was usually outside the headmaster's office for some offence or other, interspersed with regular trips to the infirmary for cuts and bruises, concussions, and even the odd broken bone. He looked up now to see one of the older boys, Bainbridge. Dare swallowed. Most of the boys were afraid of Lawrence Grenville, the Marquess of Bainbridge, who was a glamorous and rather daunting figure in the school, but he'd always been very decent to Dare, and not let the bigger boys trouble him. As Bainbridge often chose to stay at the school during holidays rather than go home, they spent a fair bit of time in each other's company.

"Yes," he replied, aware he sounded a bit odd, his voice faint. "Here again."

"Got sent down?" Bainbridge enquired.

Dare shook his head.

"Close shave?"

Dare shook his head again and cleared his throat. "They're dead. My parents, I mean. They... drowned. In Italy."

Why the geography mattered he wasn't certain, but for some reason he felt it needed saying.

Bainbridge stared at him. "Oh. Both?"

Dare nodded.

There was an awkward silence.

"That's... rough."

With nothing further to add to Bainbridge's statement that seemed the least appropriate, Dare shrugged. Bainbridge frowned, studying him for a long moment before he spoke again.

"Got a bottle of brandy in my room. Good stuff. French. Want some?"

For a moment Dare could only gape at him. Bainbridge never... *never* invited the younger boys and....

"Yes," Dare said quickly, realising he'd been too stunned to reply at once and not wanting to lose the opportunity.

"Right. Come on, then."

Dare nodded and hurried after his idol. Just wait until Raphe and August heard about this.

Chapter 1

Fifteen years later...

My dear Nic,

I write to send you my sincere felicitations on your marriage. A duke's daughter, no less, and none other than Bedwin's eldest. You must have balls of steel, my friend. Well, if any man could do it, it was you.

I thought I'd best put your mind at ease, lest you were losing sleep over how I might call in that favour you asked of me. It will be nothing to cause you undue stress, I assure you. Only a place for a weary traveller to rest his head when I finally decide to set foot upon English soil once more. For you know as well as I, no welcome will be forthcoming anywhere else.

—*Excerpt of a letter to Mr Nicolas Alexandre Demarteau, signed... Wolf.*

9th April 1839, Royle House, Derbyshire

Dare climbed off his horse with a groan of effort. His limbs were cold and stiff, his clothes soaked through despite the greatcoat he wore. It had been a long and arduous journey, mostly in the pouring rain, and everyone was tired and fractious. Not least

Lawrence Grenville, Marquess of Bainbridge. Riding to your father's deathbed was not likely to put any fellow in the best of spirits. If anyone ought to be pleased by the event, it was Bainbridge. His father, the Duke of Axton, was an utter devil, and quite possibly mad, who'd made his son's life as difficult as possible. Bainbridge would take the title too, of course, making him the duke. Dare wasn't certain what the fellow thought about any of it, however, other than that he despised his sire, and with good reason. No one ever knew what Bainbridge was thinking, not even Dare, who was the closest thing the man had to a best friend.

Dare met Raphe's eye as he handed his horse over to a groom. Raphe looked grim too. None of them knew quite what to do with Bainbridge if he got into one of his black moods; Dare usually became responsible for him, and the results. August hurried over to them and they watched as Bainbridge stared up at the vast building that was Royle House.

"What now?" August said, as they considered the sombre, dark figure before them who was staring at his home as if facing the gates of hell.

"God knows," Dare replied with a shrug. "But let's get out of this damned rain at least."

Raphe nodded his agreement and three of them escorted Bainbridge inside the house. Little more than ten minutes later, they were back outside again.

"The old bastard," Bainbridge raged, striding up and down in the torrent which seemed to have gained force in the short time they had been indoors.

"Not dead, then?" August asked tentatively, for which he was sent an incinerating look from Bainbridge.

"Why'd he send for you then?" Dare demanded, annoyed at having been dragged away from London where he'd been having a thoroughly nice time for an unpleasant slog through the sodden

English countryside, which had taken the best part of four days. All for nought, too.

"It was that arse, Pennington," Bainbridge fumed, naming the duke's steward. "The old man had an apoplexy and couldn't speak or move, everyone assumed that was his lot. Oh, no. Not he. He rallied, and with strength enough to tell me I was a damned vulture and to get the hell out of his house or he'd shoot me. I swear the devil won't take the old goat."

Bainbridge snatched the reins of his horse from the groom who'd brought the poor creature back round and leapt up into the saddle.

"Where are we going then?" Raphe demanded.

Everyone looked to Dare.

"Well, you're all welcome, of course, but the place will be all shut up."

"Didn't you write and tell them you were coming?" Raphe looked at Dare in astonishment.

"No, why should I? I wasn't coming, I was staying here," Dare retorted, stung.

"For the love of God, man," Bainbridge yelled. "Your property is barely five miles away. You didn't have any intention of visiting it, at least?"

"No." Dare was getting irritated himself now, not least because he knew he was in the wrong. He ought to have written, ought to have gone back and seen how everything and everyone was going on, only.... "No, I dashed well didn't."

"Bloody buggering bollocks." Bainbridge turned his furious blue eyes upon Dare, looking very much as though he'd rip his head off at the least provocation, and then, in typical Bainbridge fashion... he burst out laughing. It could have gone either way, as they all knew, and their collective relief was palpable. Bainbridge threw his head back, letting the rain fall on his face. "For the love of God, Dare, you're a pain in the arse and no mistake. Let's see this blasted house of yours, then, for I need a drink and soon and there's nothing closer."

Dare sighed, but there was little point in remonstrating. For one, Bainbridge was right and Dare's estate, shut up as it was, still seemed preferable to spending any longer in this miserable weather. So he mounted and led the way back to his home.

Rowsley Hall was one of the oldest grand houses in the country and had been the Roxborough family home since its first incarnation in the twelfth century as a Norman hall. Now, as Dare approached it on a dreary, wet April afternoon, it looked as if every one of its seven hundred years sat heavy and burdensome upon its crenellated walls. It stood on a raised platform of limestone, above the western bank of the River Wye. Their horses' hooves rang out as they crossed the picturesque bridge over the river, and Dare's stomach tied itself into a knot. It was stupid. He knew it was stupid. But no matter how many times he told himself so, coming home made him feel all on edge. Returning made him feel like a boy again, rattling about in the great house all by himself and afraid of the many ghosts that lurked in the darkness.

There was no one to greet them, no one to take the horses, and Bainbridge make a sound of disgust as they walked their tired mounts around to the stables themselves and saw to their care. Everywhere there were signs of neglect, piles of rubbish and debris left to moulder. The place appeared deserted, ghostly as the light waned and the grey afternoon sucked what brightness remained into an early twilight.

The interior of the building was not the least encouraging either. All the furniture was shrouded, carpets rolled up, and it seemed even colder inside the great walls than it did outside.

"Abandon hope, all ye who enter here," Raphe murmured, and Dare had to suppress a shudder, for that was exactly how he felt every time he set foot inside the door, as though all life and hope had been drained from him.

"Christ, Dare, how could you let it come to this?" Bainbridge demanded. "When was the last time you were here? Do you never speak to your steward?"

"I… er. No," Dare replied with a surge of guilt, remembering all the unopened letters on his desk at home. "At least, not for a while."

There really wasn't any point. Each letter was just an account of Dare's dwindling finances and the increasing demands of an ancient building that needed more money than he could even conceive of simply to keep it standing.

"Define 'a while,'" August said, peering into a corner and then leaping backwards as a rat scurried out and darted across the floor.

"Sometime last century judging on the state of the place." Bainbridge shook his head. "For the love of God, is there at least something to drink in this pit of doom?"

"The study," Dare suggested, and led the way through a series of dark rooms until they reached the impressive oak panelled room.

This too was shrouded with dust covers and cold, and a shiver ran down Dare's back as he took note of the immense oak desk and the chair behind, swathed in a white cloth. The last time he'd seen his father, he'd been sat behind that desk. Not that his sire had seen him, or known he was there. Dare had peered around the corner to catch a glimpse of the great man, and had remained unobserved, but that was how it always was. He suspected his parents went months at a time without even remembering the fact they had a son. So long as he was alive and capable of carrying on the line when he was mature enough to do so, that was really all they expected of him. Perhaps once his father had hoped for more, but he didn't think so. His father despised him for almost killing his mother when he was born and made no secret of the fact. As for his mother, she couldn't even bear to look at him. Dare could not remember a time when they'd been anything other than a grave disappointment to each other.

The decanters were empty, and so Dare hurriedly lit a candle and went off to the cellars to find provisions, leaving his friends to remove the dust covers and light the fire. As he reached the kitchen, he noticed a slight rise in the arctic temperature and the aroma of meat cooking. With some relief, he discovered the place had not been wholly abandoned. This room was as neat and shiny as it had always been in his memory… quite unchanged, in fact.

"Oh, you're back, are you?"

Dare swivelled about to see a woman of perhaps sixty years sitting in a chair by the fire. For a moment his hopes rose as he expected to see their old cook, but no. The old cook was rotund and jolly, as a cook ought to be. This woman was thin and angular, her salt and pepper hair plaited and turned into a tight little coil at the back of her head. Good Lord, was that…?

"Mrs Grigson," Dare said, shocked to see she of all people had remained when everyone else had gone. The old witch always made him feel like he was a grubby boy who'd been caught stealing jam tarts. Of course, she often had caught him doing just that, and he *had* been a grubby boy. With difficulty, he reminded himself he was Viscount Roxborough now, and stood a little straighter. "I am glad to see you."

She snorted at that and gave him a look that could have stripped wood.

"Bet you are," she said, her voice heavy with irony. She reached down into her voluminous skirts and there was a metallic jangle as she lifted a huge set of keys, dangling it with a mocking smile. "The cellar key is there. When you stopped paying the servants, things started to go walkabout. I did what I could."

"S-Stopped paying?" Dare said, staring at her.

Mrs Grigson heaved a sigh, staring at him as if she'd expected no better. Well, no one ever had before, so why would she?

"About six months ago. Your steward left then, too. He wrote and told you, thought it best to let you know you were nigh on bankrupt. I suppose you never read the letter. Well, we'd had to let most of the servants go long before that, but when the wages stopped, the few who'd remained out of some misguided sense of loyalty were off. Some went up to Royle House. I suppose you'll be wanting to eat?"

Dare stared at her for a moment as he tried to absorb this information. Not that it came as a surprise. It had been inevitable, a path he'd been treading since the day his parents had died. He'd just not realised he'd reached the bitter end. Rousing himself, he turned his attention to the more immediate matter of food. "Ah. Yes. I appreciate I gave no notice of my—"

"You alone?"

"No, Bainbridge and a couple of friends are with me."

This information did not seem to impress her. "Well, there's not much in. I can give you some cold ham and chicken pie, and there's bread and some good cheese."

"A feast," Dare said with a hesitant smile, relieved they wouldn't starve at least.

The old housekeeper looked at him and gave a disgusted sigh. "Well, I'll get Parker to bring it up."

"Parker is still here?" Dare brightened at the information. He'd been fond of the old butler, one of the few people at the Hall who had ever been kind to him.

"Aye, more fool him."

Deciding there was nothing more to be gained here beside the knowledge he was utterly despised—and he'd not needed reminding of that fact—Dare carried on his way to the cellar.

17

"You're an arse," Bainbridge said later, once they had adjourned to the library after demolishing the plates of food Mrs Grigson had provided and made inroads into their fourth bottle of Burgundy.

"Remind me, why we are friends?" Dare said, stretching out his long legs before the fire.

For April, the weather seemed dashed cold and grim, and it seemed to have settled into his bones. He could not get warm.

"Because I'm a delightful addition to the wasteland that is your life."

Dare turned to Bainbridge and looked at him, considering this with apparent gravity.

"No," he said at length. "That's not it."

"Because you would be bereft without my sunny disposition and benign influence."

Dare choked on his wine. "*Benign*? Benighted, more like, and as for sunny…. Good God, Bainbridge. Keep on like that and I might give more credence to those stories about you and your family being mad as a box of frogs."

"We *are* mad as a box of frogs," the fellow said amiably. "And if it's not for those reasons, it must be because I paid your damned tailor for you."

"Ah!" Dare said, wagging a finger at Bainbridge. "Knew there was a reason."

"Idiots," Raphe muttered, not looking up from a rather battered copy of *Don Juan*.

"Well, at least there was food, and we have a fire," August said, who was inclined to be good-natured and cheerful.

Dare snorted. "Yes, and when we run out of fuel, we can start burning bits of the house as they fall off."

There was an odd cracking sound and a large chunk of plaster detached itself from the ceiling and fell on his head. Dare yelped as a plume of white dust and debris billowed about him and then staggered to his feet, coughing.

Everyone exploded with laughter as Dare stood there looking like a badly wrought statue.

"I could have been killed!" he exclaimed.

Bainbridge caught his breath for long enough to speak. "That's what you get, old man, for speaking of your home so callously. There's blood and bone in places as old as this, not to mention ghosts. You hurt their feelings."

Everyone stopped laughing to stare at Bainbridge in astonishment. He was not given to flights of fancy. Alarm ran up Dare's spine as the words rang through him, tugging on the guilt he'd buried so many years ago when he'd turned his back on Rowsley and everything it stood for. There *were* ghosts here, of many varieties. It was the main reason he'd stayed away. Yet he had a wave of foreboding at Bainbridge's words, the awful sensation that they would follow and not let him be if he didn't save Rowsley Hall.

"Well, it's not like I can do anything about it," he snapped as something that felt horribly like remorse struggled up through years of drinking and dissipation and bad behaviour to make an unwelcome reappearance. "There's no money. My wonderful father made a damned hash of things, left the property in the hands of a bloody villain who had embezzled the lot before I was sixteen. All I inherited was more bills than I could even read within the space of a year, let alone pay in a lifetime, and they just kept sending more and more and…."

"All right, all right, old man," August said, getting to his feet. "You're getting overwrought. Come and sit down, there's a good fellow."

Dare took a breath and then exploded into a coughing fit as plaster dust caught the back of his throat. August handed him a clean handkerchief which he used to wipe the worst of the mess from his face. He snatched up the glass of wine Bainbridge proffered to clear his throat.

"There is something you could do about it," Bainbridge said, sitting back in his chair.

"What?" Dare glowered at him, praying he wasn't about to make some flippant comment, for he was very much not in the mood.

"Marry an heiress."

Dare snorted. "Even if there was a woman with a dowry big enough to fix this mess, who in the name of everything holy would have me?"

"The Cadogan twins."

Dare paused in the act of scrubbing dust off his face and sat up, staring at Bainbridge with interest now.

"I'm listening, but they're not heiresses," he said, frowning.

"Oh, yes they are," Bainbridge replied with a twisted smile. "Not that it is widely known and for God's sake keep it under your hat unless you want every fortune hunter in London to crawl out of the woodwork. But I got it from an extremely reliable source that their grandmother shared her considerable wealth between the three granddaughters. The youngest girl isn't out yet, but the twins most certainly are."

Raphe looked up, dragging his attention from *Don Juan* for long enough to attend the conversation. "They might actually contemplate you as an option, too. They're not really considered good *ton,* so it's not like they are overburdened with offers. Their mama is far too wild. Good heavens, their parents might even *like* you. You're birds of a feather."

"Really?" Dare said, brightening. "Lively girls, are they?"

Bainbridge pursed his lips. "One is. I forget... I think it's Greer and Elsa...."

"Elspeth," August corrected.

"That's it. One of them is cast in their mother's mould, that's for certain. A hoyden to her toes. The other, however, is a bluestocking, from what I've heard. Serious girl, prefers books to parties."

Dare wrinkled his nose. "Well, which is which? If I must marry, I'd rather have some fun while I'm about it. Don't want to get landed with a dashed intellectual. Too terrifying for words."

August snorted. "If they both attend a party, you'll have no trouble telling them apart. Greer will be dancing like it's her last night on earth, and Elspeth will be in a quiet corner hoping no one notices her so she can finish her book, if she's managed to sneak one in under her skirts. She's a nice girl, though. I'm fond of her. I don't really know Greer very well, but Elspeth... well, I wouldn't want anyone to take advantage of her."

"I'm not a monster, am I?" Dare demanded, stung by that comment. "I may not have a feather to fly with, but I'm not the sort of fellow to treat his wife with disrespect. Good Lord. A *wife*."

He shook his head, stunned that he would even consider the notion. Not that there seemed to be any choice. Bainbridge's comment about angry ghosts and upsetting the house might have been in jest, but Dare didn't think he'd sleep again until he knew the damned place wouldn't fall down.

"No," August said at once. "No, I never meant—"

"Right," Dare said, waving away August's apology. "Well, you know the girls, so you can introduce me, and I'll do the rest. With luck, we can be married by summer. I'll drink to that."

"And so shall we all," Bainbridge said with a grin and lifted his glass in a toast.

Chapter 2

Dear Eliza,

I do hope you and your new husband are having a wonderful time. Have you visited Rouge et Noir yet? Is it very glamorous?

I just wished to reassure you that everything is running smoothly at the school. I have still not admitted to my parents that I have accepted a full-time position here, though. I am afraid they believe I am just helping out in your absence, but I am enjoying myself so much.

There are, as predicted, a few troublemakers in the school, but there have been far fewer problems than we might have anticipated. Much of this is thanks to Agatha, who is a wonderful influence on those who might be swayed into following into bad behaviour. She has a remarkable gift for diffusing difficult situations, though she is not entirely innocent of mischief herself. Hers is of a different variety, however, as she has taken to sneaking out at night to visit Louis César. The last time, he brought her back the following morning, and it was rather amusing to see him trying to be dreadfully cross with her when everyone could see how touched he was at her having wished so badly to see him. He visits almost daily now to keep her from doing it again.

I must sign off as I am to attend a party tonight, despite all my protests that I do not wish to go. I would not mind so much if I could just sit with the wallflowers and read a book, but Mama will insist that I 'enjoy myself'. She has never understood that sitting quietly with a book is enjoying myself!

The poor dear, she so wishes for me to have fun.

—Excerpt of a letter from Miss Elspeth Cadogan (daughter of Jerome and Bonnie Cadogan) to Lady Elizabeth Demarteau

25th April 1839, Mrs Hely-Hutchinson's Spring Ball.

Elspeth tapped her toes and sipped at a cool glass of lemonade, watching her sister as she danced with yet another young man. She was over the far side of the ballroom and not quite visible, so Elspeth could not tell who her partner was. Greer really was indefatigable, you had to give her that. Elspeth wondered why her sister found such enjoyment in these events, when they generally left *her* with sore feet, a headache, and the feeling she'd have had a far nicer time at home. It wasn't that she didn't like dancing, she did, but only with friends. When she was partnered with a man who might consider her as a potential wife, she got horribly self-conscious and usually ended up saying something idiotic. Thank heavens Mama and Papa had agreed not to reveal the truth of their hefty dowries to keep the fortune hunters at bay. At least if any man pursued them, they knew it was because he truly liked them. There weren't too many of those, though. Mama was wonderful and fun and full of love and joy, but there were not many men like their papa who wanted such a vivacious creature for their wife.

Wives were supposed to be quiet and demure and elegant and modest, and a thousand other qualities that made both Elspeth and her twin furious if they considered them. They were hard indeed upon Greer, with her natural exuberance. Elspeth did not particularly want to marry, or at least if she did, it would have to be someone intellectual. A professor, perhaps. She imagined someone tall and thin who forgot to eat because he was too busy working. He would be sweet and kind and wear spectacles, and they would read together by the fire of an evening, occasionally speaking a few lines aloud that they knew the other would appreciate. Of course he would be all in favour of her love of teaching and educating young minds. Yes. A man like that would make a comfortable husband, but not yet. In two or three years, perhaps. She could not endure too many more seasons than that. She didn't much like town at all, preferring the peace of the countryside, but at least whilst she was here, she could make herself useful at Eliza's charity school.

Lady Elizabeth Adolphus—oh, no, Lady Elizabeth *Demarteau*—was away on her honeymoon in France, and Elspeth had told her parents she was stepping in to help the place run smoothly in her absence. That was a plumper of considerable proportion. Despite a few minor problems, the staff had all managed marvellously well, and Eliza ought to be proud of everything she had created there. Still, Elspeth hoped she was contributing valuably by helping those children who showed the most aptitude with extra lessons in maths. The truth was that the place would run along perfectly well without her. The truth also was that Elspeth fully intended to teach there, full time, needed or not. She just hadn't told her parents that yet.

Her poor mama and papa, on whom she doted, simply did not understand her. She and Greer might be twins, though Elspeth was the eldest by perhaps half an hour, but they were not the least bit alike. Greer was like their parents. They loved parties, loved entertainments, and filling their home with friends and family and chaos and… and that was nice. *Sometimes.* Other times it all felt a bit… too much.

Still, at least Mrs Hely-Hutchinson could always be relied upon to serve marvellous refreshments. The lemonade was cool and refreshing, and the vast array of plates piled with dainty *amuse-bouche* were utterly delicious. Elspeth had already eaten far more than was good for her, considering there would be a lavish supper later too. Still, she was bored and fidgety, though she did not wish to dance. Perhaps it would be worth running the gauntlet and risking her mama seeing her and finding her a dance partner, just to taste a few more of those delicious lobster patties.

Elspeth was considering this when Greer flopped down in the chair beside her with a rustle of petticoats.

"Lawks," she exclaimed, and took the glass of lemonade Elspeth held, draining it in one go. "Oh, that's better. I was spitting feathers."

"Greer!" Elspeth said, glancing around anxiously to see if anyone had heard her. "You're not supposed to talk like that, and do sit up straight, you look like a rag doll that's lost its stuffing."

Greer pulled a face but sat up and handed the empty glass back to Elspeth.

"Thank you," Elspeth replied dryly. "Who were you dancing with?"

"Leo Hunt."

"Oh, is he here? I've not seen him or Arabella."

"You wouldn't. Arabella is making sheep's eyes at the Comte de Villen, and Leo is trying to keep her in hand."

Elspeth chuckled. "Well, I can't blame her. He is terribly handsome, and actually rather nice."

"Do *you* like him?" Greer asked, turning to look at her in astonishment.

"Me?" Elspeth exclaimed and then gave an emphatic shake of her head. "Good heavens, no. I mean, I do like him—as a friend—but can you imagine being married to such a man? No, thank you. He has women throwing themselves at his head from all corners, and he does not strike me as having faithful husband potential. Truthfully, he doesn't strike me as a potential husband at all, for anyone. I can't imagine what kind of young women could hold his attention for above a week at a time."

"He needs to marry, though. Everyone says so."

"Yes, I know. A scandalous past to quiet, though no one seems to have any idea what the scandal is. Well, we shall see. I pity his poor wife, whoever she may be, but it will not be me." Elspeth looked at Greer with interest. "Do you like him?"

Greer shook her head. "No. I agree with you. I want to fall in love and be loved wildly in return, like Papa loves Mama. Nothing less than that will do. I'd rather be alone than settle for anything else."

Elspeth smiled. Despite her rather frivolous nature, Greer was far more principled than people gave her credit for.

They looked up and Elspeth smiled as she saw August Lane-Fox approach them.

"Mr Lane-Fox, good evening."

"Miss Cadogan, Miss Greer, you are both looking lovely this evening. I wonder if I might introduce you to my good friend, Daire Kelburn, Viscount Roxborough. Daire, this is Miss Elspeth Cadogan and Miss Greer Cadogan. Ladies, Viscount Roxborough."

Elspeth swallowed as the Viscount nodded a greeting to them both and sent them a dazzling smile. Good Lord, a smile like that ought to carry some sort of warning. It was warm and inviting, his mouth the kind she suspected laughed often and easily, and his eyes were full of mischief. He reminded her of a grown version of Felix Knight, Florence's little brother, who was always in one scrape or another. The same boyish desire to be naughty glinted in his hazel eyes. She had heard stories about Lord Roxborough, and his mischief was somewhat more scandalous in nature. He was certainly no boy, either, not with those broad shoulders and long, long legs. Hastily she dragged her eyes from his tightly fitted trousers, which highlighted a quite magnificent pair of muscular thighs. She wondered at Mr Lane-Fox introducing them. Elspeth had always wondered why Mr Lane-Fox would be friends with such loose screws as Roxborough, Baron de Ligne and—God help them—Lawrence Grenville, the Marquess of Bainbridge. The marquess was rumoured to be mad as a march hare, and the other two were the most dreadful libertines. By contrast, Mr Lane-Fox was a quiet and unassuming fellow, and really quite sensible. It made no sense.

"Ladies, it is a pleasure to finally make your acquaintance. August here has told me so much about you."

Elspeth glanced at Mr Lane-Fox, who blushed a little and shifted from foot to foot.

"Might we have the pleasure of dancing with you both?" the viscount asked politely.

Greer glanced at Elspeth, a wicked glint in her eyes, and spoke before Elspeth could react.

"We would love to dance. Mr Lane-Fox, lead on."

Oh! The dreadful creature. She knew full well that Elspeth would far rather have danced with her friend than the scandalous viscount. Elspeth glared at Greer and grasped her wrist, but Greer tugged free with a giggle and took August's arm. "Well, do come along, sister. Don't keep Lord Roxborough waiting."

Elspeth gritted her teeth as Greer bounced away, and then looked up to see the Viscount frowning too, watching his friend lead Greer away. Well, then. Just as she suspected.

He turned back to Elspeth and immediately rearranged his face into one of pleasure at their forthcoming dance.

"It's all right," Elspeth said with a smile. "She's engaged for the next one, but I think the country dance after that is still free if you want to try again."

He had the decency to look puzzled, at least. "But I wish to dance with you, Miss Cadogan."

"No, you don't," she said, shaking her head. "And it's quite all right, really. I'm not the least bit offended. I don't want to dance with you either."

Oh, dash it. She ought not have said that last bit. No doubt she'd wounded his masculine pride, or some such nonsense.

"You don't wish to dance with me?" he repeated, something that might have been amusement glinting in his eyes.

"No. I'm sorry, but I don't. It's nothing personal. I just… don't wish to dance."

He stared at her for a moment and then nodded. "Very well. We need not dance. Would you mind if I sat down?"

"You want to sit down?" Elspeth studied him with suspicion. He appeared the picture of innocence, yet every suspicious instinct she had prickled to life.

"Unless my company is unwelcome too?" he said, something in his expression daring her to tell him it was exactly that.

He *wanted* her to tell him to go.

Well, in that case.

"Please do, my lord," she said with a pleasant smile.

He settled himself beside her. Elspeth chewed at her lip, uncertain what to do now. Oh, what was she saying? She knew exactly how to scare men off. Elspeth turned to him, her expression eager and enquiring.

"Have you read *Le Père Goriot* by Honoré de Balzac, my lord?"

29

The viscount looked back at her, his hazel eyes wide and guileless. A slow smile curved over his mouth and she could not help but stare at it.

"Miss Cadogan," he said, and Elspeth had to fight a shiver at hearing her name spoken so softly, his voice deep and intimate. "Do I *look* like I've read... whatever the title was?"

"Ah, but one should never judge a book by its cover."

His lips twitched and he leaned a little closer.

"So I've heard," he whispered, and the look that followed it seemed to scroll over her, taking her in from head to toe.

Elspeth blushed and knew at once he was speaking of her. For she might look just like every other debutante here—beautifully dressed, and coiffured, young, and pretty—but she had a marvellous knack for sending young men scurrying away from her, and everyone knew it.

He knew it.

Well and fine. She *wanted* him to scurry away from her.

"Well, it is true, you know. I once picked up a splendid looking book, all bound in blue leather, with gold lettering and blue and gold headbands. A handsome edition to be sure, and do you know... it was the dullest thing in all creation. I was most dreadfully disappointed. But that is often the way of things, is it not?"

Rather to her surprise, he did not get up and stalk off in a huff but threw his head back and laughed.

"Oh, a hit!" He put his hand to his heart and gasped. "I say, that was very good. You rightly judged that I'm not the brightest fellow and chose to frighten me off with intellectual talk, and when that didn't work you insulted my appearance. Always the way to shift a peacock, eh? To criticise his plumage."

Elspeth stared at him, torn between astonishment and mortification. "Oh, but I wasn't…. It was a book, not you and—"

"Oh, no." He wagged a finger at her. "It was very well done. Don't pretend you didn't mean it when you did. You wanted to get rid of me, and with any other fellow it would work nicely, I'm certain. Sadly, you misjudged. I have the skin of a rhinoceros and not much in the way of a conscience. I will go, however, if you simply say, 'go away, Lord Roxborough.'"

Thoroughly rattled at having been shown up for her rudeness, Elspeth felt she could do no such thing.

"I should never dream of saying such a thing to you," she said, blushing furiously now and wishing she'd not spoken a word to him. It jolly well served her right.

"Well, come, come, surely you're not defeated? Come about, Miss Cadogan. I await your next sally."

Elspeth winced and turned to face him. "My lord, forgive me. I was abominably rude, and I beg your pardon for it."

To her chagrin, he waved this away with annoyance. "Never mind that. If you don't find a more ingenious way to get rid of me, I shall be compelled to do something to provoke you."

"You are quite provoking enough without putting any effort into it," Elspeth snapped before her brain caught up with her wretched tongue. She clapped a hand over her mouth.

The grin that was sent her way was enough to make her heart skitter about in her chest. Oh no. He was dangerous, this one. No wonder he had such a dreadful reputation for being a troublemaker and a rake. That smile was irresistible, inviting her to join in the fun.

"You know, everyone told me you were dull and bookish, but I think they got you all wrong."

Elspeth swallowed in alarm as she saw something that looked horribly like admiration shining in his eyes. *Oh, help.*

"They were *not* wrong, my lord," Elspeth said stiffly. "I am bookish. I would far rather be at home reading a book than here, dancing or… or talking to you."

He studied her for such a long time, Elspeth's palms sweated inside her silk gloves as she became increasingly self-conscious.

"You know, I'm not entirely certain that's true."

"How the devil would you know?" she retorted, glaring at him. "Or are you really so arrogant as to believe every woman in the world would rather be in your company than anything else?"

There was that disarming smile again. Elspeth turned away so she needn't look at it.

"I didn't mean the bit about talking to me, as it happens, but the dancing. Though I think perhaps you are enjoying my company a tad more than you let on. Is it not just a tiny bit liberating to be invited to be rude to me?"

"No." She folded her arms, refusing to look at him.

"I think it is."

"You think? My word, you do surprise me. Congratulations."

"Oh, I say, that was a good one."

Elspeth huffed. She stared at the dancers, ignoring him, though she could feel his eyes upon her. He was smiling, damn him. She could *feel* him smiling. The desire to turn her head and see that smile again was… was….

No.

She would ignore him. *La la la.* What was the name of this tune again, she couldn't remember? *He wasn't there.* Oh, look, there was Greer and Mr Lane-Fox. They danced very well together. *He's not there. He's not there.*

"Stop smiling!" she exclaimed.

"I do beg your pardon. I shall stop at once. It was very bad of me." He immediately arranged his face into something ridiculously solemn and, much to her annoyance, Elspeth could not help the bubble of laughter that escaped her.

"Oh! You're impossible."

"So I've been told. Are you going to tell me to go away now?"

"No," she said through gritted teeth. The desire to tell him to go away was burning on her tongue, but somehow that seemed like losing this… this… whatever this was.

"Ah, so you do like my company," he said triumphantly. "I knew I would grow on you."

She turned and stared at him, expressionless.

"Like mould?" he suggested, batting his eyelids at her.

She rolled her eyes and turned away before her traitorous mouth turned up at the corners.

"Tum, tum, ti tum tum… What *is* this tune called? I can't remember. It's very catchy. I shall be humming it all night."

"I can't remember either," Elspeth said, irked to have to admit it.

"Are you certain you would not like to dance?"

"Will you stop talking if I dance with you?" she demanded.

"I'm tempted to say yes, if it means you'll agree, but then you will soon discover it's not true and I should not wish you to think me a liar."

Elspeth snorted.

"Oh, I have a list of terrible character flaws as long as your lovely arm, I admit, but that isn't one of them."

"No," she said with a sigh. "I imagine that's how you get away with such dreadful behaviour, because you always agree it was very bad and smile charmingly and everyone forgives you, though the lord knows why."

"You think I have a charming smile?" He sent another such expression in her direction.

"No! I... *Argh!*"

He chuckled. "And what do you know about my bad behaviour?"

"Enough."

"No, no. It's not all true, you know, and it will explain a great deal if I know just what you have heard. For surely it is not possible you hated me on sight?"

Elspeth turned and quirked an eyebrow at him.

He laughed again, a merry sound that was far too pleasing to the ear. "You know, I was rather dreading this evening, but I'm enjoying myself immensely."

"I'm so happy for you," she replied dryly.

"Well, hunting for a suitable wife is a little daunting for a fellow, but I had no idea choosing one would be so easy."

Elspeth froze. Surely. *Surely*, she had misheard. He could not possibly have meant.... Slowly, she turned to stare at him. He was watching her, one corner of his mouth quirking up a little.

"*Me?*" she said in outrage.

"Why not you?"

Despite remembering every one of her late grandmother's many lessons on deportment and how a proper young lady ought and ought not behave, Elspeth's mouth fell open and she gaped at him.

"My lord," she said, relieved that her voice was steady and calm despite the fact her heart was hammering in her chest like a panicked bird in a cage. "I am glad you have found my company so diverting, and I apologise again for my earlier rudeness. Well, and my more recent rudeness too, but I am afraid I must make something abundantly clear to you. I will not—under any circumstances—even in the event of a cataclysm that destroys the entire human race and leaves only thee and me remaining, ever, *ever*, consent to be your wife."

"But I'm growing on you," he said, his eyes sparkling with amusement.

"Like mould," she reminded him. "The nasty black, fluffy stuff that grows in very unpleasant places." Elspeth flushed as she realised that made her the unpleasant place but she could hardly take it back now.

He considered this for a moment. "I'll take it."

She threw her hands in the air.

Apparently sensing he had pushed her as far as was prudent, he got to his feet.

"You never did tell me to leave," he said with a wink, and sauntered off with the air of a man well pleased with himself.

"What are you looking so damn smug about?" Bainbridge demanded as Dare returned to stand beside him.

At that moment August returned from his dance with Greer, rather breathless and a little pink in the face.

"I introduced him to the twins, and I rather wish I hadn't," August said with a scowl. "I thought you were interested in Greer?"

"And so did I," Dare admitted, shrugging. "But that was before I met Elspeth. She's... fascinating."

"Don't tell me you've actually fallen for the chit?" Bainbridge stared at him in disgust.

Dare tutted. "Don't be an arse, Lawrence. Of course not, but I do like her. A sparky little thing. Far more about her than a mere bluestocking. Whoever gave her that label was doing her a grand disservice."

"You have fallen for her!" Bainbridge accused.

"I have not!" Dare retorted impatiently. "Not that it matters either way. She said she'd not marry me if a cataclysm wiped out the rest of humanity and only we two remained. I *think* she was exaggerating. Actually, I think she rather enjoyed my company, but she'd rather die than admit that, and I don't have time for a lengthy courtship. If I don't get some funds soon, Rowsley Hall will be nothing but a pile of stone and worm-riddled wood."

"Then don't court her. There are other ways of getting a girl to marry you."

"What do you mean?" Dare asked, frowning.

"Oh, no." August shook his head. "No. No. Nothing underhand. I won't be a party to it."

"Then run along like a good fellow, August. You need not know a thing about it." Bainbridge waved him away.

"But I do know!" August said heatedly.

"Well, I don't. What are you—" Dare's face cleared as he cottoned on. "Trap her, you mean?"

Bainbridge shrugged. "Happens all the time. You need only get caught alone in a room together...."

"Not very sporting, Laurie," Dare said, troubled by the idea.

The marquess just tutted at him, impatient now. "Then woo her properly and get her to fall in love with you."

"I don't have time!" Frowning, Dare considered his options.

August wagged a finger at him. "No, Dare. It's underhanded. I won't have it," he said, and stalked off in disgust.

"He's right." Dare sighed despondently.

He really had liked Elspeth, far more than he'd imagined he would. He didn't particularly want to marry her, or anyone, but if he must marry someone... well, at least she was interesting. She didn't ought to be dull, though she was likely to scold him a great deal. For some reason he could not fathom, the thought only made him smile.

"But what if it weren't underhanded?" he mused aloud.

"What do you mean?" Bainbridge asked.

"Fair warning," Dare said with a grin. "I'll tell her what I'm about. If she can escape me, so be it. She's clever enough to do it, but if I get her... well, at least I was honest about it."

Bainbridge rolled his eyes at him. "God, you're tiring."

"No, I'm not, I'm... honourable. Sort of," Dare said, and then grinned.

He had a suspicion that Elspeth might quite like pitting her wits against him, and if she didn't...Well, she could always tell her father and her uncle to see him off. There. Sorted.

Dare wandered off to get himself a drink, feeling the first stirrings of hope alight in his chest.

Chapter 3

Miss Cadogan,

I fear I made rather an error in judgement in introducing my friend Lord Roxborough to you the other night. Please do not mistake me. He is a decent fellow and has been a jolly good friend to me, but I think I have not done you a kindness. I beg you to have a care with him. The fellow is up to his neck in the River Tick and is in desperate need of a wealthy wife.

I have no idea if it is true that you have inherited a fortune, but Roxborough believes it. He will make you his wife, and I very much fear by fair means or foul. Do not allow yourself to be alone in his company.

—Excerpt of a letter from Mr August Lane-Fox to Miss Elspeth Cadogan (daughter of Jerome and Bonne Cadogan).

29th April 1839, The Countess St Clair's spring garden party, St James's, London.

Dare walked through the throngs of people in the extensive and beautiful gardens at the home of the Earl and Countess St Clair. The Dowager Countess had begun the tradition of a summer garden party some decades ago, and the current countess had continued it, deeming it such a success that she had another, slightly smaller affair in the spring. They had erected a large marquee tent in case of inclement weather, but for once the English climate was behaving itself admirably. The afternoon was warm and sunny with the occasional fluffy white cloud scudding across the vivid blue to add to the picturesque quality of the day.

It was a glorious scene, with everyone dressed in their finery. The ladies looked like overblown flowers themselves, with their huge skirts fluttering in the light breeze that danced about the garden, tugging mischievously at their petticoats. Dare had to acknowledge a little surge of excitement as he scanned the gardens for one pretty bloom in particular. Though he hesitated to admit it, he had been looking forward to this for days.

He saw her across the garden. A charming yellow bonnet with pale lemon-coloured flowers and bows hid most of her golden hair, and her dress was yellow too, decorated with flowers and lace. It sat low on her shoulders, exposing her elegant neck and creamy skin, and she held a small lace parasol to protect her from the afternoon sun. She stood beneath a magnolia tree, and the pink and white petals fell about her like confetti.

Dare stopped and simply stared, enjoying the enchanting picture. Perhaps she felt his gaze upon her for she looked up, turning her head until she saw him, and froze. She looked in that moment like a doe, startled by a hunter, ready to bolt. He didn't move, only quirked his mouth in a crooked smile.

She frowned and looked away from him, but when the people she was speaking with walked away, she remained where she was. Waiting for him.

Dare was not about to waste the opportunity.

"You look like the sun fallen to earth," he remarked, pleased when she rolled her eyes at him.

"Very pretty, my lord, but I beg you not to waste your time and energy."

"How could any time spent with such an invigorating companion be wasted?" Dare replied, quite serious, though it surprised him to realise it. "You make me exercise my brain, Miss Cadogan, which it will come as no surprise to you to learn, is in dire need of exerting itself, used as it is to an indolent life and being very little called upon."

"Oh, do stop!" she said, and Dare frowned at her, realising she sounded properly cross this time and... something else.

"Miss Cadogan?"

"I know what your game is."

She glared at him and... had he hurt her feelings? But how?

"Oh, everyone knows I excel at games," Dare said lightly, puzzled as to what he'd said to put that edge of unhappiness in her eyes. "Of all kinds."

"Yes, the more disreputable the better."

She turned away from him, making a show of inspecting the beautiful magnolia tree, though Dare doubted she saw it, she was too irritated.

"Men have always enjoyed being disreputable, I'm afraid, and I am a sorry example, I grant you. I am like... like one of Lady St Clair's roses been left unattended to grow into chaotic disorder. I need someone to prune me back into shape."

She snorted at the comparison. "Do not tempt me to get close to you with pruning shears, my lord. You may not appreciate the consequences."

He laughed at that, pleased to discover some of her previous spark returning.

"I think it might be worth the odd cut to my person to have your undivided attention, and perhaps you may discover you enjoy shaping me into something more pleasing to your eye."

"You are less a rose and more a bramble, I fear. The more I cut you the stronger and more invasive you become."

"Ah, but even brambles have their good points, despite the thorns. Just think of what delicious, sweet fruits there are to be savoured," he said, aware his voice had dropped to something low and far too intimate considering where they were.

There was a flush at her cheeks now, and he wondered how much of it was due to the warmth of the afternoon and how much his antagonism. He was having a marvellous time sparring with her.

"I'd likely get one with a maggot," she retorted.

He couldn't help but laugh. By Jove, she was funny.

"May I be blunt, my lord?" she asked, moving to face him.

Dare considered this for a moment. "I doubt it. I see you more in terms of a surgeon's scalpel, a precision blade poised to cut open a fellow from nose to navel and expose his innards for all to see."

She wrinkled her nose at that and snorted. It was strangely endearing.

"Oh, do not underestimate the appeal of a heavy blunt object, Lord Roxborough. If I had one to hand, I should put it to good use, I assure you."

"No assurance necessary. I can see from the gleam in your eye you are a bloodthirsty creature and should enjoy spilling my brains in a gory mess upon the floor."

"Doubtful," she said tartly. "There's little enough in that fatuous head of yours to spill out, methinks. What remains is likely so soaked in brandy it's nicely pickled, about the size of a walnut, perhaps. I shall put it in a jar with some vinegar and keep it beside me always as a reminder of a happy day."

Dare gave a roar of laughter, rather delighted by her. "God, you've a violent turn of mind. I thought young ladies were supposed to be serene and calm, and full of the gentler emotions."

She leaned closer to him, so close that he could see her eyes were green with a golden halo about the pupil. The colour so struck him he had to force himself to attend to her words.

"Other young ladies. Not this one, Lord Roxborough, so I suggest you tear up your carefully laid plans and choose another poor fool, for I won't be manipulated."

"Plans?" he said, admittedly surprised by that. "What plans?"

The look she gave him might have shrivelled a man with a conscience or anything resembling feelings to trouble him. As it was, Dare just looked back at her, the picture of innocence.

"Your plan to trap me into marriage so you can get your hands on my dowry."

"Not *just* your dowry," Dare replied without so much as a blink, wondering if she would hit him. He would not blame her if she did.

As it was, her mouth dropped open and she seemed to be lost for words, which was disappointing. He was relieved when she rallied, looking him up and down as if he'd just crawled out of cheese.

"You are a vile excuse for a human being."

With that she turned and stalked away from him. Dare followed, the gravel path crunching beneath his feet.

"Oh, come, come, Miss Cadogan. I'm not so bad. I admit I need a wife...well, no, I *need* money, and the only way I can get any is to marry well, so a wife is inevitable."

She turned a volcanic gaze on him, and he grinned at her.

"You don't even deny it?" she said, staring at him in outrage.

"No, why should I? I'm a scoundrel, I grant you, but not a liar. I had every intention of giving you fair warning, I promise. I do mean to trap you into marriage, however, assuming you won't come willingly. You see, I am a sportsman, so I must give you a fighting chance. Though, may I ask how you discovered the plot? I suspect August. The poor fellow has a surfeit of decency. It's very trying to him, not to mention the rest of us."

"Indeed, I wonder you can bear to keep company with someone who actually has a shred of honour."

"Oh, no, doing it too brown, Miss Cadogan. I do have honour. It's a little battered about the edges, I admit, but it's there right enough. Just... wait a moment, will you? A fellow can't talk to you when you're striding about like a dashed... well, a thing that strides about. It's not terribly ladylike, you know."

"I don't care!" she said and picked up her speed. "And I do not wish to talk to you."

"I quite understand, but give me five minutes," he begged, attempting his most charming smile.

Not so much as a hesitation, though he noticed she was following the path around the less populated outside of the garden, not heading to the centre where they might be overheard.

"Please," he added. "Then I'll go away, I promise. For now, at least. Can't not see you again if I'm going to trap you into a scandal, that would be awkward."

With a rustle of yellow skirts and lace petticoats she came to a halt and swung around to face him, doing up her parasol with a snap. She looked as if she was contemplating beating him about the head with it.

"Three minutes," she said.

Dare beamed at her. "Excellent. Right, well... I only wanted to suggest that we might not make such a terrible match. I don't much want a wife and you don't seem to want a husband. So... perfect."

43

She gaped at him.

Clearing his throat, he thought he'd best elaborate. She was clearly an intelligent woman, and there was no reason on earth she would want to marry him. Except that if she really didn't wish to have a husband to trouble her, marrying him might give her the freedom she desired, the liberty to behave in a way an unmarried lady could not. That she would likely run rings about him if he even tried to lay down the law was another good reason not to bother attempting it. He needed no reminders of that fact she was far cleverer than he was. Dare would leave her be because it was too unnerving to do otherwise. "I only mean that I shouldn't interfere with… well, whatever it is you don't want me to interfere with. You could go your way and I'll go mine."

"And you'll go merrily along, never bothering me a jot—"

"No," he began, pleased she'd got the gist of it, but she wasn't finished.

"—and spending my money until it's all gone and I've not a feather to fly with, *and* an idiot for a husband. Yes, an appealing picture, I can't think why I don't agree at once."

"Oh, well, come on. I'm not that bad, and I only want the money to—"

"Goodbye, Lord Roxborough. Your three minutes is up."

"That was barely two!" he retorted, indignant.

"I don't care," she said, flashing him a brilliant smile. "Go and fall in that ornamental fishpond, there's a good chap."

"We're not done," Dare grumbled.

"*I* am done."

"I want to marry you, Miss Cadogan."

"Well, I do not want to marry you."

"You might, if you got to know me."

"You are delusional, you poor, poor man."

"I have a plan…." he mock-whispered from behind his hand, wondering if that would pique her interest.

"Fine. Enjoy yourself. Do your worst."

Her green eyes flashed with some emotion he could not quite decipher.

"Oh, you did *not* just dare me," he said, a thrill of delight lancing through him.

She was not done with him, no matter what she said. She stopped in her tracks and looked over her shoulder at him.

"I do. I dare you," she said. "You couldn't trap me in a million years. You don't have it in you. Your poor little brain could never conceive a plan that I would not see through. Good day, Lord Roxborough."

"Well," Dare said, watching her go with an odd, almost electrical sensation fizzing about in his chest. "Well, we shall see about that."

Chapter 4

Monsieur Le Comte,

Thank you for visiting ~~yeser~~ yesterday. I am sorry you cannot come again today. I hope you are well. Please come and see me ~~very~~ soon. Do you think my writing is pretty? ~~Pretty awful. Haha.~~ I am ~~practissing~~ practising my writing and spelling. My teacher keeps ~~coreting~~ correcting me. ~~Bring some more sweets. Why may I not ask for sweetmeats? Why is everything I want to ask rude?~~

I look forward to seeing you.

—Excerpt of a letter from Miss Agatha Smith to Louis César de Montluc, Comte de Villen.

5ᵗʰMay 1839, Rotten Row, Hyde Park, London.

It was a glorious morning. Elspeth let out a happy sigh as her mount trotted through Hyde Park, heading towards Rotten Row. Everywhere was green, that first surge of verdant intensity that showed spring's enthusiasm to burst and bud and bring forth all around. Here and there clumps of jewel like daffodils nodded their heads in the breeze and birds sang jaunty songs, as well pleased with this early morning world as Elspeth was. She loved this time of day, not long after dawn, just as the sun was climbing and sending its first touch of warmth across the land. It was peaceful, with no one else in sight except....

Oh, drat the man!

Elspeth swallowed an oath as she saw Lord Roxborough riding towards her. His mount was a splendid black beast, huge and powerful, and she didn't doubt he'd borrowed it from Lord Bainbridge for he certainly couldn't afford such an animal. He was alone, and Elspeth thanked her good sense in having brought a reliable groom with her. Sanders had been with the family since she was a babe and would not be bribed to go away. It would have been far too easy for Roxborough to ruin her if the two of them were alone together.

"Good morning, Miss Cadogan, and a beautiful morning it is too. Though not, I think, as lovely as the picture before me."

Elspeth rolled her eyes.

"Oh, stow it. What are you doing here? I cannot believe you got out of bed at this hour of the morning just to irritate me. Surely you have better things to do, like destroying your liver. You'll give yourself a mental collapse rising before noon. Do you think it wise to risk it?"

"Not at all," he said, as jovially as if she'd greeted him with enthusiasm instead of such appalling rudeness that she was quite shocked herself. "Do not worry yourself unduly on my account. I gave my liver a thorough beating last night, and I've not been to bed yet."

The wretch winked at her.

She wrinkled her nose in disgust. "You astonish me. A man without so much as a farthing to his name, out all night gambling and carousing. It's so tempting to marry you, my lord. I cannot think why I do not accept you at once."

"Now, now, love, don't be so harsh. I'll have you know I was neither gambling nor carousing. I went to the theatre—Bainbridge has a box of course—and then we returned to his home for dinner and drinks. You see, I did not spend so much as a farthing, nor did I do anything reprehensible. Well, except perhaps criticise the chef, but there was far too much salt in the soup."

Elspeth narrowed her eyes at him. "Except sponge off your friend. Yes, I see. My lord, may I make one thing perfectly clear?"

"You may try," he said seriously, tapping his temple with one finger. "But I suggest you only use small words. I'm not terribly bright and I've not been to sleep for some time."

"I shall keep it quite simple enough for your limited intelligence, I assure you. For I am only reminding you that I am not, and will never be, *your love.*"

"Well, that's not very romantic," he said indignantly. "Just think what our children will say when I tell them about our courtship. They'll think me a poor sort if I cannot address you as a swain ought."

"You are not my swain!" Elspeth retorted. "And there will be *no* children!"

"No children?" His face fell. "Well, I think you might have discussed the decision with me first, dearest one. I mean, I was so looking forward to little blonde girls with ringlets, toddling about and calling me... Papa...."

"*Argh*! You are without a doubt, the most irritating, irksome, vexing.... Are you even listening to me?"

He jerked in the saddle, blinking as he snapped out of some abstraction.

"What? Oh. Er... vexing? Yes, I apologise. I know I am, but I really can't help it. It's in my nature. It's always been so, ever since I was a boy. 'Go away, Daire, you're a dashed nuisance,' are probably the first words I ever remember hearing," he said with a laugh.

Elspeth frowned, wondering if that were true. If so, it was not actually very funny. She sighed, wondering what to do with him.

"Do you want me to go?"

She turned back to him, wondering why she didn't just snap, 'yes, you devil,' and have done with it.

"You remember the magic words, don't you?" he said, looking adorably sheepish.

Elspeth gave herself a mental slap.

"You mean, if I say, 'go away, Lord Roxborough,' you will go?"

He nodded. "Of course. If that's what you want. I mean you have your faithful groom with you this morning, so there is no opportunity here for me to cause a scandal. And I assume you've not changed your mind about marrying me?"

He raised an enquiring eyebrow.

"No."

"Well, then." He glanced back at her, mischief glinting in his eyes. "Or... I could race you up the Row."

Elspeth felt a little quiver of anticipation at the idea.

No, she told herself sternly. *You'll only encourage him. If you're seen together, people will talk and then if something happens, they'll be all too ready to believe it. But....*

She pursed her lips, considering.

"Oh, come on. There's no one about to see. Where's the harm? Have a little fun for once in your life."

"I have fun," Elspeth retorted, glaring at him.

He said nothing, but disbelief was written all over his face.

"I do!"

"I'm sure you do," he said soothingly.

She wanted to hit him. He began to whistle a jaunty tune, looking thoroughly at ease and content. How did he manage that, she wondered? Was he really as happy and at peace with the world as he appeared to be? It was something she'd never been very good at. If only he wasn't so... so.... She sighed. He looked very fine this morning. His dark coat hugged a splendidly athletic figure. Elspeth knew he was a sporting gentleman. He boxed and rode, and the exploits that did not involve less than respectable women were usually centred around some feat of strength or a race. He was quite the Corinthian when he wasn't either in his cups or suffering a concussion from some ill-advised adventure.

"Oh, very well," she said, shocking herself as she'd not intended to say any such thing. "But on one condition."

"Name it," he said, his eyes bright.

"You must ride to win. Don't pretend to let me beat you or any such nonsense."

"As you wish." The devil grinned at her. "Though Bucephalus here will take one stride to your pretty mount's two."

Elspeth gave a shrug, knowing she would not best him. "I don't care if you beat me. I only want the race to be fair."

He nodded his acknowledgement and they trotted to the head of the row.

"When you're ready, then," he said.

Elspeth nodded.

"Right then. Ready, set—"

Elspeth's horse sprang forward, and she laughed at his look of outrage.

"You duplicitous female!" he yelled after her.

She didn't care. The pretty palomino mare she rode pricked her ears as Elspeth chortled with glee. The two of them raced down the Row, sand flying, the cool morning air rushing past her as the sound of hooves and of her own blood rushing in her veins sang in her ears. She turned her head as a large dark shape appeared in the corner of her vision. Lord Roxborough was beside her, his laughing eyes warm and approving.

He grinned and the powerful black beast surged ahead, leaving her behind and reaching the head of the Row long before she did. Roxborough was walking his horse in a circle as she reached him and, though she knew she ought not—for he did not need the encouragement—she laughed and laughed. Goodness, but that had been exhilarating. She could not remember the last time she'd had such fun.

"Well, minx, that was not terribly sporting."

She shrugged, grinning at him. "I couldn't win fairly."

"Neither can I," he said softly. "Not if you won't give me a chance, at least."

Her good humour evaporated in an instant and she turned her horse, heading back towards where her groom was waiting for her.

"Why should I? You only want my dowry. I know what this is, remember. I'm not a fool."

He tsked and trotted up beside her. "Don't be naïve. You have far more appeal than that, and I am sure you must know it. I am a man, and you are a beautiful woman, and far more fun than I had anticipated. I'm not some stern husband who would curb all your fun and make you sit quietly at home sewing samplers. I think we might rub along rather well."

Elspeth snorted.

"Rub along rather well?" she repeated sourly. She put a hand to her heart and affected a swoon. "Well, my darlings, I was simply swept off my feet by your father when he said he thought we might 'rub along rather well.' It was *sooo* romantic."

Roxborough snorted with amusement. "Is that what you want? Romance?"

"No," she snapped. "I want love and sincerity, and a man who doesn't give a damn if I have five shillings to my name or not."

"I can give you sincerity," he said with a crooked smile. "And I do think we might be friends. It's more than many people achieve."

"Go away, Lord Roxborough," she said, her voice stony.

To her surprise the words seemed to shake him, as though he'd not really believed she'd say them. He rallied and lifted his hat, giving her a smile, but it didn't reach his eyes. She watched him ride away and refused to acknowledge the little pang of regret that accompanied his departure.

Still the 5th of May 1839, The Cross Key's Club, Charles Street, Mayfair, London.

"Afternoon, Roxborough."

Dare looked up from his brandy as the Comte de Villen took a seat beside him.

"Villen," he said and then snorted. "I feel like I'm calling you a villain whenever I say your name."

The comte smiled and Dare could hardly blame the women of the *ton* for giggling and getting all silly when they spoke of him. No man ought to look like that. It was dashed unfair. He wondered if he would have more luck with Miss Cadogan if he looked like a cross between a beautiful angel and the handsomest of wicked devils too.

"What's it like?" he asked.

The comte looked up with a frown. "What?"

"Looking like...." Dare waved a hand at the man's face. "That."

"Honestly?"

"Of course."

"It can be very useful when I want something."

He sent Dare a smouldering look from under thick, dark lashes, his blue eyes an incredible colour even in the dim light of the club. Dare was rather astonished by the blush that heated his face in response.

"Bloody hell. I wish I could do that," he said sincerely.

Villen snorted. "Other times it can be a pain in the arse."

Dare raised his eyebrows. *"Really?* And your English is excellent."

"People always say that when I curse," the comte mused. "And yes, really."

The Frenchman stretched out his long legs and accepted the bottle of Bordeaux that was delivered to the table with a wine glass. Dare watched as he poured a little out and held it to his nose, savouring the scent. He smiled and then took a sip, giving a sigh of pleasure once he'd swallowed.

"Magnifique," he said, filling his glass.

He offered the bottle to Dare who shook his head. His guts had not yet recovered from last night's overindulgence. The brandy he was sipping like an old lady nursing a thimble of sherry was purely medicinal.

"Rumour has it you are courting Miss Cadogan."

Dare looked up. "Well, that didn't take long."

"You are surprised?"

"No. I suppose not."

"Is it true?"

Dare narrowed his eyes at him. "Maybe."

"I like Miss Cadogan," the comte said mildly.

"I say, are you warning me off?" Dare demanded, irritated and wondering why the comte cared. Did he have an interest there? Good God, he hoped not. He'd not stand a chance with bloody Apollo in the running.

"There's no need. Miss Cadogan has friends enough to do that for her, but I am curious as to why the sudden interest."

"None of your business, I should say," Dare retorted.

The comte smiled, a lazy expression that belied the keen intelligence shining in the man's eyes. "Quite so."

Dare relaxed, relieved Villen wasn't offended and wondering why he felt so prickly about it, anyway. He was only courting her because of her stupendous dowry. It was only that when Miss Cadogan had told him to go away this morning, he'd.... Oh, he was just being stupid. Of course she'd told him to go away. He'd told her she could, hadn't he? Everyone told him to go away eventually, so it was hardly a surprise. He'd just... just... Dash it all, he'd been enjoying her company and he'd rather hoped.... Yes, well, he was a blithering idiot.

"I'm going to have a bite to eat here, assuming they can manage such a thing without cremating the meat, and then I am going to visit my ward."

"Your ward?" Dare repeated with surprise. "And I always thought the food here rather good."

The comte quirked an eyebrow at that but did not comment. "My ward, yes. If I do not visit her at regular intervals, the little beast does something shocking. She is attending Lady Eliza's school for girls."

"Oh," Dare said, not much interested, but wondering where the comte had picked up a ward from. Unless it was an illegitimate daughter. More than likely.

"Miss Cadogan is teaching the children there."

Dare sat up straighter. "Oh?"

"I thought that might interest you." Again the lazy smile as the comte swirled the wine in his glass, tilting it and watching the liquid slide down the sides in little streaks. "An excellent vintage, full bodied. It's got legs."

Frowning, Dare did not bother asking how wine could have legs. He wasn't the least bit curious. "Why would you help me?"

"I never said I was going to."

He blew out a breath and sat back in his seat. Shaking the fellow by his immaculate cravat would not help.

"Do you like her?"

Dare slanted him a look. "Yes."

"Why? Most men seem to give the Cadogan twins a wide birth. One is a hoyden, the other a bluestocking."

"She's not a bluestocking! I mean, she's more than likely got ten times the brain I have, but she's not all dull and prissy. She's got spirit, a little spitfire when you provoke her just the right way, and she's funny too. You should have heard her this morning...."

Dare cleared his throat and tried to ignore the surge of heat creeping up the back of his neck.

"Yes, I do see," The comte murmured politely, his lips twitching a little as he poured himself another glass of wine. "Would you care to join me in some overcooked beefsteak? Then you could come along and meet my ward. If such a thing would interest you?"

Dare hesitated, wondering if he was being mocked, but the man seemed sincere.

"It would," he said at last. "And, well, that's very decent of you, Villen. Thank you."

"Oh, for heaven's sake, call me Louis-César. No, in fact, just Louis will do. If you can mangle my family name so badly, I dread to think what you could do with two first names."

"Dare." Dare put out his hand. "Dare by name."

He shrugged at the man's enquiring look. They shook hands.

Chapter 5

Dear Em,

No, I still have not got my hands on a copy of The Ghosts of Castle Madruzzo. It is so frustrating as everyone is talking about it now, and no one knows who the author is. It is becoming a huge success and I began reading it ages before it became famous. I promised papa I would not be frightened to death, or turn into a dreadful, spoilt little beast if he allowed me to read it. He just said he believed the first promise and it was already too late for the second, but I still couldn't read it. It's monstrous unfair. Pip has read it. He agreed it was marvellous and won't tell me a thing about it.

Brothers are horrid.

—Excerpt of a letter from Lady Catherine 'Cat' Barrington (youngest daughter of the Marquess and Marchioness of Montagu) to Miss Emmeline Knight (Daughter of Lady Helena and Mr Gabriel Knight).

5th May 1839, on the road to The Phoenix Charitable School for Young Ladies, Chelsea Village, London.

Dare looked across the carriage to see Louis rubbing his hand over his chest with a pained expression.

"Indigestion?"

"And this surprises you? *Mais, c'était immangeable.* I only wonder that you are not prostrate on the floor after that... that...." He shuddered. "And you ate enough for two men, like you'd not seen a morsel of bread for a week or more."

He shrugged. "I was hungry, and it was all right. The meat was a bit tough, I grant you."

"A *bit* tough?"

Dare watched, amused as Louis muttered to himself, a stream of incomprehensible French. Admittedly it hadn't been the best food he'd ever eaten but Louis seemed to take it to heart. Like such a meal was an affront against the laws of nature or some such. He'd waved away the apricot tart as though it had personally offended him because the pasty was soggy.

Funny people, the French.

Their carriage stopped outside the gates of a large redbrick building. Dare jumped out and waited for Louis, who stepped down from the carriage and then staggered backwards. It was no wonder, as something barrelled through the gates and flung itself at him.

"*Mon Dieu,* Aggie! You nearly killed me, and after the lunch I've endured, it wouldn't take much."

"Sorry," it said sheepishly, staring up at him with an adoring expression.

It was a small, skinny girl, with wild dark hair and large blue eyes. Dare looked between them, considering whether there was a resemblance.

"No," Louis said succinctly, catching Dare's expression. "I am not her father, and no, it's none of your business, but this is Miss Agatha Smith. Say good afternoon to Lord Roxborough, child."

Agatha dutifully executed another curtsey. "Good afternoon, Lord Roxborough."

"Miss Smith," Dare said, giving her an overly formal and elegant bow in return.

Miss Smith giggled.

"You are a hoyden and a disgrace," Louis remarked, amusement in his eyes. "And do stop crushing me, you make Elton cry when I come home all rumpled."

Reluctantly the girl unpeeled her arms from about his waist. Louis' expression softened, and he ruffled her hair affectionately. "How are you, brat?"

"Very well, thank you, Monsieur le Comte," she said, giving a slightly haphazard curtsey.

"Very good, you are improving, and I thought your letter exceptionally well done. Very pretty writing. Oh, that reminds me." He turned back to the carriage and took out a small box wrapped in pink tissue paper and tied with a blue ribbon. "Don't eat them all at once, you'll be sick."

Miss Smith tugged at the ribbons and opened the paper.

"Coconut ice!" She gave a little yip of pleasure and tugged him down so she could kiss his cheek. "Thank you!"

She took his hand, dragging him towards the school.

"Is Miss Cadogan here today?" Louis asked.

"Oh, yes. I've just finished a maths class with her. She said I did very well, and I excel with numbers."

"This surprises me not a bit," he remarked. "Anyone who can cheat at cards like you do needs a firm grasp of numbers."

She gave him an indignant glare. "I don't cheat."

Louis raised an eyebrow at her.

"Much," she amended.

"Miss Cadogan teaches maths?" Dare said, hesitating on the doorstep of the school.

"Oh, yes, she's ever so clever," the girl enthused. "And she makes everything seem so clear. She's even been teaching some of the grown-ups. The cook and the gardener 'ave—*have*—both been taking lessons with her."

Anxiety prickled down Dare's back. Miss Cadogan was a maths teacher?

"You're doing very well, Aggie," Louis said, and Dare was struck by the affection in his eyes.

Why on earth was he bothering with the child if she wasn't even his? It seemed odd to Dare, bearing in mind his own parents hadn't remembered his existence above twice a year. A gift on his birthday and at Christmas, though it would have most likely been the steward or someone in his father's employ who'd chosen and sent whatever it was. Most often a large selection of books that Dare had no interest in reading. Those books had piled up about his room, mocking him.

"Perhaps I ought not bother her…." Dare said, the familiar whiff of a school building reaching his nose and making his stomach tighten. "She wasn't best pleased with me this morning. I'll… I'll see her another day."

Louis gave him an odd look. "Are you sure?"

Dare nodded and thrust his hands in his pockets. "Quite sure. Thanks for today, and sorry lunch didn't agree with you."

"Do you want to take the carriage?" Louis offered. "Just send it back when you're done."

"No, I could do with a walk," Dare replied cheerfully, at least he hoped he looked cheerful. "Walk off that lunch."

He patted his stomach and Louis groaned.

"Please, do not remind me. Very well, *à bientôt.*"

Dare waved and walked back down the path.

He'd just got to the gate and pushed it open when he saw her, standing at the edge of the garden. She was staring back at the school with a frown of concentration. Dare hurried on, hoping he could leave before she saw him. He pulled at the gate which gave a slight creak.

Glancing up, he saw the sound had caught her attention.

"Oh!" she said in surprise. "You."

"The very same," he said awkwardly. Damnation. Now she would hate him even more and think he was following her about. Which he had been, but…. He raised his hat and pulled the gate wide, intending to make his escape before she could tell him what a sorry excuse for a human being he was. "Good afternoon to you."

He had just closed the gate behind him when she spoke.

"Wait."

Dare watched cautiously as she came closer, staring at him through the bars of the gate.

She said nothing, and he felt the oddest sensation creep over him as he stood waiting. It was akin to the sensation he'd sometimes had as a boy, standing before his parents, praying they might find something in him that pleased them and knowing it was a forlorn hope. He didn't like it. He didn't like it one little bit. Anger and resentment rose in his chest.

"It's all right, you don't need to say it again. I'm going, aren't I?" he said, aware he sounded terse but unable to stop himself.

"I'm sorry."

Dare stared at her in suspicion. "What for?"

He couldn't think of a single thing she ought to apologise for, so it must be a trap.

"For… For sending you away so rudely this morning."

Good God. "Think nothing of it. I can hardly blame you. I'd be an idiot to expect perfect manners from a woman I intend to force to marry me. I might be dim but I'm not that much of a fool."

"You still intend to, then?" she asked, frowning at him. It made two little lines appear between her pale brows and he was suddenly struck with the longing to smooth them away.

He shrugged. "I've not much option. You don't *want* to marry me, do you?"

She shook her head.

"Well, then."

"How much?" she asked him.

"What?"

"Your debts? How much do they run to? Is it gambling, or—"

He stiffened with indignation, which was ludicrous. She would have heard enough ridiculous stories about him to assume the worst.

"Or?" he demanded.

She put up her chin. "Women. An expensive mistress? H-High flyers?"

Dare snorted and shook his head, wondering why he felt so bloody depressed. "Goodbye, Miss Cadogan."

"Wait!"

He turned again, impatient now, wanting to get away from those beautiful green-gold eyes that looked at him and saw a worthless, hopeless… oh, what was the use?

"What?" he snapped, not caring that he was being rude.

She frowned at him, interest in her expression.

"I'm alone in the garden," she said quietly. "I'm just a little curious why you've not… taken advantage of the situation."

Dare laughed, realising she was right.

"So you are," he said, and walked away.

8th May 1839, Lady Helena Knight's ball, Grosvenor Square, London.

Elspeth frowned as she stared out of the window. The evening was mild, and it was not yet full dark as their carriage made the journey to Lady Helena and Mr Knight's lavish home. Lady Helena was giving a ball tonight and, in usual circumstances, Elspeth would be steeling herself to endure the evening, perhaps grasping the opportunity to sneak into the library and borrow a book to keep her company for the evening. Tonight, however, was different. She wanted to see Lord Roxborough and he was bound to be here.

She could not shake the sensation that something was wrong, ever since her strange meeting with him at the school three days ago. When she had spoken to Louis César, she had gained the impression that Roxborough had come with the express purpose of seeing her but had changed his mind. Louis had asked if she was being courted, and if she liked his lordship. Elspeth had retorted rather tartly that she was being hunted not courted, and no, she did not. Except there was something bothering her. She *did* rather like Lord Roxborough. Oh, not as a husband, good heavens no. That would be disastrous for everyone concerned. No, but he was charming, and funny too, in an annoying sort of way. She enjoyed sparring with him. It was liberating to tell someone they were an idiot and talking rubbish and not have them take offence. Yet… he *had* been offended. When she had asked about his debts, he'd become all stiff and prickly and stalked away, and she'd been alone in the garden too. If ever he'd wanted an opportunity to trap her....

Oh, it made no sense. He had been quite open about the fact he was up to his eyes in debt, and everyone knew he was a loose screw. So why had he looked so hurt? Guilt stirred in her chest. No matter how she told herself she was being ridiculous when he would trap her into marriage for the sake of her dowry, it would not go away.

Well, she would speak to him tonight and see if she could get to the bottom of it. She must only ensure she did it in full view of the ballroom and not be so stupid as to go onto the terrace with him or into a quiet room.

Half an hour later and Elspeth was still scanning the ballroom, looking for him. As a gloved hand touched her arm, Elspeth turned to see Florence Knight and her younger sister Evie.

"Good evening, Elspeth," Florence said. "Oh, what a beautiful gown. You do look lovely."

"Thank you," Elspeth replied, looking down at the pale grey satin gown. It was rather lovely, and she knew she looked well this evening, having gone to more trouble than usual—which did not signify in the least. "You both look beautiful, too."

Evie snorted and then blushed as her sister glared at her.

"You do, Evie." Florence insisted.

"I agree," Elspeth said. "That green gown is a splendid shade on you, it brings out the colour in your eyes."

Evie shrugged, clearly disbelieving, and looked about the ballroom. At sixteen, she was out rather earlier than Florence had been allowed, as her parents believed she needed more time to acclimatise herself to the world of balls and socialising. She was a plump girl, and whilst not plain, she was not remarkable and when she was constantly standing next to her beautiful older sister she faded into the background. Elspeth had wondered if she resented being compared with Florence but could find no sign of it. The two girls seemed close.

At that moment, a deep masculine laugh caught her ear, and her heart did an odd little somersault for no good reason… no reason except that she recognised the voice.

"Would you excuse me, please?" Elspeth said, hurrying away from the sisters in the direction from which the sound had come.

"Drat," she muttered as she looked around the crowded ballroom.

Everywhere were ladies in silks and satins of every shade, and men in their severe black–and–white, but the man she was looking for was not there. Oh, there was Louis César. Perhaps he would have seen him.

Elspeth hurried through a gap in the crowd before it could close and Louis disappeared again. Unusually, he was standing alone, keeping to a shadowy corner of the room, partially hidden by an arrangement of large potted plants. She got the feeling he was hiding.

"Good evening, Monsieur le Comte," she said politely.

"Miss Cadogan," he replied, with apparent pleasure, though she was never quite certain what Louis was feeling. "You are a vision of loveliness, as usual."

"Thank you," she said, feeling she really ought to return the compliment. She would have if it wouldn't have appeared she was flirting with him. He was breathtaking, however, and it was hard not to take a moment to appreciate the fact. "Are you enjoying the evening?"

"It is a splendid affair," he replied, which Elspeth realised was not really an answer.

"I was wondering if you had seen Lord Roxborough?"

Louis turned to give her a direct look, those vivid blue eyes considering and full of intelligence. It was very hard not to blush.

"You want to see him?" he asked mildly. "I was under the impression you did not wish to encourage his suit."

Elspeth tsked at him. "He hasn't got a suit. He has a plan to compromise me and get his hands on my dowry."

Louis shrugged. "I cannot help but feel there is more to it than that, but nonetheless, my question remains."

"Oh, I don't know," she said impatiently. "I had words with him the other day, and when he came to the school I—I think I hurt his feelings. It's utterly ridiculous when he doesn't give a damn for mine."

"Doesn't he?"

"He wishes to trap me into marriage," she reminded him.

"Yes, so he says."

"Well, then. Why should I feel so guilty?"

"I have no idea," Louis replied, amusement glinting in his eyes. "What exactly did you say to him?"

"I asked how much his gambling debts amounted to, or if perhaps it wasn't just gambling debts, but an expensive mistress."

Louis's eyebrows rose.

"Yes, yes, I know," Elspeth said irritably. "A lady ought never even consider such things, let alone ask a gentleman for such information, but I don't think that was why he was upset. I think... I think he was hurt that I considered him in that light, but everyone knows he's a scoundrel, so why would I not?"

"Why, indeed," Louis murmured, frowning.

"Don't you know?" she asked desperately.

He shook his head. "I'm afraid I do not know him well at all. He's a mere acquaintance, and no, I am not about to ask him."

66

Elspeth sighed. "Oh, very well."

"There, there, Miss Cadogan. Do not look so downhearted. I have gained the impression that Lord Roxborough has a rather irrepressible spirit. I do not believe he will remain downcast. Perhaps if you were to allow him a dance this evening, that would smooth his ruffled feathers?"

Elspeth nodded, wondering rather gloomily if the man would ask her now, and why the devil should she care if he didn't?

"In the meantime, might I ask for the pleasure of the next dance for myself?"

Elspeth looked up, frowning at Louis as she'd not been attending.

"A dance, Miss Cadogan, if you would be so kind," he repeated.

"Oh! Oh, yes, of course. I'd be delighted," she said automatically.

Louis snorted and gave her his arm. "Yes, I can see you are brimming with enthusiasm."

"At least you know I won't gaze at you like a lovesick kitten for the duration."

He laughed at that as he escorted her onto the dance floor. "Which is why I like you, Miss Cadogan. You are an eminently sensible young woman."

Elspeth sighed inwardly. Only a few days ago she would have agreed with that description quite happily. Now... not so much.

Dare glowered at Louis-César and Elspeth Cadogan dancing a waltz together. They made quite a picture, with Louis' dark godlike appearance in striking black and white, and Elspeth's fair golden beauty in a pale grey satin gown. Something in his gut tightened and told himself not to be a twit. Louis wasn't looking for a wife, so even if Elspeth was smitten—like half the bloody *ton*—it would do her no good. They were talking as they danced, looking quite at ease together. Louis said something and Elspeth laughed, and Dare's stomach twisted into a knot. Well, she would laugh with Louis. He was a clever chap, always witty and amusing. If asked, Dare would have said he liked Louis too. Right at this moment, though, he wasn't so sure.

Louis saw him as they made a turn and Dare made himself hold the man's gaze and not look away. Louis nodded and swept Elspeth off on another circuit of the ballroom. Dare realised he was holding his wine glass far too tightly and tried to relax his grip. He was being an idiot. It did not signify who Elspeth liked, or even if she liked *him*; he just had to get her alone and into a compromising situation. This evening was as good an opportunity as he was likely to get. Unfortunately, Bainbridge couldn't come, so he had no one to help but... but surely, he could think of something. Perhaps he really could seduce her? She did not seem entirely revolted by his charms, and he had made her laugh more than once. Humour was always his best friend. He might not be able to spout poetry or make clever remarks, but he could always make girls laugh, even if it was at his own expense.

Dare considered the idea of seducing Elspeth Cadogan and abruptly halted the image that formed in his mind of her in his arms, of his mouth upon hers, his hands spanning that neat little waist. Everything south of his brain was perking up with far too much interest and that would not do, not in these trousers. Dare let out a slow breath and considered instead where the deed would take place. The library, perhaps. She might go there of her own accord. From what he had gathered from others, she often sneaked away. If he was less than discreet in following her, some busybody was bound to notice and come to see what they were up to. She would hardly throw herself into his arms. He could force the issue, but.... Nausea roiled in his guts. *No.* No he could not. He was being a big enough blackguard without such vile behaviour. She already thought him a fribble and waste of time, not that he could blame her for that. He swallowed down the sense of regret that had hit hard when he had realised she believed his debts came from gambling and whoring. Well, why shouldn't she think that? Besides, it didn't matter what she thought of him, only that she married him. He needed to save Rowsley Hall, and then perhaps he'd be able to sleep peacefully again. His parents might have despised him, and he might have spent every moment at the Hall feeling abandoned and miserable, but that did not wipe out generations of history. Dare knew he was part of history, part of an unbroken bloodline. He was Roxborough now and his family had created the Hall, each generation adding to its magnificence. His father might have brought the place to ruin, but Dare was damned if he would be the one responsible for finishing the job.

The dance had ended now, and Dare looked about to see where his quarry was heading next, except there was no need, as Louis César was escorting her directly to him.

"Dare, good to see you," Louis said with a smile. "I believe Miss Cadogan is free for the next dance, and I know how much you wished to ask her."

Dare wasn't certain whether to curse Louis or thank him, but was thoroughly vexed by the rush of heat that climbed up the back of his neck. His only consolation was realising that Miss Cadogan was more than a little pink herself. That could be dancing the waltz with Louis, of course. He'd seen more than one woman looking flushed and dazed after such an experience... which did not help his mood a bit.

"Miss Cadogan. Good evening," he said, wishing he didn't sound so stiff and formal.

What the devil was wrong with him?

"Lord Roxborough."

"If you'll excuse me."

"Oh, but—"

Both he and Elspeth spoke at once, identical expressions of panic in their eyes as Louis turned to leave. The man paused, looking from one to other of them in surprise. His lips twitched slightly, but he just inclined his head and carried on his way, leaving Dare and Elspeth standing together in awkward silence.

"You don't have to dance with me if you don't want to."

Miss Cadogan did not look at him, her eyes on the ballroom and the people moving to take their places.

Dare snorted. "Yes, well your enthusiasm towards the idea has left a mark, Miss Cadogan. I should not want to cross swords with you again."

"Whyever not?"

Dare turned to look at her with a frown. "Whyever not, what?"

She tutted impatiently. "Why would you not wish to cross swords with me? I thought you enjoyed it."

He shrugged, knowing this was calculated to be the most annoying of responses but not much caring.

"That is not an answer."

Dare was tempted to do it again, just to rile her, but then her hand curved about his forearm and his entire body lit up with the contact. "My lord, have... have I offended you in some way?"

Eyes of green and gold stared up at him and Dare was lost, sinking into that astonishing colour, into that expression of... what *was* that expression? Pity perhaps or, was that concern? *Concern?* For *him*? Good God, she meant it. She actually cared that she might have hurt his feelings.

"Lord Roxborough?"

Dare shook himself, aware he had been staring at her. "No. Of course not."

He smiled. She cared. Something foolish and happy flitted about in his chest. Oh, he wasn't kidding himself that she was in love with him, or even in like with him. Could one be *in like* with someone? He hoped so, for it was all he could reasonably expect from her. Not despising him seemed like a good start from the admittedly low bar he'd set himself, but concern... well, he'd never expected that.

"Are you sure? For I truly meant no offense. I know I ought not speak of gambling debts and mistresses, but if I cannot speak honestly to a man preparing to trap me into marriage, then I'm not sure who I can speak to."

"You may say exactly what you wish to me," Dare said, feeling much better for no reason he could put his finger on. "I promised to be honest with you, so I see no reason why you ought not return the favour."

"Oh, good, but I really didn't—"

"I don't have any tender feelings, Miss Cadogan. I'm sure everyone has told you that much. So you couldn't possibly have hurt them, now, could you?"

She didn't look entirely reassured by this, so he carried on talking. "They're taking places for the quadrille. Shall we?"

"Actually, I'd rather not," she said, and all his pleasure evaporated at once as he realised she still would not dance with him. "I'm frightfully thirsty. Might we go to the refreshments room?"

Dare brightened. Well, she wasn't trying to ditch him, that was something. "Certainly. Would you like to go via the library?"

She gave him a withering look that made him want to smile.

"Oh, yes," she said in a breathless voice that made something inside him react, though he knew she was mocking him. "Do take me to the library, Lord Roxborough, so we might be alone together. I'm quite certain *no one* will interrupt us."

She batted her eyelashes at him so comically he gave a snort of laughter.

"Ah, well, it was worth a try."

"You really must believe me stupid if you think it will be that easy to compromise me."

"Not in the least stupid," Dare replied, guiding her through the crowds. "Far cleverer than me, at any rate, but I thought perhaps you might take pity on me or give me points for perseverance."

"Points? Since when have we been working on a points system?"

Dare shrugged, enjoying himself now. "Well, it might give me something to aim for. How many points should I need to make myself an acceptable prospect for matrimony?"

"Oh, good heavens. You're serious. You poor dear," she said, shaking her head at him.

Ah, now *that* was a pitying expression.

"Yes, and why not? Shouldn't you encourage my efforts at good behaviour?"

"Why?" she demanded, looking faintly disgusted.

Dare paused to allow a stream of giggling girls to hurry past them, on their way to the dance floor. "Well, because if I transformed into a fellow that resembled a good husband, you might wish to marry me, and then I'd not need to do something that will make you angry."

"Creating a scandal and forcing me accept you as my husband, you mean?"

"Yes, exactly. So, how many?"

She stared at him for a moment. "Ten million, six hundred and forty-nine thousand, three hundred and twenty-eight."

Dare let out a low whistle. "Right, then. And how many points do I have?"

"*Have?*" she said, her eyes growing wide.

"Yes!" He stared down at her, a little indignant. "Oh, come on. Even a terrible fellow like me must have a few points."

"Minus eight."

"Well, I call that very shabby, Miss Cadogan. Very shabby indeed. You might offer a fellow a bit of encouragement."

"Encouragement is the very last thing you need, my lord."

"No, that's simply not true. It's very daunting, you know, for a chap like me, trying to make himself an appealing prospect."

"I can imagine," she said dryly.

"No, dash it all. It's true," he said, wondering at what point he'd stopped joking and become serious. "I mean, look at you, you're...."

He waved a hand at her, suddenly lost for words.

"What?" she asked, with obvious trepidation.

Her shoulders had gone all stiff and there was a frosty look in her eyes.

"You're...." he began, wondering why his voice sounded so odd. "You're beautiful and clever and funny and... and I... and I...."

She flushed and turned away from him, and when she spoke, she sounded rather cross. "You are Lord Roxborough, notorious scoundrel who wishes to get his hands on my dowry, yes, I know. So there is no point in pretending to make love to me."

"But Miss Cadogan, I wasn't—"

She turned on him, her cheeks still hot. "No. It's not fair. You promised to be honest and not... not pretend. If you must pursue me, then at least don't dress it up as something it's not."

Dare stared at her.

"But you are beautiful," he said, nonplussed.

"So what if I am? What does it signify to you? If not for my dowry, you'd not give me a second glance. Would you?" she demanded, crossing her arms. "Would you? *Admit* it, drat you."

Dare hesitated. He was very certain his answer was going to make a great deal of difference to what happened next, and he really did not want to mess it up. Being put on the spot always made his brain spiral into a panic, but he did his best not to let it and to answer the question as honestly as he could.

"I don't know if I would have given you a second glance," he said carefully. "I've not been looking for a wife and, if things weren't so very bad, I probably wouldn't be now, but... but I have seen you now, Miss Cadogan. I see you very clearly, and I know I'm not the cleverest chap in the *ton* but, well, I'm not so bloody stupid that I don't know a good thing when I see it. You are a very, very good thing, and if I were not desperate for money, I should still pursue you, knowing what I do now."

She stared at him, and if anything her cheeks burned a deeper shade of pink than they had before.

"Oh," she said. The tight lines that had bracketed her mouth faded and her expression softened. "Oh."

Dare felt some of the tension leave him, and realised he might have said something right for once in his life.

"Shall we get that drink now?" he asked, offering her his arm again.

She nodded, the movement a little jerky, but she took his arm and Dare escorted her to the refreshments room.

Chapter 6

My Lord Frederick,

Thank you very much for lending me the lovely books ~~what~~ which arrived this morning. I did enjoy Sleepy Hollow which was ~~blee~~ every bit as horrid as you said it would be in your letter. Has Cat read it? I'm sure she would enjoy it too.

It was a great surprise to hear from you as I did not think you liked me very much. I did not mean to laugh at you when you ~~fell on your ar~~ tripped over at your sister's wedding. It sort of slipped out. I am sorry.

If ever you should like to visit the school, I would be happy to show you around.

—Excerpt of a letter from Miss Agatha Smith to Lord Frederick Adolphus (younger son of the duke and duchess of Bedwin).

Still the 8th of May 1839, Lady Helena Knight's ball, Grosvenor Square, London.

Louis dared a glance over his shoulder and let out a sigh of relief when it revealed no sign of his pursuers. They would not be far behind, however. He hurried on, along the grand gallery, looking for somewhere to wait, out of sight, until they had passed him by.

A faint sound of humming reached him, and he looked into one of the alcoves he was passing and paused as he noted a young woman. She was very young, plump and rather sweet, and she turned the colour of a cooked lobster as he caught her in the act of lifting a pastry to her mouth. There was a plate beside her with a delectable selection of little treats.

"I beg your pardon," he began, and then paused as the sound of footsteps echoed along the parquet. He looked about for a means of escape, but found none. *"Dieu."*

"Monsieur le Comte?"

Louis looked around to see the girl had opened a secret door in the panelling. She gestured to it. "If you want to avoid them…."

"Mille mercies, mademoiselle," he said with feeling, and hurried into the dark space. The girl closed the door on him, and Louis let out a breath. He stilled as the footsteps he'd heard grew closer.

"Oh, Evie, did you see the Comte de Villen come this way?"

Just as he'd suspected. Arabella Hunt, and the girl in the alcove was Evie? He had not seen her before. She looked rather too young to be out yet.

"Oh, no. Sorry, Bella. I've not seen him," Evie replied cheerfully. "Were you looking for him?"

"I told you he went the other way," said another voice impatiently.

Louis did not recognise that one, but it could have been any of half a dozen girls he'd been dodging all evening.

"It doesn't matter," Arabella said with a sigh. "I was hoping he might dance with me. He hardly ever asks anyone, but he danced with Elspeth tonight, of all people. She doesn't even like dancing. It's so unfair. He just refuses to notice me."

"Perhaps you ought not chase him so?"

"Oh, I know that, but… but I'm sure he's lonely and I… I just want…. Well, I hoped I might make him smile, that's all."

Louis frowned, feeling rather guilty and not a little discomforted by her words. Surely it wasn't that obvious?

"He smiles, doesn't he?" Evie said.

"It doesn't reach his eyes. Have you never noticed?"

There was a short silence.

"Well, it's not like you are short of offers," Evie said brightly. "You look splendid tonight."

"Thank you, Evie. You look very pretty too. That green suits you very well."

"Oh, do come along, Arabella, we'll never find him if you stand here gabbing all night."

"All right, all right, I'm coming. See you later, Evie…."

The footsteps faded and a few moments later the door opened again.

"It's safe to come out now," the girl said, her eyes glinting with amusement. Louis' eyes adjusted after his plunge into darkness, and he regarded his rescuer with interest. Arabella was right, the dress became her. Though she was rather a plain little thing, she had remarkable eyes, as emerald green as her gown. Ah, she must be one of Lady Helena's daughters.

"I am in your debt, Miss…?"

"Miss Evie Knight," the girl said, giving a quick curtsey. "And you are very welcome. I saw how you were pursued earlier in the evening and wondered how you bore it. I see now that you don't."

Louis snorted. "You must think me very ill-mannered."

"Not in the least. I should imagine it is very tiresome. At least if someone comes to talk to me, I know they want to speak with me, not just gaze into my eyes or something revolting."

She gave a little snort of amusement. God, she was young. Louis wondered if he'd ever been that young. If he had he couldn't remember it.

"Are you hungry?" She lifted the plate of pastries and Louis stomach growled. She grinned at him.

"I did not have time to eat before I came out," he said, a little embarrassed.

"No, and you've been too busy trying not become an *hors d'oeuvres* yourself to visit the refreshments room."

She gave an impish smile that made her cheeks dimple and Louis laughed.

"Quite so, and yes, please. I am famished, as you may have gathered."

The girl sat back down on the carved wooden bench and placed the plate beside her, gesturing to Louis to take the remaining space. "Do sit down."

"Thank you, though...." He looked up and down the corridor.

"Oh, don't worry, people have been walking up and down all evening. It's not the sort of place for an illicit rendezvous and no one in their right mind would believe you were pursuing me, of all people."

"Of course not," Louis said in disgust. "You are far too young."

"Yes, that's the reason," the girl murmured ruefully.

Louis frowned but did not contradict her. He did not wish for his remarks to be misconstrued as flirtation, and young girls were notoriously impressionable.

"That is a handy hiding place," he said, gesturing to the hidden door.

"It is. Though it's a new house, it is full of surprises. Like my mother," she added with a grin. "My father built it for her, you see."

"A romantic story, I gather."

A wistful look entered the girl's eyes and she sighed. "Yes. He was born in the workhouse and did not dare consider her, for she is a duke's daughter and was considered far above him, but Mama was having none of it. She pursued him most shockingly. I'm afraid you would not have enjoyed such a hunt."

Louis laughed.

"I'm not wholly averse to being pursued, it just depends on who is doing the hunting." He paused and cleared his throat. "I apologise, this is not a suitable topic of conversation."

"Don't be silly. I brought the subject up. Try the lobster patties, they're utterly divine," she said, gesturing to the plate.

Louis did, popping one into his mouth and chewing. He gave a sigh of contentment. "You're right. That is *délicieuse*."

"Oh, I wish I could speak French properly," she said. "Our governess says my accent is execrable. *Delishouse*."

Louis winced.

"There, see? She's right, too!" She laughed merrily, and Louis could not help but smile.

"*Délicieuse*," he repeated, slowly this time, and then several more times as she copied him.

Evie repeated it after him, her gaze trained on his mouth, a little frown of concentration puckering her brow.

"*Pas mal*." He nodded with approval and she beamed at him.

"Well, I wish you would teach me French. It's far better hearing it from a real Frenchman than from Miss Rigsby. She tells me my accent is appalling, but I'm not convinced hers is a great deal better."

Louis snorted. "Well, if we are at the same event again, I shall happily teach you in return for a safe space to hide and a plate of food."

"A deal," she said, beaming at him and holding out her hand.

Louis raised his eyebrows in surprise. He'd been joking but... oh well. Where was the harm? "A deal, Miss Evie."

They shook hands and she offered him the last pastry. "Go on. I've already eaten too much, and you look like you need it more than I do. Must keep your strength up if you're to outrun all those debutantes."

Something mischievous glinted in her eyes and Louis could not help but laugh. He took the pastry.

"Thank you, and now I had better go. Sadly, I cannot hide the entire evening."

"Not if you are to find yourself a wife," she agreed with sympathy. "That is why you are here, isn't it?"

Louis shrugged. "I suppose so."

"Does no one catch your eye?" she asked, frowning at him. "There are some very beautiful girls here. Arabella is a lovely person, too. She's ever so kind and caring, you know, not just a pretty face."

"I know. I just... well, I don't want to get married at all."

She looked surprised at that, and he could not help but feel a little astonished he'd told her.

"Then why come at all?"

"It's... complicated."

She snorted at that. "Yes. I don't doubt it is. Well, enjoy the rest of your evening and... don't get caught."

He laughed and bowed to her. "Thank you for your hospitality, Miss Evie. Until next time."

12th May 1839, Private View of the Old Masters Exhibition, Royal Academy.

Dare looked around, scanning the throng for Miss Cadogan. What had possessed him to come to such an event as this he dared not consider. It wasn't as if he could compromise the delightful Elspeth Cadogan when the place was fit to bursting with people and there was no place for devising a scandalously illicit rendezvous. It was disquieting to realise that he didn't care. Something hopeful and happy was jittering inside him and no matter how often he told himself not to be such an idiot, he could not quell it. He was excited to see her. Their meeting at Lady Helena's ball had gone far better than he'd dared to hope. By the end of the evening something seemed to have changed and he got the feeling she did not despise him after all. Oh, he wasn't stupid enough to believe she wished to marry him, or that there was any hope of her actually falling in love with him, but... well, she did seem to not dislike his company. Not disliking a possible husband might not seem like much encouragement to some fellows but to Dare, especially in the present circumstances, it seemed like a something of a triumph. She'd even smiled at him, an event which he thought might have damaged his poor brain as he could not think of anything else ever since.

"I really don't know why I let you persuade me into this," August grumbled.

"Because you like fusty old paintings, and this is your idea of a splendid afternoon out. Besides, you had an invitation, and I'd never have got in otherwise."

August turned to look at him, his expression grave. "I will not aid you in ruining that poor girl, Dare. You have been a good friend to me, and I am aware I owe you a great deal, but it's wicked and wrong, and I won't have it."

Dare turned away from his friend, something unpleasantly like shame twisting inside of him. Christ, if he couldn't look August in the eye, how would he ever look at Miss Cadogan again if he got his way? She would hate him forever. Was saving Rowsley Hall worth it? It wasn't as though he even liked the place. He'd certainly never been happy there. Was it worth saving, knowing he had wronged a woman like Elspeth, forced her to be his wife, and that she would despise him until the day he died? Dare swallowed. His parents hadn't had enough interest in him to despise him, but he doubted it was much more enjoyable than being ignored. Dare hated to be ignored.

"What if I don't intend to trap her?"

The words tumbled out in a rush before Dare could stop them or think better of them, but he knew as soon as he heard them it was true. He couldn't do it.

August turned back to him, his expression clearing. "Really, Dare? Oh, thank goodness. I am relieved. I felt sure you would see it was a vile trick in the end. I knew you were too good-natured to go through with it, but I admit, you had me worried there."

Dare shrugged.

"I can't do it to her. I like her," he admitted, feeling like an idiot boy confessing a *tendre* for the girl next door.

August grinned at him. "Oh, dear. Cupid's arrow struck deep, did it?"

"Shut up, you stupid bastard," Dare grumbled, folding his arms. "It's not like that. I still intend to marry her, and I do need her money, but…. Well, dash it all, August, I don't want to marry a woman who will hate me for the rest of my days. I don't expect her to fall head over ears, but perhaps we could be… *friends*."

He winced, realising how pathetic that sounded. Glancing at August however he was surprised to see a look of approval in his eyes.

"I think you should woo her properly, and for God's sake be honest with her. You might be surprised."

Dare snorted. "Oh, I might, indeed. I can't wait to discover what manner of surprise it is too, for watching her turn her back on me and run off to a far better prospect won't be the least bit shocking to anyone, least of all me. She's too sensible to do anything else."

"Dare."

Dare looked back at his friend, a little taken aback to see sympathy in August's expression. "What?"

"Don't be so hard on yourself. You're a good man. A bit of a clown at times, I grant you, but you deserve to be happy. Perhaps if you behave properly and show her you are really not such a bad fellow, she'll give you a chance. Now look, she's over there, so pull yourself together and go and court the girl with the seriousness the situation merits."

Dare opened and closed his mouth, uncertain of what to say. August's words had rather startled him and now Elspeth was there and looking so damned beautiful he felt a surge of apprehension. What if he couldn't do it? He'd done nothing seriously in his life before. What if he didn't have charm enough to win her around? What then?

"Go!" August gave him a little push and Dare turned to scowl at him but kept walking. His mouth was dry, and he didn't have the least idea of what he was going to say, but then he was standing beside her, staring up at some huge painting. Dare looked at the painting. For lack of anything intelligent to say, he peered at the title and read it aloud.

"*The Penny Wedding* by David Wilkie."

"It's rather good, isn't it?" Elspeth said, apparently not disturbed by his presence.

Dare relaxed just a little as he hadn't been told to take a running jump. Yet.

"They look like they are all having a jolly time," he observed, taking the time to study it properly. There were several guests in a large ramshackle building. Some were dancing to a fiddler who was clearly playing a jaunty tune, and others were still feasting, but everyone seemed to be having fun.

Elspeth nodded. "It's a tradition in Scotland, I believe. Everyone gives a penny towards the expense of the wedding, and anything left over goes to the happy couple."

"A penny, eh? I might be able to manage that," he said ruefully.

To his surprise she laughed. "And look how happy they all are, my lord. I believe the painter is making a point. That riches do not necessarily bring happiness."

"No, I don't suppose they do," he said with a heavy sigh. "They're awfully good at keeping bailiffs happy, though."

"Is it so desperate?"

Dare forced himself to look at her. His chest felt tight as he met her eyes, green and gold and looking directly at him, seeing him. What *did* she see, he wondered? He'd never spent much time in polite society, certainly not with proper young ladies. He was always too aware that everyone thought him a joke. Not that he ever did anything to contradict them. Oh no, he'd given them what they expected, behaving badly, causing chaos and generally being a pain in the arse.

"Oh, let's not talk of that," he said, and then cleared his throat. "Do you like paintings, then? I assume you must as you are here."

"I do," she said, and her eyes sparkled with amusement as she added, "do you?"

"Oh, er... certainly," he began, and then sighed. "Miss Cadogan, you know as well as I do I haven't the slightest idea how to tell a good painting from a bad one, and I only came to see you."

She looked away from him, but he caught the glimpse of a smile and thought mayhap the comment did not displease her.

"Perhaps you could teach me a thing or two," he suggested. "If you showed me around, I might learn something."

Miss Cadogan looked back at him, considering. "You know, I think a good painting is one that pleases you. Everyone has different taste, a different idea of what is good or bad, and one need not be a scholar or an art critic to find pleasure in them."

"Well, then," Dare said, looking around the walls. It was a little overwhelming in all honesty. There were so many paintings, sky hung, one on top of another reaching so far up the higher levels were difficult to make out. "I like that one."

Elspeth looked to where he pointed and smiled. "That's *Dignity and Impudence*. It's by Landseer."

They walked closer to the rather amusing portrait of two dogs looking out of a kennel. One was a large bloodhound, the other a little West Highland terrier.

"It is rather droll. It's been painted in a parody of the Dutch portrait tradition, where the subject is usually framed by a window with an arm or a hand extending over the edge. See how the bloodhound's paw hangs over the edge of the kennel."

"Oh," Dare said in surprise. "I just thought they looked to be good dogs. The kind to keep a fellow company."

"Do you have dogs?" she asked.

Dare shook his head. "No, I desperately wanted a dog as a boy, but I was always at school and.... No. I've never had one."

"Wouldn't your parents have looked after it when you weren't at home?"

"My parents were never at home," he said with a laugh. "Always off on their travels."

"But they must have returned for the holidays?"

Dare shook his head. "No. Just me rattling about Rowsley Hall like a pea in a drum. I should have liked a dog then."

She frowned at him and Dare studied the painting, wondering what it was about the way she looked at him that made him feel so peculiar.

"Why not get one now?" she asked. "You're a grown man, you can do as you please."

Dare shrugged. "I have thought of it but, well, I'm always in town. It wouldn't be fair, but… but perhaps if we were married…."

He stopped as an image formed in his mind of a summer day at Rowsley Hall, walking the gardens with Elspeth and parcel of dogs and children and…. His breath caught. Remembering himself, he turned back to Elspeth to see her watching him with a curious expression.

"We are not getting married, my lord," she said, and though her tone was firm, it was gentler than before.

He laughed and shook his head. "Well, no, but if we were, I'd like a dog, perhaps two. Should you mind that?"

She shook her head. "No. I like dogs. Cats as well."

"Oh, well we can get a cat too, if you want. So long as we get them with the puppies, they'll be fine friends."

"My lord I… I don't think this is…."

She stared at him and there was the strangest sensation in Dare's chest again, almost a pain. It took him several moments to identify it.

Longing.

"Miss Cadogan," he said, his voice a little unsteady. "I know we got off to a bad start and... and I've behaved very badly, for which I should like to apologise, but... but the thing is I like you. I like you very much, and I really don't wish to trap you or make a scandal or anything of the sort, but I want, very much, to call on you. Do... Do you think that would be all right?"

He thought he heard her breath hitch and she turned away from him, staring back at the painting. Dare waited, wondering if he had a hope in hell.

"You still want my money, though, don't you?" she said, and the words were laced with sadness.

"I want you more."

As declarations went it was hardly romantic. Certainly, it was indelicate, but it was also true, and he thought perhaps she heard the sincerity in it as she turned to look at him, her lovely eyes wide.

"I do," he said, meaning it. He wished to God he didn't need her money Whether or not she had a penny, he wanted her. He wanted her badly.

He watched as she licked her lips, aware she was nervous. Dare couldn't help staring at her mouth, at the soft, plump pink curve of her lower lip. He wanted to kiss her so much he could hardly breathe.

"Well, my aunt, Lady St Clair, has organised a picnic at Holbrooke House this weekend. We will be away for a few days, but... perhaps...."

Dare held his breath, waiting for the end of the sentence.

"Possibly one day next week."

He let out the breath in a rush, giddy with relief, smiling so broadly he must look a complete fool. No change there, then.

"I shall look forward to it very much indeed. Next week seems a devilish long time to wait, but I will endure."

Miss Cadogan bit her lip, looking very much as if she was wondering what on earth she'd just done but she nodded. "I should get back to my father. He'll wonder where I've got to."

Dare smiled, reluctant to let her go but afraid he might spoil everything and make her rescind his invitation if he pressed her to stay. Yet, he did not need to speak as she hesitated, turning back to him.

"The Comte de Villen has an invitation to Lady St Clair's picnic," she said in a rush. "So you... you might come too, if...."

She blushed scarlet and turned away, hurrying back to her father.

He stood rooted to the spot for some time after that, unable to remove the daft grin from his face. Even when she was long gone from his sight, he lingered still, staring at the portrait of the two dogs, one solemn and grave, the other full of mischief. Something small and happy unfurled inside him, a tentative seed of hope daring to take root. She wanted to see him. The invitation for next week had been more than he'd ever expected to gain but she didn't want to wait a whole week any more than he did. He laughed aloud, only realising he'd done so when the lady beside him turned and stared at him as if he'd run mad. He didn't care.

Gesturing to the painting of the two dogs he said blithely, "It's a parody of the Dutch portrait tradition, you know."

Dare sauntered off through the crowd, humming merrily as he went.

Chapter 7

Dear Miss Smith,

You are most welcome for the books. Will you be going to the picnic at Holbrook House this week? I understand your guardian has been invited. Cat and Emmeline will be there. I do hope you can come.

I wasn't really cross that you laughed at me falling ~~on my ar~~ over and I'm sorry I shouted at you. That was badly done of me. The books were an apology if you hadn't guessed. Only a fellow doesn't like to look a fool in front of a girl.

I hope to see you at Holbrook.

—Excerpt of a letter from Lord Frederick Adolphus (younger son of the duke and duchess of Bedwin) to Miss Agatha Smith.

14th May 1839, Holbrook House, Sussex.

"This is awfully decent of you, Louis," Dare said as the carriage rumbled through the streets of London.

"My pleasure," Louis said. "I hate going to these affairs alone, so you are doing me a favour, besides you do not yet understand what you have let yourself in for."

Dare frowned, realising he recognised where they were. "This is Chelsea Village."

"Yes," Louis said dryly. "We are taking Aggie with us."

Dare's eyebrows went up. Four hours in a carriage with a small girl was not what he'd signed up for.

Louis smirked. "Still think I'm all heart?"

"Well, that was a dirty trick," he said, though he could not help but laugh. He was in too good a humour to complain about anything, even a child whining about being bored or travel sick. "Still, so long as she doesn't throw up on me, I shan't complain."

"You are very good," Louis said, his tone soothing. "However, Aggie is good company and does not whine or complain. I don't think she'll be sick, though we've never taken a long journey together," he added, frowning a little over that.

Ten minutes later and Aggie was ensconced in the carriage too. The child was alight with excitement but, as Louis promised, she did not misbehave or whine. After a couple of hours had passed and even the adults found the journey tedious, Dare suggested a game of cards.

"With pleasure," Louis said, sitting up straighter. "But watch this one. Don't you fall for those big blue eyes, she's a Captain Sharp and don't think otherwise."

"I ain't going to cheat you," she protested hotly, and then took a breath at Louis's mild look of interest. "I will not cheat," she repeated with dignity.

"I am very pleased to hear it. I have no doubt you can beat us both soundly without resorting to such dishonourable tactics."

"Is she that good?" Dare asked in alarm.

"Don't play for money," Louis said in an undertone.

Dare laughed.

They played for the best part of an hour and Dare was a little startled to discover that not only had Louis not exaggerated Aggie's skill, Louis was something else entirely. He was damned impossible to beat, a fact that was making his young ward wild with frustration.

"I'm so glad we aren't playing for real money," Dare said fervently. "Between the two of you I'd be bankrupt, not that it would take much."

Aggie glared at her guardian and folded her arms. Louis looked serenely back at her, the picture of innocence.

"Devil," she muttered.

"Baggage," Louis returned amicably. He sighed and put his head back against the squabs, closing his eyes.

"Well, deal another hand, then," Aggie protested. "You've got to give us a chance to win back our losses."

Louis sighed. "You didn't really lose anything, Aggie."

Aggie huffed with annoyance. "If that had been a real game, I'd be fifty quid down."

"Fifty *pounds*," Louis corrected. "And it serves you right for playing for such high stakes and not quitting sooner. Learn the lesson. Never play if you can't afford to lose."

"You ain't—*aren't*—any fun."

"Oh, hush child, I have a headache."

Dare watched as the girl peered at him. "Are you poorly? You're an awfully funny colour."

"I'm never unwell," Louis groused, but now she came to mention it Dare thought he looked pale.

"I'll play another hand if you like," Dare offered, hoping to pass the last hour or so amicably.

"All right," Aggie said grudgingly, but cast another anxious glance at Louis. "You're not going to be sick, are you?"

Louis cracked open one eye to cast her a look of revulsion and closed it again.

"Hmph," Aggie said, and turned her attention to the game.

They made it to the Royal Oak in Holbrook village where Dare and Louis were staying. Aggie would stay with the other children at Holbrook and was beside herself with excitement at the prospect of seeing her friends. Dare was a little surprised Louis wasn't staying at the house too and said as much.

"I believe the last time I was here I fell from grace," Louis remarked. "Not that I had far to fall. Truthfully, I was surprised to be invited, as Cassius is still away. I'm uncertain the earl likes me, so I am more than happy with the invitation without the privilege of being asked to stay at the house."

They readied themselves for the afternoon's picnic and returned to the carriage. Dare looked at Louis critically.

"You know, you really don't look well. You didn't go eating at the Cross Keys again, did you?"

"*Mon Dieu,* do not remind me of that," Louis said with feeling. "I would suspect poisoning from that appalling experience, except even I do not think the ill effects would last this long, as inexcusable as they were."

"You Frenchies have delicate constitutions, that's what it is." Dare grinned at him, for which he received an arctic glare.

"*Non,* just not the stomach of a rhinoceros," Louis said acidly.

Holbrook House was magnificent and the gardens a glorious sight to behold. Dare considered the place with a stab of envy. The money it must take to keep a place like this running to such a standard was staggering. He considered Rowsley Hall and felt an uncomfortable twist in his belly. It was far older than Holbrook and could be just as magnificent, if only he had the money to bring it back to what it had once been. If only his parents hadn't been so besotted with each other, and travelling, his father might have noticed the bloody steward was a crook before he'd turned up his toes. A swell of anger and resentment rose inside him and Dare forced it back down, just as he always did. The past was dead and gone. *They* were dead and gone. He alone had the problem to deal with. He alone. Well, didn't that make a bloody change? Aware he would grow maudlin if he didn't stop thinking about it, Dare reminded himself he was here to see Miss Cadogan and his spirits—never long depressed—rose considerably. He was in a beautiful spot, to see a beautiful girl, and he'd be a dashed dull dog if he couldn't find pleasure in that.

The weather was that peculiarly English perfect spring day that was neither too hot nor too cold, but bright and glorious. The cobalt sky was dotted with fluffy white clouds and a gentle breeze ruffled parasols and lace trims but did not disturb anyone's elegantly arranged coiffure. Heartened to believe he had a great deal to look forward to, Dare set off to find Miss Cadogan.

Louis let out a breath. He was hot and his head ached like the very devil. He just wanted to lie down somewhere quiet. Having been surprised to have been invited to this event at all, however, he did not dare make an excuse not to come for fear of causing further offence. Blasted Madame Lafitte had made both him and Nic look the very worst kind of libertines on their last visit, and he suspected the Duchess of Bedwin had played a hand in getting him invited at all. For some reason he could not understand—bearing in mind she was quite obviously in love with her husband—the woman seemed to have a soft spot for him. Indeed she treated him like one of the family and made no bones about the fact she thought he needed mothering. She somewhat baffled him, but he must remember to thank her for intervening on his behalf.

Still, he did not feel up to the prospect of greeting his hosts just yet and walked to a shady part of the garden, praying no one would see him and he could find a place to sit quietly. It was with great relief that he found a bench, tucked away in a hidden spot, and sat himself down.

He awoke with a start sometime later.

"Oh, I am sorry. I wasn't certain whether or not I should disturb you, but you've missed lunch."

Louis blinked, disorientated for a moment. Green eyes stared at him from a rounded, pink-cheeked face.

"Miss Evie," he said, sitting up straighter. He sucked in a breath as his head pounded and his stomach roiled.

"A hangover, is it?" she asked with a sympathetic smile.

"No. Not a hangover. I don't know what it is." Though he'd never felt so bloody awful, even with a hangover. He put a hand to his temples and rubbed.

"Well, don't worry, I shan't disturb you. I only brought you something to eat, as you'd already found a place to hide, and I did promise."

Louis looked at the plate in her hand and bile rose in his throat. *Merde. Oh, no. No, no, no.*

"I do beg your pardon, Miss but... but...." He leapt to his feet, moving as far from her as he could get before his stomach rebelled and he was violently sick.

Louis leant against the tree beside him as his head swam. He ached all over and staying on his feet seemed to take considerable effort.

"*Merde*," he muttered with feeling.

"Oh, you poor thing, you are unwell. Here, take my hanky."

Louis groaned as he realised Miss Evie had not done the decent thing and gone away to leave him to his misery in peace.

He took the handkerchief all the same and wiped his mouth.

"Thank you," he said. "I should consider it a great favour if you'd forget you ever saw this."

"Don't be a twit. Everyone gets sick," she said briskly. "Was it something you ate?"

"I don't think so."

"Come along. I'll take you back to the house and find you somewhere quiet to lay down and a cold cloth for your head."

"There's really no—"

A cool hand pressed against his forehead. "Good heavens, you're burning up. Come along now."

"No, I do not wish to cause trouble. This has been quite mortifying enough. I shall take my carriage back to the inn."

Louis turned and straightened as best he could, only to meet the girl's stern gaze.

"Do you really want to spend ten minutes in a stuffy, jolting carriage?"

Louis swallowed hard. No. No, he really did not.

"No, I didn't think so. Now, do come along and stop being so silly. I'll take you in the back way, so no one will see. I know this place like my own home, for we nearly always come for their summer house party."

In ordinary circumstances he might have bristled at being managed by a chit of a girl of sixteen. As it was, he did not have the strength to argue. Louis nodded and took a step and then stopped, closing his eyes as his head spun in a sickening fashion.

"Here, lean on me."

Too sick to protest, Louis allowed the girl to drape his arm over her shoulders and took some of his weight.

As good as her word, Evie escorted him into the great house, found a small quiet parlour in the back where he would not be disturbed, closed the curtains, and bade him lie down. Meanwhile she bustled off and came back shortly after with a servant in tow. They brought him a jug of cold water, some willow bark tea, a basin should he have further need of it, and a cold cloth for his head.

"There," she said, once she had bullied him into drinking every drop of the tea and placed the cloth upon his forehead. She was a remarkably managing female for one so young. "Now you get some rest and don't worry about a thing. I shall explain everything to Lady St Clair."

Louis made a sound of distress.

"Do stop fretting. All will be well. Now, is there anything else you need?"

"My ward," Louis said. "Miss Agatha Smith. She's here and...."

"Say no more," Evie said with a smile. "I shall find her and let her know. Don't worry, I will make sure she is entertained. Do get some rest now. I shall come back later and check on you."

With that she left, closing the door behind her. With a sigh, Louis closed his eyes and gave in.

Much to his frustration, Dare learned that the Cadogan family had not yet arrived. As he mixed little in polite society, Dare didn't know anyone here that he wished to speak to and those he knew would be unwilling to make further introductions as his—and his friends'—reputation proceeded him. He'd thought he might find Bainbridge, as he and the St Clairs' son Cassius had been at school together, but Dare could find no sign of him. Louis was nowhere to be seen either, so Dare milled about on his own, admiring the scenery and enjoying the lavish lunch that was provided.

Once lunch was over, he made his way into the house and see if there was any word of the Cadogan family yet from the servants. In the grand entrance hall, he found a footman who told him the family had arrived a little over half an hour ago and would be down shortly. Relieved, Dare thanked the footman, who hurried off about his business. He was about to make his way back outside when a high-pitched shriek came from behind the door he was passing. Afraid someone was being attacked, Dare hurried inside.

"Aggie!" he said in alarm on finding the girl alone. She looked flushed and her eyes glittered feverishly. "Whatever is the—"

"Oh, do help! *Please!*" she cried, breathless with anxiety. She was tugging at a heavy ladder which gave access to the towering bookshelves that ran the length and breadth of the room and right up to the high ceiling.

"Whatever are you doing? If you want a book that badly, surely there's one on the lower—"

"That's not a book!" she snapped in frustration.

Dare followed the direction she pointed in, up to the highest shelf and a tiny white kitten that was balanced on the edge. It gave a piteous mewl and wobbled.

"Oh!" Aggie cried.

"All right, all right, don't panic," Dare said, lifting the ladder and moving it over to the kitten. "How on earth did the idiotic creature get up there?"

"Oh, a boy in the stables said I might have one and so I took him so I could show Monsieur Le Comte and ask if I could keep it, but I couldn't find him anywhere. So I thought to leave her here whilst I looked, for she was getting fed up with being held. I think she must have climbed up the curtains and—"

"Fine, fine, I get the picture," Dare said, climbing the ladder.

As he reached the top, however, the stupid feline took fright and did not recognise the face of a heroic rescuer. Instead it arched its spine and spat furiously, backing up. Too frightened to be as nimble as a cat ought, it slipped on the high shine of the bookshelf and tumbled off the edge.

Then things happened very quickly.

Aggie screamed and Dare lunged sideways, too far and too fast for his own good. He caught the squirming kitten by the scruff of the neck and dropped it to the girl, who was holding out her skirts. The kitten bounced harmlessly down. With his hand now free, Dare made to grasp at the shelf, but the shiny surface aided him no more than the cat and his grip slithered off the edge. And then he was falling....

Elspeth hurried down the stairs. Her family were still dressing, but she had managed to get ready in record time, much to everyone's amazement. She did not know why she was being so ridiculous, but her heart was thudding with anticipation. No matter how many times she reminded herself that Lord Roxborough was a worthless devil who was up to his neck in debt and had promised to ruin her to ensure he could get her dowry, she still wanted to see him. Though it was insane, she had believed every word he'd told her at the Academy exhibition. He had apologised for his behaviour and he'd said... he'd said he wanted her more than he wanted the money. Her heart fluttered in her chest as she remembered the look in his eyes when he'd said that. There had been such sincerity, such longing, for *her*.

Elspeth had never seen a man look at her like that before and that it was a man like Lord Roxborough, so big and handsome and virile....

She let out a breath and forced herself to concentrate on the stairs before she tripped and broke her stupid neck.

Elspeth had just reached the grand entrance hall when a door flew open, and a girl barrelled out of it.

"Miss Cadogan!" she cried, running towards her and clutching a tiny white kitten. "Oh, help, help... do help him! I must get someone to fetch a doctor."

"Aggie?" Elspeth exclaimed in surprise, but before she could question the girl, she had run out into the garden.

Elspeth hurried in the direction Aggie had indicated and stepped into the library. Her breath caught at the sight of the big figure crumpled on the floor, surrounded by books.

"Lord Roxborough!"

Elspeth ran to his side and knelt beside him as he groaned and lifted a hand to his head.

"My lord, whatever happened? Are you hurt? Oh, do speak to me. Is anything broken?"

He blinked, staring at her, his hazel eyes widening.

"Elspeth?"

"Yes, I'm here. Are you hurt?"

She held her breath as he gazed at her and she saw that same look again, the depth of longing enough to make her want to cry.

"I'm dreaming," he murmured, sounding somewhat dazed. "I must be. You can't possibly be real, for I've seen nothing as lovely as you in all my life. I can't stop thinking about you, Elspeth, about how different my life would be if you were in it. I'm so tired of being alone. I don't want to be alone anymore."

"Oh," she said, melting under the force of such a declaration.

He lifted his hand, tracing the curve of her cheek with a fingertip and with such reverence it made her feel like she was truly everything he had ever dreamed of. Her heart thudding with too many emotions, Elspeth covered his hand with hers and turned into it, kissing his palm. His breath hitched at the touch of her lips against his skin, and she smiled, hardly able to breathe herself, the moment was so very overwhelming.

"It's all right," she said. "You're not alone."

"Elspeth," he whispered, and her name was a plea, a prayer, filled with yearning, with desire, with everything she never dreamed she wanted to hear so badly until this very moment.

His hand moved from her cheek to the back of her neck, pulling her down and she went willingly. The touch of his lips to hers was electric, like being woken by a lightning strike, her entire being energised, jolted from a life where she must have been always half asleep for now... now she was entirely awake.

His mouth was soft and warm and so tender, so right, that when his tongue sought entry, it did not occur to her to deny him, not for a moment. It still did not occur to her that this was foolish and reckless and wrong when he pulled her down, into his arms and deepened the kiss, nor when she found him above her, his hands moving over her as she gasped with pleasure. She was intoxicated, drunk on him and her first taste of desire, wanting more, never wanting it to stop.

Dare was lost, drowning in a sea of want and need. Perhaps it was the blow to the head that made him lose his senses, for his mind was thick and sluggish, or perhaps it was all her. It was like being caught in a fever dream. He was beyond reason. His sanity— or the ragged article that passed as such—had simply waved a white flag the moment he'd seen her face full of concern for him. No one but her had ever looked at him like that in all his life. He'd cracked his head too many times to count, and broken bones, half-drowned himself one time, and not once had anyone ever come running and looked as if they might cry because he was hurt, because they feared losing him. But she did.

He needed her, needed to see that concern in her eyes and know there was someone in the world who thought he was worth something. Someone who would worry for him and look for him if he were late home, or fuss over him when he was poorly. There were his friends, of course, but they were not tender creatures, all of them forced by family or circumstance to band together and find some comfort in not being alone when they were named as the odd ones, the bad ones, the troublemakers.

"Daire," she said, and the breathless sound of his name, his real name, not the stupid nickname he'd earned, was enough to make his heart swell.

"Darling, darling, say you'll marry me. I can't bear it. I'll run mad," he murmured against the elegant curve of her neck. Oh, lord but she smelled like vanilla and sunshine and tasted like every good thing he'd ever wanted and never got. "I need you. I need you to save me from this god-awful loneliness. I want you so much… please, Elspeth."

He didn't even know what he was saying, didn't care, only that the words were dragged up from some secret place that he never allowed himself to consider, let alone reveal to anyone else.

"Oh, Daire, I… I can't think when, when… oh." She gasped as his hand palmed her breast, squeezing gently and rubbing his thumb over the taut little nub of flesh he could feel beneath her gown.

He paused, staring down at her, at those lovely green-gold eyes, hazy with desire, and realised they were on the floor of the library. Some shred of sanity fought its way through a thick fog of lust and emotion.

"My God, Elspeth," he began, appalled at what he'd done, but before he could rectify things, the door swung open.

"It's here, I swear it. Cass showed it to me one summer when we were boys and—"

A sickening sensation rose in Dare's gut as he looked up and saw Bainbridge leading in what seemed to be half the bloody garden party. Everyone froze, staring down at him, on top of Elspeth, with his hand full of her breast. It did not need a lot of explanation.

Bainbridge, the utter bastard, grinned at him. "Well, well, Dare, old man. It looks like wedding bells are ringing any day now. Congratulations."

Chapter 8

Dear Madam,

Please accept my sincere apologies for Agatha's absence from the school. As you know I sought permission for her to accompany me on a visit to friends in Sussex. Sadly both myself and Agatha were taken ill with influenza and have been extremely poorly. Please rest assured that the best care has been taken of her and that I will escort her back to the school as soon as she is well enough to travel.

—Excerpt of a letter from Louis César de Montluc, Comte de Villen, to Mrs Thompson, head mistress, Phoenix School for Girls, Chelsea Village.

20th May 1839, St Clair's London Residence, St James, London.

"You don't have to go through with it, darling. No one should have to marry a man they don't love, scandal or no. We shall all support you no matter what, you know that."

"Listen to your mother, Elspeth. I know it will be hard on you, but we have powerful friends, and I will do everything I can to limit the damage. We will protect you against the worst of it."

Elspeth looked up at her Uncle Jasper, the Earl of St Clair. He was still a very handsome man and his unusual turquoise eyes glinted with emotion. Her poor mama had been crying all morning, and even Greer had stuck to her like glue, holding her hand. Her papa looked as if he wanted to kill something with his bare hands. He would too, given half the chance. They had been wonderful, kind and supportive, without the slightest hint of condemnation for her idiotic behaviour. They would indeed do whatever they could to protect her from the most obvious public snubs, but they could not stop the gleeful little comments spoken in whispers just loud enough to be heard, nor the sneers and half-concealed looks of contempt which would inevitably come her way.

The thing she could not believe, the thing that made her so wild with fury, was how easily she'd been taken in. She'd dared him to do his worst, bragged that he wasn't clever enough to best her, but he hadn't needed brains. No. He'd only needed to turn those soulful puppy dog eyes on her and say a few sweet words and she'd melted like the veriest ninny. She'd known she was green where men and seduction were concerned, but she had not been prepared for how it would feel, had not understood the power of such a devastating attraction that the mere touch of his lips would have her beneath him, willing to do whatever he wanted. No, not willing, *demanding.* Her cheeks burned and she felt sick. Oh, God, she hated him. She hated him for catching her with such ease, for lying and manipulating her, for making her feel such a fool. He'd said he would be honest with her, but there was no honesty in this.

She looked up as her father crouched down before her. His expression was one of such concern her throat grew tight. "Elspeth, darling, listen to me. We could go away. A trip abroad. You'd enjoy that. We could go to France and Italy and see beautiful places...."

"It will still be here when I get back, Papa. Even if we stayed away for a year, two years, five even. It will still be here, and it will damage Greer too, and poor little Alana." Elspeth swallowed and shook her head. "No. There is no other choice. I have been a fool and I must pay for that, but at least now I know. I shall go into this marriage with my eyes open to the kind of man he is. I shan't be hurt again."

Her father's jaw tightened, a muscle ticking as his eyes darkened with fury.

"No," he growled. "That you won't."

Elspeth reached out and took his hands, squeezing them. "He's not a cruel man, he won't hurt me, and he does not yet know what he has taken on. I shall not be a victim, Papa. I have more spirit than that."

"We know that, darling," her mama said, her voice thick. "Only... Only I had so hoped to see you as happy as we have been."

She sobbed and her father leapt to his feet, pulling his wife into a firm embrace.

Elspeth smiled. "No one could be as happy as you two." They looked up as the door opened and her Aunt Harriet came in, her expression as grave and worried as everyone else's.

"They're here."

Elspeth nodded and got to her feet, smoothing down her skirts. "I'm ready."

Dare felt sick to his stomach. He'd tried to speak to Elspeth after they'd been caught, tried to apologise, to explain, but there had been too many people and his head had been splitting. A concussion, the doctor had told him later, and he'd spent most of the next three days in bed whilst Bainbridge made the arrangements for their hasty nuptials. A special license and a ceremony at the St Clair's home, if her father and her uncle didn't dismember him and scatter the bits about London the moment he crossed the threshold. He could hardly blame them.

The events of that fateful day were still hazy, at least the bit where he'd woken and seen Elspeth. He remembered the wave of longing, the need for her, but what in the name of God had possessed him to treat her so... so disrespectfully? On the floor of the library, damn him to hell! He ought to be horsewhipped. He almost wished someone would, maybe then he'd feel a little less wretched. Guilt swam in his guts, for he'd got just what he wanted. The vast dowry meant he could restore Rowsley just as he'd hoped to, clear his blasted father's debts, and perhaps live a more settled life. Once again, he saw the vision in his mind of the house that he had always loathed for the years of misery he'd spent there, transformed into something else. For the briefest time, he'd had a glimpse of something that looked like home, with Elspeth, with a family... with him *belonging*. That was all it had been, though: a glimpse of a dream. She would hate him now. She would believe he'd trapped her just as he'd promised to do, and she would never trust him again. He wanted to weep.

As it was, he steeled himself and stood before the vicar.

Elspeth never so much as looked at him, but gave her replies without a quaver. He could only admire her, she was so strong, so self-possessed. Dare. by contrast, horribly aware of the tide of resentment and fury cast in his direction, stammered and stuttered through his parts, wishing fervently that God would smite him for having the temerity to marry such a creature as the one beside him.

Finally it was done, and the vicar said, "You may kiss the bride."

Dare turned, only expecting to give her a kiss on the cheek, or perhaps even lift her hand to his lips, but she turned away from him.

"Well, that's done, then," she said, as unmoved as if she'd just finished some tedious legal business to buy a piece of land, or a horse. "I'd best see if my bags are packed. If you'll excuse me."

Dare watched her go and felt his heart sink to his boots as her father and uncle approached him.

"A word," her father said.

Dare could do nothing other than nod and follow them out of the room.

Elspeth sat in the carriage that would take them to the hotel for their wedding night, opposite her husband. Her *husband*. Good God. She was Lady Roxborough. It was a struggle to know if she ought to laugh or cry. If she did either, she had the horrible suspicion she would not stop. She dared a glance at him as his attention was focused on something outside the window. God, but she'd been the biggest fool on earth to think that man could ever be serious about needing her. He looked exactly like what he was: a big, handsome, worthless frippery fellow, who cared not a jot for anyone or anything except his own pleasure.

Well, if he thought being married to her was going to be a walk in the park, he had another think coming. He had ruined her life. She couldn't even teach anymore, for the circumstances of her scandalous marriage were too public and would bring shame upon the school. The idea of damaging everything Eliza had worked for was too appalling for words. Perhaps in time she could return to it, but not for years, and he would pay for that. She would make him realise no amount of money was worth marrying a woman who held you in contempt.

He cleared his throat and Elspeth forced herself to turn towards him. Now that she looked carefully, she saw he was pale, dark circles beneath his eyes. No doubt facing her parents and her aunt and uncle had been a strain, even for a heartless bastard like him. To think she had believed she was falling in love with... with that.

"I thought we would spend a couple of nights at Browns and then journey down to Rowsley Hall."

"Did you?" she replied coldly.

There was a slight pause before he carried on. "Well, yes. It's in Derbyshire. I expect you know that, but I think you'll like it. At least, I hope you will. It's a rambling old place and—"

"I'm staying here."

The words hung between them and the air seemed to thicken.

"What do you mean?" he asked cautiously.

"Are you hard of hearing, my lord? You may have got what you wanted from me, and there is nothing I can do to stop you spending my money as you please, but I am going nowhere with you. The season is in full swing and I intend to remain and enjoy the rest of it as best I can. You may do as you like. Stay, go, I don't care."

"Elspeth, please...."

"Please?"

Her voice trembled with rage, and all the hurt and anger she'd buried down so deep she would be able to go through with the farce of a ceremony came bubbling to the surface.

"'Oh, please, Elspeth, I want you so much,'" she said, mocking him now and pleased to see he had shame enough to blush.

"I did. I still do," he said stiffly.

She snorted at that. "A pity, for you'll not have me, or do you intend to compound your villainy by taking me by force? I can tell you my father is just longing for my say so to thrash you into next week."

"I wouldn't! I would never...!" he exclaimed, so obviously outraged that one tiny layer of misery and fear slid free.

She had not believed he would treat her so badly as that, but then she had believed a great deal about him and been proven a fool for doing so.

"Elspeth, I know we've got off to a bad start, and I know it's all my fault, but we are married now. Could we not at least try to be friends?"

Elspeth turned away from him as she felt tears prick at her eyes. She shook her head. "I'll never forgive you. Not for trapping me, because you told me you would. I was the fool for forgetting that, but you made me believe...."

She snapped her mouth shut and thanked providence as the carriage drew up outside the hotel.

"It was an accident, Elspeth. I did not arrange that scene. I know it must seem as though—"

A footman opened the door and Elspeth got out. She would not stay to listen to more lies, to look into his eyes and see what she thought was sincerity when it was just as false as the rest of him. She had been fooled once and that was her own stupid fault. It would not happen again.

3rd June 1839, Lady Repton's Ball, Berkeley Square, London.

Dare had spent his wedding night asleep on the sofa of their luxurious suite, and the night after that, and all the nights following for two weeks. Not that he actually slept, he was too miserable for that. The days had a certain routine to them, which involved Elspeth leaving midmorning, alone save for her maid and a footman, and coming back laden with gowns and hats and gloves and shoes and all manner of things. Not that he begrudged her anything—he wanted her to have whatever she wished—but he did not think such things had been important to her before and knew she was only making a point, daring him to stop her.

He had dared to do many stupid things in his life, but he wasn't utterly suicidal.

Of an evening they went out, together, though Dare felt quite invisible. He'd hoped that, if he was patient and reasonable, she would see he was not such a devil as she had thought and would allow him to talk to her. He had tried to talk, to explain, but she always cut him off, leaving the room if he attempted a conversation. He was being punished, and he accepted that he deserved it. He had begun this, after all. Dare had threatened to trap her and had done so. Frankly, he was lucky he'd not been strangled in his sleep. Yet, even knowing this, it was hard.

Tonight they were at Lady Repton's ball, a lavish affair indeed, with the highest echelons of society attending. Normally, it was an event Dare would avoid like the plague. Normally, he knew damn well it was an event that would see Elspeth sitting in a corner, tapping her toes and hoping to remain unnoticed by all but her closest friends, those in whose company she felt happiest. Not so now. Tonight, and at all the other events they had attended together, she was as bright and vivacious as her sister always was, as her mother had always been. She drew people to her, attracted them with her laughter and her wit... everyone but Dare. He knew better than to approach her and give her a target in public. She might make a fool of him in private, but he had pride enough not to allow her that. So, he watched her dance and laugh and turn people's heads, and kept his distance. Always on the outside looking in.

"Still holding your balls in a vice, is she?"

Dare turned to see Bainbridge's sardonic gaze follow Elspeth about the room.

"Don't," he said, not in the mood for his friend's rather harsh view of the world.

"For God's sake, Dare, just make her listen to you! Get angry if you must, but sit her down and explain yourself."

He snorted at that. "Ah, yes, prove to her I'm a bully as well as a liar. That should do nicely."

"Well, what's your plan, then? Assuming you have one," Bainbridge demanded, folding his arms.

Dare shrugged. "I don't, really. Only I hope that this anger will burn itself out. It's not who she is. She's been trapped and so she's rattling the bars of her cage."

"Damnation, you're not a prison guard."

"Aren't I?" Dare demanded. "I've ruined all the things she loves. She was a teacher, Bainbridge, at that charity school of Lady Elizabeth's, but now she can't go back because she's not respectable enough. She's had to leave her family home, and she's married to a man she wouldn't look twice at if...."

He snapped his mouth shut, too overwrought to say any more than that.

"Dare," Bainbridge said, and the raw sympathy in his cynical friend's eyes was almost more than Dare could stand. "She's lucky to have you. I know that, and eventually she'll figure it out too, if she's as clever as you say she is."

"Oh, she's clever. Clever enough to recognise a bad bargain, but you know I... I...." Dare shook his head.

He'd thought perhaps he could endure it, for a while at least, but it hurt too much to be ignored again, to ache for someone to love him when that someone would rather he wasn't around, would rather have fun somewhere he couldn't follow.

"No. It doesn't matter. I thought I could do it, but I can't. I can't do it again, Bainbridge. I was a bloody fool to ever think it was a good idea to trap her, but I didn't know her then, didn't know what... what might be possible, but I do now and... and I can't...."

Bainbridge took his arm, guiding him away from the crowds as he was getting emotional, and people were beginning to notice.

"Do what again?" Bainbridge demanded.

Dare swallowed hard and shook his head. "Never mind. Do me a favour, will you? See she gets back to the hotel safely."

He had to get away. If he was to be ignored, then at least let it be at a distance where he felt less like a child with his nose pressed to the glass of a sweet shop window. He was used to absence, used to being alone. That he could deal with.

"What? Why?" Bainbridge ran after him as he hurried out of the ballroom to the entrance hall. If he stayed here any longer he would cause a scene, and he'd done Elspeth enough damage already without that. "Where are you going?"

"Home," he said with a bitter laugh, and walked away.

Chapter 9

Dearest Greer,

How strange it is, after all our years of bickering, to realise how dreadfully I miss you. I am utterly miserable. I am punishing my husband, day and night for what he has done to me and yet it brings no satisfaction, only leaves me hollow and wretched, yet I cannot forgive him either. He looks at me with such grief in his eyes and my heart aches and wants to forgive all, and then I remember it is all a game to him, another manipulation. I can never trust him, and that breaks what remains of my heart. For heaven's sake do not tell mama and papa for they shall be distraught, and I cannot bear for them to be punished for my foolishness.

Only Greer, my dearest sister, curb your wild ways and have a care for your future, for there is no mistake graver than marrying a man you regret being tied to for the rest of your days.

—Excerpt of a letter from Lady Elspeth Roxborough to her twin, Miss Greer Cadogan.

Still the 3rd of June 1839, Lady Repton's Ball, Berkeley Square, London.

Where the devil was the wretched man? Elspeth cursed. She'd spent the entire evening avoiding her husband, but she was tired now, weary in a way she'd never experienced before. It was a kind of hopeless lethargy that seemed to settle deep in her bones and make this awful pretence of merriment a heavy weight to bear. She just wanted to sleep and forget the horrible mess her life had become for a short while before she must do it all again.

"He's gone."

Elspeth looked around to see the Marquess of Bainbridge regarding her with an unfriendly expression. He lounged against the wall, a lazy posture that did not fool her, and instead resembled nothing so much as a great cat lying in wait for its prey. She had never liked the man, though she did not know him at all other than by repute. Daire had introduced him the day they'd married, and Bainbridge had looked as little impressed by her as she'd been by him. He had a reputation for being unpredictable, possibly even unstable, but he was certainly known to be cynical, a libertine, and the very definition of a hell-born babe.

"Who has gone where?" she asked, ensuring her voice remained cool and disinterested.

"Your husband. You've made him so miserable he's gone away rather than endure another strike from your claws, you spiteful little cat."

Elspeth gaped at him, at the unfairness of his words.

"I've made *him* miserable," she repeated, so breathless with indignation it was hard to speak at all.

"Oh, come on, my Lady Roxborough, you looked happy enough in his embrace when we stumbled upon you. You wanted him well enough then, I reckon."

Her cheeks flamed with fury and humiliation, but she put her chin up, refusing to be cowed by him and his vile insinuations. "Ah, yes. Your well-timed entry into the room. How could I forget? Fortuitous indeed, was it not?"

Bainbridge laughed at that and pushed off the wall, standing straight. "I cannot deny it. Yet strange as it seems, it truly was not planned."

Elspeth made a sound of disgust and went to turn away, but Bainbridge stopped her, taking her arm. She gasped at his temerity in touching her, but he let her go at once.

"Wait," he said, his voice harsh. "You need to listen to me."

"Indeed, I do not——" she began, but he spoke over her.

"Damnation! Someone must make you so you'll listen to me if even if I must shout over the blasted room to make myself heard. Never doubt my propensity for causing a scene, my lady. I promise you'll be sorry for it."

Furious, but not doubting him in the least for she'd heard stories aplenty, Elspeth stilled, glaring at him. She did not need her reputation sullied further than it had been by whatever this man was going to say next.

"Speak your piece, then, but be quick about it," she snapped.

He gave her a mocking smile and inclined his head a little. "A thousand thanks for your indulgence."

"*Speak.*" Elspeth clenched her fists, angry enough to strike him if he didn't stop tormenting her.

"Very well. That fateful day, Dare was in the library to help some fool child with a kitten of all things, and yes, I know he tried to tell you and you scoffed at the story. Honestly, I don't blame you, but if you knew Dare a little better, you'd realise it is exactly the kind of stupid situation he would get himself in. In any case, the kitten had somehow climbed to the highest shelf and the child was working herself into a passion over it. Dare climbed the ladder, grabbed the stupid feline as it fell and, in doing so, overbalanced himself. He fell and hit his head. The blow knocked him out cold. The child was distraught, thinking he'd killed himself."

Elspeth frowned, remembering Aggie crying that she must fetch a doctor, and the little white kitten. Something uneasy stirred in her heart. She had assumed Dare had paid the child to put her up to it. She liked Aggie very much, but the girl had lived on the streets and had a slightly skewed view of morality that Elspeth had not yet begun to unravel and understand. It had seemed entirely possible Dare had talked her into playing a prank. Bainbridge ploughed on, though, his words hard and uncompromising.

"After you were discovered and all hell broke loose, we called a doctor who said he had a concussion. He was in bed for the next three days with a blinding headache. If not for that, he might have called on you and made you listen to reason. As it was, he didn't see you until the day you married, where you ignored him, and your father and uncle put the fear of God in him. Since then you've made him so bloody wretched, he's drowning in guilt for having ruined your life, and as miserable as sin because the poor fool actually cares for you."

"I—" Elspeth began only to have Bainbridge silence her again.

"No. You listen, I speak. You've had your say, Lady Roxborough. You've made my best friend so miserable he's gone back to that blasted house he loathes being alone in so much rather than stay with you. I know he threatened to trap you—that was my idea, incidentally—and I know he *did* trap you, but strange as it seems, it was by accident, not design. He's a good man," he added gruffly, as if he was unused to saying anything nice about anyone or anything. "The very best of men, and you may not realise it, but you're bloody lucky to have him. I truly hope you're not the cold bitch you've made yourself out to be these past weeks, and were only punishing him because you misunderstood."

Elspeth stared at him, wanting to believe him so much she barely flinched at being called a cold bitch, but it was all so fantastical. How could it be a coincidence when he'd warned her time and again he would do just this? And yet....

"He made me believe he cared for me, that I meant something, and then...."

Her voice quavered and she closed her mouth, refusing to get emotional in front of this awful man, but to her surprise his hard expression eased.

"Then he does," he said. "Dare is a bit of a loose screw, I grant you. He's always in one scrape or another, and he acts before he thinks, but he's not a liar. He's too honest for his own good, that's the trouble. If he told you something you may rely on it being true, and there's not many people in this world you can say that about."

Elspeth swallowed. She didn't know what to think. This man was Daire's friend. Daire might have put him up to it. The whole thing might just be another great lie to manipulate her, except... except Aggie *had* been there with the kitten, and Daire *had* looked as if he'd fallen and... and he'd looked so wretched these past days. Her heart felt squeezed within her chest. What if everything he'd said, all those declarations about needing her and wanting her, what if it had all been true?

I need you. I need you to save me from this god-awful loneliness. I want you so much... please, Elspeth.

He was lonely, she had known that. He was lonely and she'd shut him out, cut him dead, not allowed him even a chance to explain. Her stomach twisted with regret and uncertainty and... and what if she believed this was all true, only to discover he had fooled her all over again? It had hurt so much to believe that she'd fallen for soft words and softer looks, and they'd been nothing but a fabrication. It had hurt very deeply.

"I want to believe you," she said, wishing it were any other man but this one she were facing.

If only August had been there that day, she might believe what he told her, but he'd gone away to the country the day before the party at Holbrook.

Bainbridge shrugged. "It's the truth, but I can't make you believe it. I don't blame you for being sceptical about anything that comes out of my mouth, but for God's sake talk to him. Give him a chance. You're going to be married a long time, better that you do it with some kindness between you. If you make it a battle of wills... well, everyone will suffer."

There was something in the way he said it that made her believe he meant that very deeply, and then she remembered. His parents, the Duke and Duchess of Axton, had been at daggers drawn their entire married lives. Their arguments had been legendary until the duchess had died.

Elspeth nodded. Bainbridge was right. One way or another they had to find a way forward, whether or not he'd trapped her. She must give him a chance to explain, to make her believe, or to make amends. It would take time to trust him, but perhaps something could be salvaged from this mess, perhaps... perhaps everything he'd said had been true and there was a chance for something more than that. It seemed too much to hope for after these past weeks of unhappiness, but she held onto a tiny seed of hope and prayed she would not regret it.

"I will speak to him," she said.

Bainbridge let out a breath. "Good. That's good."

They stood awkwardly together until he spoke again. "He asked me to see you safe back to the hotel."

Elspeth blanched at the idea of sharing a carriage with this man.

"There's no need," she said at once. "I have friends here who will see me back."

"Then I shall take you to them and ensure that they do," he said, in a voice that brooked no argument. "I promised."

Elspeth sighed, recognising one of those male kinds of promises that were of the honour or death variety. "Very well."

Bainbridge held out his arm to her, and reluctantly, Elspeth took it.

"Are you certain you are well enough for this?" Louis reached out and tucked a dark curl behind Aggie's ear.

The child was still pale and wan, but her blue eyes glittered with determination.

"I am," she said. "I must. Lord Roxborough was very kind to save little Bianca, and he didn't trap poor Miss Cadogan into marrying him. I must tell her that."

Louis smiled, wanting to hug the girl to him, but uncertain if that was appropriate. He had appointed himself her guardian, but was not her brother nor her father. She had no one else, however, and he remembered the aching loneliness of never being held, having no one ever touch him with affection. Damn whatever was appropriate. He put his arm about Aggie and tugged her closer, leaning down to kiss the top of her head.

"You are a very good girl, and I am proud of you."

Aggie looked up at him, her lower lip trembling. "B-But it's all my fault," she said, her voice unsteady. "If I'd not taken the kitten without asking you first, if I'd not left her in the library unattended…."

"You came to find me," Louis said gently. "And she is such a beautiful kitten, how could you resist when you were offered?"

"I've never had anything so pretty and soft," Aggie whispered.

119

"I know, child. This is none of your doing. If we'd not both been so poorly, we could have said something sooner, but we knew nothing was amiss, and you were so very ill."

Louis's heart clenched. He'd never been sick a day in his life before, but the influenza had made him as weak and wretched as a starved kitten himself. He'd been barely conscious for the first few days and when he was well enough to realise how ill Aggie was he'd been beside himself. He'd very much feared he would lose her, and the pain of that loss had staggered him.

Their carriage pulled up outside of Brown's hotel and Aggie took a deep breath.

"Are you ready?" Louis asked.

Aggie took hold of his hand, curling her little fingers tightly about his. She gave a nod.

"Yes," she said.

Elspeth was packing as her maid announced the Comte de Villen and his ward, Miss Agatha Smith.

"Show them in," she said at once, her heart beating with anticipation. Surely, there was only one reason they would be here.

She held her breath as the Comte came in with Aggie who was holding his hand for all she was worth, her great blue eyes wide with anxiety.

"Good morning, Lady Roxborough," the comte said with a smile and a polite bow as Aggie gave a little dip of a curtsey. "I do hope you will forgive our intrusion, but Agatha here has something she needs to tell you."

Chapter 10

Dear Grace,

Of course I didn't fall in love with him, you great ninny. Yes, he is very beautiful indeed, but he is my friend, and he was so very poorly. I only kept him company and read to him a little when he was well enough to leave his bed and come to the parlour. He was so worried about Agatha I had to do something to take his mind off her or he would have fretted himself to death. Anyway, never mind that, have you persuaded your papa to let you come out early or is he still insisting you wait until you are eighteen? I should so like to have your company.

—Excerpt of a letter from Miss Evie Knight, (daughter of Lady Helena and Mr Gabriel Knight) to Miss Grace Weston, (daughter of Baron Solo Rothborn and Lady Jemima Rothborn).

4th June 1839, Rowsley Hall, Derbyshire.

Elspeth could still hardly believe she was in Derby when she had been in London just that morning. It was not her first journey on a train by any means, but it was the first time when the fun of the journey itself had not been the reason for boarding. To have realised her journey corresponded with the opening of the Midland Railway had been such a happy coincidence, she decided it must be a good omen and took it as such. Of course, getting a ticket at such short notice had not been easy for the inaugural voyage, but her uncle, the earl, had dealt with that for her. Her family were still sceptical about her decision, but they could see she had made up her mind and so had moved heaven and earth to make it happen. Even so, she had only just made it in time, and it seemed to take all the journey to allow her heart to settle into a quieter rhythm.

Now, as the carriage she had hired at the station drew her and her maid closer to Rowsley Hall, it seemed to pick up again, beating erratically.

"My lady, you realise we'll be here before his lordship? If he came by carriage, he won't be here before tomorrow evening at best, probably not until the day after."

Elspeth looked to her maid, Bertha Jones. She was a slight, serious girl of about the same age as Elspeth, and had not been a lady's maid for very long. Elspeth liked and trusted Bertha, and the girl had staunchly supported her through these past weeks, for which Elspeth had been so grateful that she'd taken Bertha to her heart and into her confidence.

"Yes. I don't know how we shall be received either, so we must be prepared, I suppose. I have no idea if he even let them know he was married. They may suppose me an imposter," she added with a laugh.

"I doubt that," Bertha said. "No offense intended, my lady, but why would anyone pretend that? Everyone knows his lordship hasn't a feather to fly with. Indeed, they say Rowsley Hall is falling down around his ears and all the staff were let go. I shouldn't expect too much in the way of comfort or welcome, come to that."

From anyone else it might have seemed as if Bertha was being the harbinger of doom, but Elspeth knew she only wished to ensure her mistress was not hurt again by getting her hopes up.

Elspeth reached over and took the girl's hand. Bertha squeezed her fingers, a silent show of support that made Elspeth's throat grow tight.

"We must be nearly there. The driver said it was about an hour and a half from the station and… oh!" Elspeth forgot what she was saying as she glimpsed the jagged edge of turrets through the trees. "Oh, Bertha, *look*!"

The trees thinned as they grew closer, and Elspeth gasped as she got her first sight of the house. She'd thought she was used to grand houses, having spent a great deal of time with her aunt and uncle at Holbrook House, but Rowsley Hall was a shock to the system all the same. Such a jolt to her equilibrium was it that she could do nothing but stare and stare. It was, she reflected, as her heart thudded with excitement, like falling head over heels in love. It was simply vast, a higgledy-piggledy confection of both solidity and overgrown romantic ruin, of medieval and Tudor magnificence, and of Elizabethan splendour. A castle, but not a castle. Set slightly higher than the road on a limestone outcrop, the afternoon sun glinted on the many, many windows and Elspeth knew… she had come home.

"There's just the housekeeper and old Mr Parker still here, as far as I know," the driver said as he handed them down. "Are they expecting you, Miss…?"

"Lady Roxborough," Elspeth said, realising that it was the first time she'd said that name with something akin to pride and ownership. Yet how could it be otherwise when she looked up at this astonishing building?

Everywhere she saw signs of decay and neglect, yet her heart only saw the beauty of it. Delicate white bindweed flowers choked the climbing roses that scrambled up the walls, and destructive ivy insinuated probing fingers under lintels and into cracks and crevices, yet it was the most romantic, most glorious sight she had ever beheld.

Her name had a galvanising effect on the driver, whose eyes widened with astonishment. She didn't doubt news of the scandal had reached the most remote parts of Britain by now. The story of how she and Roxborough had been caught in wildly inappropriate circumstances had no doubt travelled with the impressive speed only the most salacious of stories could attain. Still, she was a married lady now and for all anyone knew she and her husband were wildly in love and just got carried away. She winced inwardly.

"Lady... Roxborough. Well, as I live and breathe. I beg you excuse me, my lady, I... I had no idea."

"There's not the least reason why you should," Elspeth said with a smile. "Would you be so kind as to see my trunks conveyed inside? I don't know if there is anyone to help you."

"Oh, don't you fret about that, my lady. I'll see to it. You run along inside, though you might have awhile to wait before old Parker realises you're here."

"It's of no matter," Elspeth said. "We can explore."

She gave Bertha a gleeful look of excitement and her rather more prosaic maid sighed.

"The beds will be damp," she predicted gloomily. "And spiders everywhere. It'll be draughty and cold and... and I bet it's haunted."

"*Haunted?*" Elspeth stopped in her tracks, wide-eyed at the idea. Then she grabbed Bertha's hand, towing her towards the great entrance hall. "Come on!" she shrieked, beside herself with excitement.

The driver had underestimated Mr Parker. The man, who was perhaps in his late sixties but not so old and doddery as Elspeth had expected, was pristine and dapper, straight-backed and bright-eyed, and greeted them warmly.

"Lady Roxborough," he said, bowing with great deference. "May I say what a great privilege and pleasure it is to welcome you to Rowsley Hall."

"The privilege is mine," Elspeth said, meaning it. "And I am only sorry now that I did not come sooner. Were you expecting me?" she asked hesitantly.

"Indeed, his lordship wrote and informed us of your marriage. Will Lord Roxborough be joining you?"

"Oh, yes, of course. I expect him to arrive later today or tomorrow," Elspeth said, trying not to blush. "He... er, he had some business to take care of and stayed on a little longer."

Liar, liar. How odd it must appear for the two of them not to have arrived together. Perhaps she ought to have stayed in Derby for a night or two, but it was done now.

"Well, there have been rooms prepared for you, and your maid, of course. I'm afraid we have little in the way of staff at Rowsley just at present," the man said with obvious regret. "But you may rest assured that myself and Mrs Grigson will do everything we can to see to your comfort. She'll want to meet you too, as soon as she hears of your arrival."

"I'm sure you will do marvellously well," Elspeth assured him. "And we can see about hiring a full staff again as soon as I'm settled in."

These words looked to be the greatest gift the fellow had ever been given in his entire life, judging by the way his throat worked and his eyes glittered.

"Oh," he said, his voice quavering. "Oh, my lady. You have no idea how glad, how very glad I shall be to see the Hall brought back to what it was. It's such a place, when it is cared for, you cannot imagine...."

Elspeth reached out and patted his arm, touched by his obvious love for the building. "I think you'll find I have rather an excellent imagination, Parker, and I shall be relying on you for your help and advice."

"You have it," he said staunchly. "You may be certain of that."

Suddenly looking a good inch taller, Parker showed them to their rooms. Once he'd left them, with an assurance that refreshments would be delivered to them as soon as possible, Bertha sighed.

"Well," she said. "That driver will ensure everyone from here to Derby knows the new Lady Roxborough is in residence before nightfall, I don't doubt, and that poor fellow, Parker, looked like he wanted to weep with gratitude the moment he set eyes on you."

Elspeth could hardly disagree.

"He was charming," she said with a smile and a burst of optimism. "If only the housekeeper is half so accommodating, we shall get along marvellously well."

"Hmmm," Bertha said, but otherwise kept her opinions to herself.

Elspeth's meeting with the housekeeper, the next morning, did not go well.

For a start, she did not present herself to Elspeth, requiring her to ask Parker to request Mrs Grigson come to the small sitting room adjacent to her bedroom. When she finally deigned to appear, she did not greet Elspeth with either a smile or much in the way of civility, let alone pleasure. Indeed, Mrs Grigson was a rather intimidating figure. Small and angular, with not a scrap of fat anywhere upon her sparse frame, the openly hostile housekeeper vibrated with repressed energy. There was also an undeniable sense of ownership for Rowsley in her manner that Elspeth predicted would cause trouble. For all the place was falling down around them, the Hall was her own little dominion, and Elspeth sensed she fought fight tooth and nail to keep it that way.

Like all young women of her status, Elspeth had thoroughly educated in the mysteries of running a great house, but there was a vast difference between theory and practise. As Parker had been such a dear, she'd had fond imaginings of a motherly sort of woman as housekeeper, someone she could rely upon to bolster her confidence and give sound advice. Despite the energy emanating from her thin frame, physically, this woman didn't look as if she had strength enough bolster a feather duster. Elspeth was not about to judge her on her appearance alone, however, and did not underestimate the amount of resistance she would come up against when she tried to make changes. Well, this was her home now, and the sooner Mrs Grigson realised that the better.

"The long gallery was built in 1580," Mrs Grigson told her as she swept through, barely giving Elspeth a moment to take it in.

Everywhere they went, ghostly furniture huddled mournfully in darkened rooms, curtains closed against the light to protect the fine upholstery and tapestries.

Mrs Grigson had been reluctant to show Elspeth anything at all, in fact, and had forced her to insist. The housekeeper retaliated by giving the barest amount of information and walking at such speed that Elspeth almost lost her a time or two as a corridor dived off at an odd angle or a doorway appeared in an unexpected position.

"Yes, thank you, Mrs Grigson," Elspeth said, by now thoroughly winded by hurrying up and down spiral staircases and along never-ending corridors at breakneck speed. "I shall wait for my husband to show me the rest, as you clearly do not have the time to devote to the subject."

"A place like this needs a vast amount of care," the woman retorted. "Who do you think there is, with old Parker on his last legs? Me, that's who. I've taken care of the place, me and my own bare hands worked to the bone."

"Indeed," Elspeth said, holding onto her temper. "And we are most grateful for your efforts. It cannot have been easy for you, alone in this place for so long. But that time is at an end. I shall be hiring a full staff and intend to restore Rowsley to its former magnificence."

The housekeeper snorted and folded her arms. "Reckon you can get staff enough for that, do you? The young folks don't want to work in service no more. Not when there's better wages to be had in town, and that's supposing his lordship don't fritter it all away afore you can do a mite of good."

Elspeth gaped. She could only assume that being alone in this huge building for so long had affected the woman's mind, for never had she heard a servant speak of her master with such insolence. Oh, to another servant in private, of course, but to the lady of the house? Never!

"That will be all, thank you, Mrs Grigson," she said coldly.

She did not yet know what to do about this obnoxious woman. For all she knew, she was someone Daire or his family had held in high regard and her bitterness stemmed from not being paid or... or perhaps she was mad.

"He's no good, that one," the housekeeper carried on, as if Elspeth had never spoken. "Never has been. A blasted fool, his father said of him, and I've seen no evidence to the contrary. They couldn't stand the sight of him. I supposed he trapped you into it, somehow? An intelligent girl like you would have more sense than to marry a fellow with more hair than wit and not a farthing to his name."

Elspeth gasped, uncertain what part of what she'd just heard distressed her more.

"His father said…?" she repeated, trying to comprehend. "His parents couldn't stand the sight of him?"

Mrs Grigson shrugged.

"Can you blame them? Oh, you should have seen them, and this place back before he was born. They gave marvellous parties, and everyone who was anyone came. My lady was the height of fashion, and so droll! Such a beautiful couple, they were, and so in love. Then Lady Roxborough fell pregnant." Her expression soured. "She was sick almost from the day she conceived him. Having him nearly killed her. I thought his lordship would go mad with grief, but she pulled through. She was never the same again, my poor lady wasn't, so weak and forever catching cold."

"What happened?" Elspeth asked, hardly daring to discover the truth of it, but wanting to hear the rest more than she wanted to reprimand the woman for her behaviour.

"That wretched boy ruined everything, that's what happened. The doctor said the only thing that would help Lady Roxborough to recover was to go somewhere warm, so they abandoned Rowsley and went abroad, travelling through Europe, but they settled in Italy. His lordship returned once or twice on business or to deal with his troublesome son, but she never came back, and I never saw her again," Mrs Grigson said, staring out of the window into the far distance, a wistful look in her eyes. "They both drowned. A boating accident."

Elspeth stared at the woman, torn between shaking her for her callousness and weeping. "And Daire—Lord Roxborough, where was he…?"

"Oh, at school," she waved a dismissive hand. "He'd sometimes come back here for the holidays and cause havoc. Wild, he was, breaking things and playing pranks, screaming about ghosts at all hours and frightening the poor housemaids out of their wits."

"But was there no one, no family to take him? Did… Did no one care for him?" Elspeth demanded, hardly able to bear hearing the answer.

The housekeeper returned a quizzical expression. "I told you, he was at school, and when he wasn't we fed and clothed him and looked after the little brat."

"And did anyone *care* for him?" Elspeth almost shouted this time, her anger with this woman and the callous treatment of her husband more than she could endure. "I don't mean food and shelter! I mean, did anyone love him, play with him? Did he have anyone at all?"

Mrs Grigson bristled. "We did the best we could, and would have done more if he'd been easier, but no one could manage him. He was all but feral. Well, Parker, I suppose… but that's only because he could wrap the foolish fellow about his thumb."

"Oh, God," Elspeth whispered. She put a hand to her stomach to quell the rising nausea and sat down hard on the nearest chair. The white cloth covering it billowed out with a plume of dust, but she didn't care. All she could hear was Daire's voice….

I need you. I need you to save me from this god awful loneliness. I want you so much… please, Elspeth.

He'd been telling the truth, and she… and she had punished him, shutting him out all over again. She swallowed down a sob and told herself it wasn't too late, she could make amends and they could try again. They could.

She would make it better, no matter what.

Chapter 11

Dear Evie,

Are you quite certain the comte is well again? I have been so terribly worried. Do you know when he is coming back to town?

—Excerpt of a letter from Miss Arabella Hunt, (Daughter of Nathanial and Alice Hunt) to Miss Evie Knight, (daughter of Lady Helena and Mr Gabriel Knight)

5th June 1839, Rowsley Hall, Derbyshire.

Dare was disgustingly drunk. The small—very small—part of his brain that was functioning, or trying to, knew that much. He wasn't certain he had ever been so drunk in his life and, considering the competition to be found in his past, that was saying something. Bottles littered the inside of the carriage and they rolled and chinked, one against the other, whenever the wheels jolted over a pothole or they turned a corner. Better this way, though. Sober he was wretched, drunk he was simply numb. Alcohol cocooned his brain and his heart in a thick fog where he could neither think nor feel with any clarity, and that was a blessing. He wasn't certain he could stand to be sober ever again.

He'd been a fool. Things had been fine before. Oh, Rowsley was dismantling itself bit by bit, but why should he care? His father hadn't cared. He'd turned his back on Rowsley and his son and left them both to rot. Dare should do the same. It wasn't his problem. He should sell the place and have done with it. Blood and bone be damned. Peeling his eyes open with difficulty, he tried to focus on the landscape outside the carriage and saw the turrets through the trees. Dare watched as it grew closer.

"Home sweet home," he slurred, snorting with amusement. "Driver! Driver!"

He bashed at the carriage roof with his fist and the driver slowed and then stopped.

Dare swung the door opened and leapt out, stumbling and reeling and sitting down hard on his arse by the side of the road. A footman hurried to help him up, but he laughed and sent the fellow on his way.

"Go on, go on." He waved them away. "I'll walk from here."

They gave him a sceptical glance, but Dare told them to leave him be, so they did. They left the Viscount Roxborough sitting at the side of the road like an abandoned piece of luggage. Apt, that. Or perhaps not. Someone would notice a missing piece of luggage, after all.

It took him a while to get to his feet, longer to retrieve the bottle that he'd left on the ground. He would have left it there but there was still an inch of brandy in the bottom, and he didn't want to risk sobering up. Eventually he made it to the bridge that spanned the River Wye and stood, staring up at the magnificence of the building above him. Dare's throat grew tight and so he raised the bottle to his ancestral home.

"Sorry, ghosts, made a mull of it. Don't suppose you're surprised. There's only me to haunt as usual, so… do your worst." He chuckled and lifted the bottle to his lips.

After the housekeeper's revelations and cruel observations, Elspeth had needed to get out. It had taken her ages to figure out how the devil to get to the gardens, but after some time spent taking wrong turns and opening doors that took her back in a circle, she made it outside. The grass was sodden and it was drizzling lightly. Parker had told her it had rained heavily for the past two weeks and only now was the weather clearing. The River Wye, which the Hall looked down upon, and which Parker said was usually rather shallow, was swollen now, rushing past the Hall with power enough to sweep away anything in its path. They'd had none of the sunshine here that they'd enjoyed in the south of the country. Still, the clouds were clearing in the far distance, a patch of blue showing tentatively against the tumble of grey skies all round.

Elspeth walked, not really knowing where she was going or seeing what was around her, although she had longed to explore. All she could see in her mind's eye was a little boy, all alone in this cavernous building, desperately wanting someone to notice him and causing havoc, hoping somebody, *anybody*, would see him. She wanted to cry and not just from sorrow, but from guilt. Snivelling, she was tugging a handkerchief from the sleeve of her gown when she heard singing. It was a bawdy song, and the owner of the voice was singing it with gusto and with a fine baritone, but from the slurring of some of the words, he was also very clearly drunk.

Elspeth hurried to the wall that overlooked the terraces of the gardens beneath and saw that the singing was coming from the bridge, and that the drunken fool had climbed onto the wall and was walking—unsteadily—along it. He turned just as the sun broke through the clouds and it shone on his hair, making the thick dark locks glint gold. Daire! Her heart lurched in her chest.

"Oh, no."

Elspeth picked up her skirts and ran. She could not risk calling out to him to get down, afraid that he would fall if she took his attention. So she ran through the gardens, cursing as she took too long to find her way down. It seemed to take forever to reach the road that led to the bridge and she stumbled in her haste to reach him. She did not know what to do, could only think of getting to him. He had just launched into another verse as she approached the bridge.

Madam in your face is beauty,
In your bosom flowers grow
In your bedroom there is pleasure,
Shall I view it, yes, or no?
Oh no John, No John, No John, No!

Elspeth stopped running, moving cautiously now, wondering if she dared catch his attention. He held an empty bottle in his hand and was conducting now, singing to the great hall at the top of his lungs.

Madam shall I tie your garter,
Tie it a little above your knee,
If my hand should slip a little farther,
Would you think it amiss of me?
Oh no John, No John, No John, No!

He took a breath, no doubt to begin the next verse, but as he did so he turned, and saw her.

Whatever he'd been about to sing the words died in his throat and he gasped. He stared at her, blinking.

"No," he said, shaking his head slowly. "Not another bloody ghost. No."

He took a step back as she moved towards him but missed his footing and slipped. Elspeth screamed as he swayed, arms windmilling, and then fell over the edge of the bridge, down into the river.

Dare shivered. His mind was a jumble of strange images, of frigid water and a sense of hopelessness, of fighting a tide that he knew he could not beat. He'd never been able to, why bother to try now? Yet something kept nagging at his brain. A bright vision of something lovely and… no, impossible. But yes, it *had* been Elspeth. Elspeth had been on the bridge. It hadn't been a ghost. She'd been there. Elspeth wasn't a ghost, she was alive and warm and so, so beautiful that it made him want to weep with longing. Elspeth had been at the Hall, she had… she *had*!

He awoke with a start. It took him a moment to realise that he was in his own bed, in his room at the Hall. The bedroom he'd had as a boy, at any rate. He hadn't been able to bring himself to move into his father's room. Too many ghosts. Dare blinked, wondering how the devil he'd got here, and when. He felt wretched, his throat was sore, and his head pounded and… a soft sigh caught his attention. Dare turned his head towards the sound and his heart gave an uncomfortable thud in his chest.

Elspeth. She was here. She was really here. Not a ghost. Not a drunken vision, but here in his room. Why was she in his room?

She'd dragged the heavy wingback chair that usually sat by the window, close to the bed, and was curled up in it, asleep. Her blonde hair was all in disarray, her cheek resting on her hand. As he watched her head slipped from her hand and she jolted awake with a little snort of surprise. She blinked, and sat up suddenly, staring at the bed.

"Oh!" she said, as she saw that he was awake. "Oh, Daire."

And then she burst into tears.

"What the devil?"

Dare did not know what to make of it. He stared at her, too shocked to move.

"Elspeth?" he said cautiously. "What's wrong? Did… Did somebody upset you? Oh, it wasn't Mrs Grigson, was it?"

Her crying got louder.

Dare flung back the covers and then realised he wasn't dressed and tugged them back again. He didn't want to frighten her.

"I'm so sorry," he said, feeling awful. "I ought to have warned you about the old bat. She scares me to death too."

"Oh, Daire!" Elspeth threw herself from the chair and at him, sobbing into his neck.

"Er...." Dare's heart was beating very hard and very fast, and he was all at sea. "There, there," he said warily, not having much of an idea what to do with a weeping wife.

She sobbed piteously, her tears soaking into his nightshirt and leaving a damp patch.

"Oh, Elspeth, what is it? I can't do anything about it unless you tell me, love," he said, feeling as hopeless as usual in the face of such distress. How did he make it better? "Is it the Hall? I know it's in a wretched state, it's enough to make me cry, I assure you. I tried to warn you. If I'd known you were coming, I would have said...."

"Oh, hush, you silly man," she said, her voice choked, but the words were clearly exasperated. Well, that was more usual, at least. "I love the H-Hall, it's b-beautiful and romantic and I wish I'd c-come when you asked me to."

"Oh," Dare said, brightening. He couldn't help but wonder if she had hit her head or something, for describing this crumbling old heap in such terms was quite mad in his view. "Oh, well, that's good. I think? But... beautiful and romantic I'm not so sure about. Have you *seen* it?"

"Oh, do forget about the Hall. I'm not crying about that or Mrs Grigson, even if she is awful, and I do hate her."

"Well, then... what?"

"*You*! Good heavens, Daire, you fell off the bridge and into the river. If it hadn't had rained so much, you'd have broken your neck or hit your head on a rock. As it was, the current swept you three miles downstream and it took us half the day to find you. You've been asleep for the past two days and I... I was s-so frightened."

Dare stared at her, not having realised, or remembered... but no. He did remember. The freezing water, fighting the current and thinking he should just not bother and give into it, and then he'd remembered her.

"I'm sorry I gave you such a fright," he said miserably.

God, what a sorry excuse for a husband he was. Arriving off his head drunk and then falling in the river in front of her. No wonder she hated him.

"No, it's all my f-fault. If I'd n-not been so vile to you, you'd not have gone away. Bainbridge was right. I'm a c-cold bitch, and I was... h-h-horrid to you."

"Bainbridge said *what*?" Dare gaped in fury, grasping onto the only bit of what she'd said that made the least bit of sense. "I'll bloody kill him."

"But it was true," she wailed, and threw herself at him again.

Dare sat back against the pillows, too perplexed to make head nor tail of it. All he knew was that Elspeth was in his arms and, by some miracle, she didn't seem to hate him. He stroked her back, up and down, deciding she was overwrought, and he'd not get anything sensible from her until she was calm again. Dare closed his eyes, savouring the moment, breathing in the scent of her as his heart ached with longing, and then he shook himself.

Stop it, he told himself. *She's just upset. There's no point in thinking she cares for you.*

That way led to heartache and disappointment and he'd had quite enough of that. If she hated him a little less, that was good, but he was done hoping for happy-ever-afters. He'd spent his entire childhood dreaming of a day when his parents would come back and realise he wasn't such a horrid boy after all and that he could be good if they would only give him a chance. Well, that had never happened, had it? He'd thought he was old enough to know better, but no. One glance of Elspeth and he'd hoped and dreamed all over again and... and it had hurt when she didn't believe him.

Not that he blamed her, not for a moment, but it had hurt him too deeply when he'd promised himself no one would have the power to do that to him anymore. He didn't want to feel like that again.

After a while, her crying stopped and he felt her relax against him, heard the deepening of her breath as she slid into sleep. Dare sighed with relief. Carefully, so as not to wake her, he laid her down on the bed beside him, and then slipped out of it. He dressed quickly and then spared a moment to watch his wife sleeping. He could not quite believe she was here. Perhaps he was losing his mind. How the devil had she got here before him?

At least if he'd gone mad, he had company. He gave a huff of laughter at that and fought the longing to get back on the bed with her and hold her close. Dare reached for the covers and tugged them over her. The old place was draughty and cold even in the height of summer and he didn't want her to catch a chill. Then he made himself turn and walk away. Once she was calm again, she'd be embarrassed if she found herself in his bed. Wife or no, she didn't want that from him, and he didn't want to be reminded of that fact. His ego had taken quite enough of a battering for the time being, and having her so close to him had already made all sorts of wrong ideas raise their heads. Best he keep his distance.

Chapter 12

Monsieur le Comte,

I am glad to hear you have recovered and that Miss Aggie is in good spirits and has returned to school. There was really no need to send such a lavish bouquet in thanks for reading to you and keeping you company during your convalescence. I assure you it was no hardship, but I must admit I enjoyed the look on our butler's face when he realised that glorious arrangement of hothouse blooms was for me and not Florence. I've never received flowers before, so it was a shock to everyone. I shall pretend to everyone who calls that I have an admirer and they will be wild with curiosity. Perhaps I will invent a handsome Italian Count with wicked intentions? For Frenchmen are ten a penny these days, you know.

—Excerpt of a letter from Miss Evie Knight, (Daughter of Lady Helena and Mr Gabriel Knight) to Louis César de Montluc, Comte de Villen.

8th June 1839, Rowsley Hall, Derbyshire.

Elspeth woke slowly. She'd barely slept the past nights, sitting up with Daire and horribly afraid he would take sick or break out with fever. The doctor had come, and he'd told her he was just sleeping off the exhaustion of his drunken binge and being half-drowned, and would be right as rain, but she'd been too afraid to believe him. He had been in that state because of her, because she'd made him so utterly miserable. How could she make it up to him?

She was disappointed to realise Daire had left her alone. Though it was hardly surprising if he did not want her company. Foolishly, when she'd been in his arms, she'd hoped he might want to kiss her again, that they might recapture something of what she had felt the first time he'd kissed her. He'd wanted her then. He'd wanted her very badly, but it was stupid to expect a seduction after everything he'd been through. The poor man was exhausted, that was all.

It was quite true and totally reasonable, but a little sliver of doubt stabbed at her heart, telling her she'd ruined everything, that she'd given him a disgust of her, and he'd never want her again. Elspeth fought down the panic that rose as she considered the possibility and told herself not to borrow trouble. Instead she got up and allowed Bertha to tidy her up as best she could. It was late morning, judging by the sunlight outside. It was a fine day, at least, and it seemed summer had arrived in Derbyshire. The sight of the glorious countryside through the window raised her spirits a little, and so Elspeth set off in search of her husband.

Thankfully, after forty minutes of fruitless searching, she came across Parker, or else there would have been every possibility she could still have been searching a week later.

"It is his lordship's habit to take his meals one of the smaller rooms, my lady," the butler told her with his usual warm manner. "He finds the atmosphere more convivial. If you would come this way."

Elspeth followed him. She had not had time to speak to him about Daire since Mrs Grigson's revelations. Daire's accident and subsequent recovery had taken up all her time, but now she wanted to know more.

"I spoke to Mrs Grigson the other day," she said, watching his face closely.

He was a very good butler, she thought, for it was hard to read him. She decided to take a chance and put her trust in him.

"I don't like her," she said baldly. "And I greatly dislike the way she speaks of my husband."

Parker stopped in his tracks, turning to look at her. There was anxiety in his expression now, and regret. She got the impression that he was choosing his words carefully, for he did not reply at once.

"I do not think it will take you long to discover that the Hall has not been a happy place for his lordship, my lady. I am very much hoping you can change that."

"So am I," she said, smiling at him. "But if I am to achieve anything, I need to understand. I shall need your help, Parker."

"You have it," he said, and she could tell he meant it.

"Thank you."

"May I speak freely, my lady?"

Elspeth sighed with relief. "Indeed, I should consider it a very great favour if you would. I very much want you to, and I promise to keep anything you say in the strictest confidence."

Parker nodded and took a breath, frowning a little before he spoke again. "Mrs Grigson is a fine housekeeper. She's worked hard to keep the Hall running and in good order in impossible circumstances, but she is not a woman with any... tender feelings."

Elspeth snorted at that, and Parker returned a rueful smile.

"We have had our run-ins," he admitted. "For she thinks me soft, but the truth is Lord Roxborough has had a very hard time of it. Is it any wonder he turned out a bit wild when there was no one here to take him in hand? I know it is not my place to judge, but the way his parents abandoned him...."

He shook his head and Elspeth felt her throat grow tight again as she saw the image of the little boy running about this cavernous house.

"He was never a bad boy, in any event. There was not a scrap of malice in him, despite everything," Parker went on. "Though he was always up to his tricks and drove everyone to distraction. A wicked sense of humour he has, and a nose for trouble even now."

Parker laughed, and she saw the warmth and affection in his eyes and was glad of it, glad that Daire had someone who'd given a damn for him. His expression grew serious.

"We've heard a lot of... *rumours* about your marriage." There was distaste behind the words and Elspeth thought it pained him to bring the subject up. "And I don't know the truth of it, and I would never pry, but I do know his lordship was hoping to marry a wealthy wife, so that he could pay off his father's debts and get the Hall back in order."

"His *father's* debts?" Elspeth repeated.

Parker nodded. "The late Lord Roxborough was a man much given to entertaining, and lavishly too. Sadly, he was also incautious in his choice of steward for the Hall. I tried to warn him myself that something was amiss but... well, I was only an upper footman in those days. It wasn't until the present Lord Roxborough reached his majority that the scale of the steward's villainy came to light. Though I'd had my suspicions, even I had never realised...."

"He stole from them?"

"Embezzled a vast fortune, sold everything that was not entailed and pocketed the money, and then disappeared," Parker said, shaking his head. "He took advantage of the master's absence and subsequent death and stole everything he could. By the time your husband was sixteen, it was all gone. He inherited debts and this vast house and the title… and not a great deal else."

Elspeth blinked, stunned.

"But… But I thought… All the scandal sheets indicated that he…." She broke off, wondering just how much she really knew about her husband.

Parker gave a crooked smile. "Dirt sticks, my lady. Lord Roxborough was forever in trouble as a boy and, once he'd gained a reputation for wildness, it was impossible to shake. It is easy enough to paint a man with his talent for mischief in the colours of a libertine, capable of all manner of vices, especially bearing in mind the company he keeps, but his lordship has never been a gambler, nor so wicked as people like to think him, despite his reputation."

Elspeth bit her lip, desperately wanting to ask if the other rumours were false too. Deciding she might not get another chance for such candour from Parker, she threw caution to the wind.

"Does he keep a mistress?"

Parker's eyebrows almost hit his hairline, but he recovered quickly. He cleared his throat, looking deeply uncomfortable.

"I am not privy to his lordship's personal affairs, my lady," he said, a little stiffly. "But I should think it unlikely."

Elspeth nodded, allowing herself a little breath of relief. He couldn't afford a mistress was what Parker meant. Or at least, he couldn't before. Now, with her money at his disposal, things might be different. Unless she could persuade him he didn't need a mistress, because he had her.

"You said he wished to marry well to bring the Hall back in order," she said, seeing the relief in Parker's eyes that they were back onto a less scandalous topic of conversation. "Is that true?"

Parker nodded. "Indeed. Lord Roxborough has never liked being at the Hall. When he visited back in April, it was the first time he'd been back in close to two years. I believe the place holds too many unhappy memories for him, but despite everything he feels a duty of care towards it, to those who have gone before him. I believe... but perhaps you ought to speak to him directly about his plans for the Hall. I am certain he would welcome your interest."

"Are you?" Elspeth asked, a little anxious now.

The butler smiled at her. "He has never had anyone show an interest before, my lady. I should think he would be very pleased indeed."

He indicated the door before her as being where she would find her husband and Elspeth took a breath to calm her heart, which skipped about behind her ribs in a most peculiar fashion.

"Thank you, Parker."

"You are most welcome, my lady."

Elspeth gave a soft knock and pushed open the door. Daire didn't look up from his place at the table, a fork in one hand whilst he sat engrossed in some sporting magazine.

"I'm not done yet, Parker," he said absently.

"May I join you?"

He jolted in surprise and dropped the magazine and the fork with a clatter.

"Elspeth!" he said. Daire stared at her for a moment and then pushed to his feet, belatedly remembering his manners. "Of course."

Parker appeared at her shoulder. "Shall I lay another place at the table, my lord?"

"Oh, yes. Yes, please do." Daire pulled out a chair for her.

Elspeth smiled warmly at him, feeling ridiculously shy. As she couldn't quite bring herself to hold his gaze, she looked about herself as she sat.

"This is a lovely room," she said approvingly, taking in the heavy wood panelling and the blazing fire in the hearth. "And much cosier than the grand dining room."

Daire nodded as he took his seat again.

"Yes, I don't like eating in there. It makes me feel like I'm the only living thing left in the world," he said with a laugh, but the comment only made Elspeth's heart ache. "Mrs Grigson thoroughly disapproves, of course. It isn't fitting for the master to eat in such a shabby little room, you know."

"Mrs Grigson can go to the devil," Elspeth said hotly.

Daire stared at her, clearly a little taken aback by that.

"Be careful what you say. I'm not quite certain she isn't in league with him." He flashed her a quick grin and turned back to his food.

Elspeth glanced at the cold collation of meat and pickles and cheese and frowned. She turned back to Parker.

"Has Mrs Grigson done anything about advertising for new kitchen staff? A cook is most urgently required," she said. "My husband cannot live on cold meat and cheese indefinitely."

Parker hesitated. "I er… did ask as to whether she had made enquiries or advertised the position."

"And?"

"I…." Parker began, clearly uncertain of how to respond, but Elspeth did not need him to.

Mrs Grigson was being difficult. She did not want to help Elspeth improve the Hall, even if it meant making her own life easier. Elspeth suspected in her eyes Rowsley Hall was a shrine to her late mistress and she wanted nothing to change. Well, she'd just see about that.

"Never mind, Parker," she said cheerfully. "I shall draw up a suitable advertisement. Do you think you could ensure it gets placed wherever it is most likely to be seen?"

"I should be delighted to. I have already taken the liberty of mentioning the fact you are hiring, my lady, and have taken on two footmen and some labourers for the garden. They begin on Monday. I will be glad to oversee the hiring of the rest of the staff, should you wish it."

"Parker, you are a marvel," Elspeth said and was delighted by the little flush of colour that rose on the old man's cheeks.

"I shall see to it at once, my lady," he said, sounding thoroughly pleased.

He gave one last tweak of table setting he had laid for her, bowed politely, and went out.

"Well, you've conquered Parker and no mistake," Daire said, sounding amused.

"He's a dear," she replied, serving herself with a thick slice of ham. "How are you feeling?"

Daire paused with his fork halfway to his mouth. "Me?"

"Of course you. You've been through a dreadful ordeal. Are you quite well?"

Daire snorted and put down his fork.

"I was drunk as a wheelbarrow," he retorted, shaking his head. "My own damned fault as usual, but you need not worry. I'm fairly indestructible."

Elspeth reached over and placed her hand over his. "I'm glad."

Daire stared at it for a long moment. He withdrew his hand.

"Fit as a flea," he said, looking uncomfortable.

"Daire," Elspeth said, desperate now to say what she had longed to say ever since she had discovered the truth. "Daire, I'm so desperately sorry."

He sent her a wary glance. "What on earth for?"

"For not believing you. Bainbridge told me what really happened that day, and then I heard from Miss Agatha too. She told me all about her kitten and how you rescued it. I ought to have given you a chance to explain, but… but I didn't, and I was so awful to you and…."

To her surprise he put down his knife and fork, casting his napkin to one side as he stood.

"That's nonsense," he said, waving her words away. "What else were you to think? I said I'd trap you into marriage and I did. For God's sake don't apologise. I deserve everything I got and more besides."

"No!" she said, standing too, but he moved to the window, staring outside. "No, you didn't. Please, Daire, won't you let me make amends?"

"Make amends?" he repeated, looking at her as if she'd run mad. "Don't be foolish. It's me that needs to make amends. Good God, I trapped you and landed you in this… this mouldering monstrosity. You should hate me."

"I don't hate you, Daire," she said, her heart beating fast.

She wanted to go to him, to feel his arms about her, holding her tight and telling her he forgave her, for she needed forgiveness no matter what he said, but she could not. There was something between them now, some sense of reserve that had never been there before, not even when they'd first met. It was as if she'd created some invisible barrier between them by her actions, and she did not know how to breach it. The temptation to just fling herself at him was unbearable, but she remembered how he'd just withdrawn his hand from her and knew that was not the way to go on.

He was staring at her, puzzled and somewhat wary. The expression put her in mind of the children she'd taught at Eliza's school. Many of them were orphans, from workhouses, or off the street, and they all had a mistrust of... well, of everyone. The teaching staff all understood that it would take time to bring them around, to prove to them that they were safe, that they were among friends. Elspeth jolted at the realisation. It was the same look of mistrust she saw in Daire, the same confusion why she would bother when no one else ever had, and a certainty that there must be an ulterior motive. She must be careful if he was ever to trust her.

"I know you did not arrange for Bainbridge to walk in on us," she said, her voice clear and firm. "You did not mean to trap me, no matter what your intention had been. The events of that day were not by design."

"What does it matter?"

He turned away to stare out of the window.

"It matters."

He shot her a sceptical glance.

"Daire, do you think we might be friends?"

She saw at once some of the tension leave his shoulders.

"Yes," he said, nodding. "Yes, I should like that. I hate to think that I've made you miserable, Elspeth. I've been so wretched with guilt."

Elspeth took a step closer.

"There's no need. We both made mistakes. We are both as bad as each other," she said with a little laugh, hoping to lighten the atmosphere.

It was the right thing to say.

Daire grinned at her. "Oh, I think you'll need to work hard before you can say that, my lady."

"Then I shall," she said, putting her chin up. "Do you think I cannot be every bit as disreputable as my husband? I assure you I can. Have you *met* my parents?"

He laughed at that and the sound, deep and rich, rumbled through her, making her thrill with pleasure at having amused him. Daire watched her for a moment, hesitating.

"Has Mrs Grigson shown you around at all?" he asked.

Elspeth pulled a face. "Not exactly, but I should love it if you showed me. It's such a wonderful building. I want to know all its secrets."

And yours, she didn't say.

"By gad, all of them?" he said, shaking his head. "I certainly don't know all of them, but the ones I do know would take a year to repeat."

"Oh, well, it's not like we haven't time. We've years and years, have we not?"

Daire frowned and then nodded. He went back to the table and stood by her chair. "Well, come and finish your lunch and I shall give you the grand tour. Or a bit of it, at least."

"Thank you, Daire," she said softly, and sat down to finish her lunch.

Chapter 13

Miss Evie,

I shall take my flowers back again, you ungrateful creature.

—Excerpt of a letter from Louis César de Montluc, Comte de Villen to Miss Evie Knight, (Daughter of Lady Helena and Mr Gabriel Knight)

8ᵗʰ June 1839, Rowsley Hall, Derbyshire.

Dare slanted a look sideways at Elspeth. He wasn't certain what to make of her. He felt certain her apology had been heartfelt, yet he did not understand why she felt so terrible. Though he'd been wretched at the way she'd treated him, he'd not blamed her for it. He'd made a mess of everything and he knew it. That she seemed enraptured by the vast money pit that was his home was even more bewildering.

She paused at a window, staring out at the view, and Dare felt his breath catch as the sun glinted on her blonde hair and highlighted her beautiful profile. Her lips were a delicious shade of pink, soft as a rose petal, and longing filled his chest. Friends, she'd said, and he'd agreed, but did she want more than that? Dare might not be the brightest fellow in the *ton,* but he knew well enough when a woman wanted to be kissed, and earlier the invitation to do so had been so blatant he'd not wanted to resist.

Yet, something had held him back. He wanted her too much. In the brief time before Bainbridge had crashed in, he'd glimpsed a world he might be a part of and he'd wanted it, all of it. He wanted the dream of her here with him, wanting to be *with* him. If he couldn't have that he didn't want any part of it, for he knew now it had the power to destroy him.

Never knowing what it was to be loved and belong somewhere was one thing, but having a taste of it before it was taken away again was quite another.

Dare moved a little closer to her to see what she was watching with such interest. Gardeners were setting to, hacking away at a large bramble that had taken hold in one of the rose beds.

"There's the ghost of a dog in that part of the garden," he said.

She turned and gaped at him. "You're roasting me."

He laughed and shook his head. "No, I swear it. It drove me mad when I was a boy. I was so desperate for a dog I used to pretend I had one, then one day I heard barking. I searched and searched but no sign of a dog. It took me a full year before I accepted it was there, but not there at all, and only then because Parker told me he'd heard it too."

"Good heavens. The ghost of a dog? I never heard of such a thing."

Dare smiled.

"There are many ghosts at Rowsley," he said, and then his face fell. "Oh, damn me for an idiot. You're not scared, are you? I... I didn't mean to frighten you."

Elspeth shook her head. "At least, yes. I am a little scared but... but they are not likely to come and find me in my room, are they?"

"No, of course not. I should never let you stay in a room that was haunted."

She smiled and slipped her arm through his, as if it were the most natural thing in the world. Dare's heart thudded erratically.

"Is that why you haven't taken the master bedroom? I was surprised to discover your room is not next to mine."

Dare ignored the crawling sensation down his spine, like little insect legs. He cleared his throat. "Oh, no. I've not spent much time here in the past and so it seemed silly to move. Besides it's the devil's own job to heat that huge room and, with only Parker to see to it, well, it was ridiculous. I couldn't have him lugging fuel for the fire about up all those stairs. Poor blighter would have a heart attack, and then where should I be?"

She gave him a shrewd look. "It's not haunted, then?"

Dare almost told her the truth, that he felt his father's disapproving presence there every time he set foot in the room and he couldn't stand it. Almost. "No, no. Though there's the ghost of a maid in the corridor that leads to the kitchen, and you can hear crying in the west wing on stormy nights, and I once saw a very fine lady strolling down the long gallery. I believe she was a great-great-great-grandmother."

"It must have been frightening for you as a boy, to know of such things."

Dare avoided the concern in her eyes, not allowing himself to believe it this time. *Yes. Yes, it was bloody terrifying, and I don't think I slept a full night in the blasted place before I was old enough to drink myself insensible.*

"Oh, well, you get used to things, you know," he said with a shrug.

"I would like to redecorate. With your permission, of course."

Dare stopped, staring still at his boots, unable to meet her eyes.

"It's your money, Elspeth," he said, feeling sick.

"No," she said. "It's our money, and this is our home. So, I think we should discuss things with each other before we make any great expenditure."

He glanced at her. "Elspeth, I only ever wanted the money to save Rowsley, not to… to raise hell or spend on any of that kind of thing. It needs a shocking amount of work and it will likely take years, but…."

"I know," she said, and there was something in her eyes that made him believe she really did know and that she cared. "I want to save it too. Could we do it together, do you think?"

"If you'd like to," he said cautiously, not understanding why on earth she would give a damn. "But it's a dreadful place to live, you know. It's freezing all year round. In the winter if you put a glass of water by the bed it will be frozen when you wake up, and you must walk bloody miles, daily. There're staircases that don't go anywhere and bits waiting to drop off the place at any given moment…."

"My Lord Roxborough," she said, her lips quirking. "I do believe you are trying to put me off."

He snorted at that. "Just being realistic."

Elspeth looked outside again. "It's a beautiful day. I wish we could go for a ride and explore the countryside."

"Perhaps tomorrow we could see about buying some horses," he said. "If you'd like?"

"Oh, yes. That's a splendid idea."

She beamed at him and something shifted in his chest.

Oh, lord. This was not going to be simple.

"Oh, she's a beauty." Elspeth laughed as the mare nuzzled at her hand, seeking another caress.

"We'll take her too," Dare said to the owner of the mare, pleased that Elspeth had found a mount that suited her so well.

He'd chosen a large bay hunter himself and was well pleased with him. They'd also bought four carriage horses and two work horses. They'd come to Sheffield, to the Smithfield Market beside the River Don. The place was packed, not only with horses being sold but all manner of livestock, and Dare was very aware of the fact that it was no place for a lady. Elspeth didn't seem to mind the rather ripe atmosphere, however, nor the noise and bustle. Indeed, she seemed fascinated.

"Well, that's done, then," he said, pleased with their purchases.

He'd missed not having his own horses. Bainbridge was generous and was always happy to loan him something, but Dare didn't like to sponge off his wealthy friend too often. Of course, now he was spending his wife's money. Lord, what a fine catch he was. He forced a smile to his face, not wanting to spoil Elspeth's enjoyment.

"I don't know about you, but I'm famished. Shall we find something to eat?"

She cast one last look at the pretty mare and nodded. "Goodbye, girl. I shall see you soon, I promise."

The mare whickered softly, as if she understood and was happy with the arrangement. Dare didn't blame the creature. He'd watched, entranced as Elspeth stroked the beast's silky neck, her elegant, gloved hand moving in a slow caress. His mind, already over-excited by a long journey with her in a closed carriage, had needed little encouragement to imagine that same hand stroking parts of him with such tenderness. *Stop it,* he told himself. *Why?* demanded another voice. *She's your wife.*

Dare didn't have an answer for the question. He wanted her, very badly, yet he felt instinctively that he would lose any power he held if he gave into lust. Falling in love with her was too dangerous, and he was too close to the edge. The more time he spent in her company, the more under her spell he became. What would happen to him when she grew tired of his company, as she was bound to do. She was clever, far cleverer than him. She taught maths and... and likely a dozen other things he didn't understand. For the moment she felt guilty for having believed the worse of him, and perhaps she desired him. He knew he was a good-looking fellow, well made. Women had told him so often enough. But that wouldn't be enough for Elspeth. She'd want to talk, intelligent conversation about books he hadn't read and things he wouldn't know a thing about or would bore him to tears. It was only a matter of time before she realised that, so... best she be kept at a distance. But she was his wife, and he couldn't *not* consummate their marriage. He'd be a laughingstock if anyone found out, besides which he'd run mad. He could hardly think of anything else when she was close to him.

"Dare, are you all right?"

"What?"

Elspeth was giving him an odd look. He sat up straighter. "Of course."

"Really? I've told you we are here three times, and you didn't bat an eyelid. You seemed to be thinking very hard."

"Ah, well, I don't exercise the old brain box often. Takes a deal of winding up and getting going," he said lightly. "Shall we go in?"

He climbed out of the hired carriage and handed her down, guiding her into the Old Queen's Head where he bespoke a private parlour. It was a charming fifteenth century building, all heavy timbers and low beams, and when the inn keep realised he had Viscount Roxborough visiting with his rich new wife, the man all but fell over himself to be agreeable.

In no time at all, they were seated comfortably in a clean parlour and provided with ale, wine, and a basket of bread whilst they awaited their meal.

"Thank you for today. I enjoyed it a great deal," Elspeth said, tugging off her gloves.

Dare's gaze dropped to her slender fingers and he swallowed, looking away again.

"Good. Aim to please," he said and took a long drink of his ale.

God above, what was he to do? He was aware of a tangle of conflicting emotions in his chest, none of which he had the slightest idea what to do with. He'd thoroughly enjoyed this morning too. Elspeth was wonderful company, so funny and quick, and she was beautiful. More than once he'd seen men turn their heads and gaze at her—his wife—and he'd felt a swell of pride and possessiveness. But it was more than that, he was happy and sad all at once, pleased and proud and... and utterly wretched. What *was* wrong with him?

"Daire?"

Her voice was soft, yet it jolted him out of the mire of his thoughts. He turned to look at her and then wished he hadn't, for he wasn't certain he could look away again.

"Daire, are you certain there's nothing wrong?"

She was staring at him, like he was a puzzle she could solve if she only looked hard enough. Well, good luck with that. All she'd get was the frustration of realising the last piece was missing. Yet she didn't seem frustrated, but concerned. There was that warmth in her expression again, the look that made him want to believe she could care for him. Yet, why should she? She was an intelligent woman. Everyone with the slightest bit of sense ditched him as soon as they could. Bainbridge hadn't, but only because he was half barmy himself, and Parker seemed fond of him, but the old boy had always been a soft touch. Women, though? His mother hadn't been able to bear the sight of him. Mrs Grigson hated him with a passion, and as for his many conquests, they didn't know him. They saw the pretty face and the fine figure and assumed he was as good as any other nobleman, so long as he paid their bills. They didn't see *him.* Thank God, or he'd never have had any fun at all.

Elspeth, however…

His breath caught as she reached out and touched his cheek, her fingers gentle upon his skin.

"Why do you look so sad? When we first met, you seemed so happy and carefree. You made me laugh so, even when I was dreadfully cross with you. Is it my fault, Daire? Have I made you unhappy?"

Her eyes glittered, too bright, swimming with tears. It took him a moment to understand the question it was so ridiculous.

"*What*? No! By Jove, Elspeth, how could you think… no!"

"Oh," she said, blinking hard. "Then… don't you want to kiss me?"

Dare swallowed. Not want to kiss her? And he was supposed to be the dim one. Yet if he kissed her here, now, he was very afraid he wouldn't stop. Perhaps they could take a room and he could… they could….

"Daire?"

"Um."

Oh, very suave, he thought savagely.

"Oh," she said, her disappointment palpable.

Damnation!

Dare reached for her, or perhaps lunged might have been a better description of the way he grabbed hold of her. It was not exactly his finest hour, but he was all in a dither and she'd been going to cry, and he panicked. So he hauled her into his lap and kissed her.

Elspeth made a muffled sound of alarm and grasped at his lapels, and for a moment he feared she would push him away. She didn't. After the initial shock, her lips softened beneath his and the tension left her body and she sort of... melted into him. Suddenly she was pliant in his arms, her mouth opening to his demand and letting him in to plunder as he would. Her hands moved up his chest, over his shoulders. One curled about his neck, whilst the other sank into his hair, such a possessive gesture a pulse of pure lust shot straight to his groin. Oh, this was going to get out of hand very quickly and the servers would be here at any moment with their meal.

"Elspeth," he said, but the word came out as more of a growl and she pressed closer, her mouth upon his again, her breasts crushed against his chest.

What had he been thinking about again? He couldn't remember. He needed to touch her, touch skin, any skin. There were too many blasted layers, that was the trouble. There were stiff corsets beneath his hands when there ought to have been nothing but soft flesh. Frustrated by the devil's work that was a lady's fashionable attire, he chose the path of least resistance and reached for the hem of her skirts. Even that took an age, for he had to find his way beneath the dress and several layers of lace trimmed petticoats. He sighed against her mouth as his hand skimmed over a slender, silk-clad leg and up over her knee to where he discovered the bow of her garter. His heart gave one, hard thump in his chest as his palm slid higher and finally, finally, found warm, satiny skin.

Elspeth gave a little squeak, and he drew back to look at her, to see if it was a sound of protest, but she only gazed at him, her beautiful eyes hazy with desire. He watched her face as his hand moved higher, exploring the tender skin of her inner thigh. Her breathing hitched as his own grew fast and erratic. He felt like a boy again, making his first foray under a girl's skirts, too eager, too curious and excited. Good Lord if this kept up he was going to spend before he even got to the good bits. She never looked away from him, watching him as he explored, his fingers inching higher, her gaze at once bold and startled. Only when he brushed the silken curls between her thighs did her eyes close, though he'd seen her pupils dark and blown, swamping the green gold. She shifted on his lap, her lovely arse nestling his cock as she leaned back against him and widened her legs, giving him better access.

Oh God, oh God, oh God.

Some instinct, honed over many years of bad behaviour, made him react the moment he heard the door creak open. With more speed than he realised he was capable of he'd removed his hand and settled her skirts. She was still sitting in his lap, her cheeks flushed, and her mouth swollen from his kisses, but he could do nothing about that, and they were married after all.

He opened his mouth to tell the serving staff to damn well come back later and closed it again with a snap as he saw the glint of cynical blue eyes that glittered with amusement.

"Bainbridge?" he said, torn between surprise and outrage. "What the devil are you doing here?"

Bainbridge closed the door behind him and smirked. "Come to see if she'd killed you yet. Thought you might need some moral support. It seems I underestimated your charms, Dare, old fellow."

Elspeth leapt to her feet, cheeks blazing now as she settled herself down again on the bench beside him.

"My Lady Roxborough, it is good to see you looking so well."

"Lord Bainbridge."

Elspeth sounded breathless and could clearly not bring herself to meet his friend's eyes, the poor girl. Personally, Dare wanted to thump the devil. Still, it was kind of Bainbridge to come all this way to check he wasn't utterly blue devilled. In truth, he wasn't sure—underneath the excitement that was still thrumming through his blood—that he wasn't. He was something. What that something was he still hadn't figured out.

Chapter 14

Dear Harry,

You will be pleased to discover your years of nagging have not fallen entirely on deaf ears. I'm coming home, sister dear. The prodigal returns, so go and fatten up a calf or something. I'm on my way back to civilisation. God help me.

—Excerpt of a letter from Mr Henry Stanhope to his sister, Lady Harriet Cadogan, Countess St Clair.

8th June 1839, on the road to Rowsley Hall, Derbyshire.

Of course they'd had to invite him to come and stay. Elspeth sighed inwardly and did her best to avoid Bainbridge's amused blue eyes as he accompanied them back to Rowsley Hall. She knew she owed Bainbridge her thanks for his rather… *frank* words to her the night before she'd left. He'd not been kind, but he'd been honest, and she'd needed to hear what he'd said. Still, had he *had* to turn up at that precise moment? Just when things had been getting interesting. She remembered the feel of being in Dare's arms, his strong thighs beneath her, his warm hand sliding between her legs and…. Her breath caught as the memory lanced through her, and she looked up to find both men staring at her. Dare's eyes grew dark, and she only felt hotter. She didn't dare look at

Bainbridge, it was too mortifying. She had no doubt they both knew just what she'd been thinking about. Elspeth stared determinedly out of the window and forced herself to think of something, anything else. It wasn't easy.

Tonight, she promised herself. Tonight she would go to her husband's room and ensure he did his husbandly duty and made certain their marriage was legal. She watched the countryside as it passed by and the carriage drew them back home far too slowly.

Tonight could not come quickly enough.

It was still far too early to dress for dinner when they returned home, much to Elspeth's annoyance. The day was determined to drag until she'd gone quite mad. Daire had gone to the stables to inform the new staff to make ready for the horses they'd purchased that morning, so Elspeth went and settled herself in the library to answer her correspondence. There was still a great deal of it awaiting her attention and it would keep her mind off… well, other things.

She had been writing for perhaps half an hour when the door opened, and Bainbridge came in.

"Oh," he said, hesitating on the threshold. "Forgive me. I did not mean to—"

"No, do come in," she said, deciding she may as well speak to him now.

"Dare and I usually inhabit this room when we're here," he said, smiling at her. "Not that it happens often."

She nodded her understanding. "He's not been very happy here, I know. I hope to change that."

He nodded, looking pleased by that. "I'm glad to hear it. You've worked things out, then?"

Elspeth nodded, though she was far from certain it was true, but she was not about to tell him her personal worries. "Yes, and I must thank you, Lord Bainbridge, for what you said to me that night."

He snorted at that and shook his head. "I was rude and obnoxious."

"And honest," she said firmly. "You were worried for Dare, and I realise now that you had every right to be. I was in the wrong and... thank you."

Bainbridge stared at her, a little incredulous. She had the feeling there was little in life that ever surprised this man. He had a world-weary air of cynicism about him that gave the impression he was tired of having seen it all before, but she had surprised him. His mouth quirked a little in the approximation of a smile.

"You're welcome," he said. "I am glad things worked out. Dare deserves to be happy."

"Yes. He does."

Bainbridge considered her for a moment more before moving to the brandy decanter. "May I?"

"Of course."

She watched as he poured himself a drink and took a large swallow. Noting her observation, he glanced back at her.

"Forgive me. I have interrupted your correspondence."

"It's of no matter," she said, sitting down beside the fire and gesturing for him to join her. "I can finish it later."

"Felicitations from your friends?" he asked.

"Yes, I was answering my friend Arabella. She writes the funniest letters and so it always takes me longer to reply as I must try to match her for wit."

"Arabella Hunt?" he said, and something about him seemed to awaken as he said the name. A spark of interest.

"Yes, that's right." Elspeth watched him, intrigued. He'd come alert, like a wolf scenting prey.

"You're close?"

"We're friends," Elspeth agreed. "Though I've not seen as much of her this season as I usually do. I've been busy at Lady Eliza's school."

"Miss Hunt is not interested in charity?" he asked, a keen glitter in his eyes that belied the lazy note to the question.

"Oh, yes. Indeed she's one of the kindest, most generous people I know, but she's not interested in teaching. She's a vivacious girl." Elspeth watched him, her curiosity piqued. Some devil in her could not help but drop a hook into the water and see if he bit. "She's very beautiful, too. I believe she's had several marriage proposals already. I think she may have taken the eye of the Comte de Villen. I wonder if he might be the next to ask."

"Oh?"

Oh, he didn't like that.

"She ought to stay away from him," he said, his tone dark. "Any man whose past is so shrouded in mystery must be hiding something."

"Really?" Elspeth asked, intrigued. "Do you think so? I like the comte, very much. He's charming, and very beautiful, of course."

"Don't let Dare hear you say that," Bainbridge said, his displeasure obvious. She did not think it was because *she* found the comte beautiful.

"Oh, I have no interest in him, I assure you, but I do consider him a friend. I know nothing of his past, however. Is *your* past an open book, my lord?"

He gave her a sardonic look.

"Indeed, and a chilling read it is, Lady Roxborough, full of madness and murder and disgrace. Our family have kept the scandal sheets in business for generations. I'm quite a catch," he said, and the mockery in his voice was unmistakable.

Elspeth shivered. She was grateful to this man, and she knew Dare held him in high esteem, but she was not certain that she liked him. She certainly did not trust him.

The door opened, and she was relieved to see Daire. He did not look pleased at finding the two of them together.

"Come, my dear. Time to dress for dinner. I've been looking for you this age."

"Sorry," she said, springing to her feet before turning to Lord Bainbridge. "I shall see you at dinner, my lord."

Bainbridge, who had stood as she'd risen, bowed, and gave his somewhat unsettling smile. "I shall look forward to it."

Elspeth nodded and hurried to Daire. She took his arm and allowed him to escort her away.

When they were a little way from the library, she glanced at her husband, noting the rigid set of his jaw.

"Is everything all right?"

"Yes, yes," he said, but sounding a little terse. She watched him until he turned back to her again. He sighed. "Be careful around Bainbridge."

"Don't you trust him?" she asked in alarm.

"With my life," he said promptly, before adding: "With my wife... not so much."

"Oh, you cannot think—" He stopped in his tracks and reached for her, his big hand cupping her cheek. "I meant no criticism of you, Elspeth. It's only Bainbridge has a shocking reputation with women, even by my standards. I should not like you to be offended by him if he… well, perhaps I wrong him. He is a good friend to me, the best of friends, but I have never had a wife before."

She turned her face into his hand, covering it with her own and kissing the palm. He sucked in a breath and the sound made her insides quiver with longing, with the desire for him to put his hands on her again.

"It will take a little getting used to, then."

"That it will," he said, and his voice had gone all deliciously deep and rumbly again, and she hoped he would drag her into a dark corner and do wicked things to her. To her great dismay, he let out a ragged breath and shook his head. "You'd best run along and get changed. I'll see you at dinner."

Doing her best to hide her disappointment, Elspeth nodded, and did as he asked.

Bainbridge endured dinner with a mixture of curiosity and something else that took him quite by surprise. He was jealous. No matter how he told himself not to be such a blasted imbecile, the feeling had taken a hold of him and would not let go. He studied his dinner, eating without tasting, as he tried to make sense of his reaction. It wasn't Elspeth. She was beautiful and charming, funny too, and any man would be proud to have her on his arm, but he didn't fancy her for himself. No, that wasn't it. Dare, then? The fellow was his best friend; the only one to whom Bainbridge had ever been really close. Perhaps he resented the fact Dare had someone else in his life. Perhaps, he mused. Yes, there might be an element of that, but that wasn't quite it. He studied his hosts surreptitiously, amused by the heated glances that passed between them. That it was early in their marriage was unmistakable. He'd never before felt so much like a gooseberry, but the atmosphere between them was thick with tension and he determined to make himself scarce as soon as the meal was over. If he didn't, Dare would likely throw him out a window. The two lovebirds would no doubt run to their chamber as fast as their legs would carry them. Yet it was the way she looked at Dare that struck him, with such... such...

Ah, he realised, as the penny dropped. That was it. Oh, not the sex. Bainbridge had never been short of willing bed partners and more sex was hardly an incentive to wed. He'd been the recipient of enough heated looks and unspoken promises to not need to marry to get anything of that nature. No. No, it was the affection in her eyes, the desire to be with the man she loved and to make him happy. He saw the same look in Dare's eyes tempered with something else... uncertainty, perhaps. Well, he was a man. Men were always uncertain about marriage. No doubt the poor devil was still reeling from the fact he'd got himself a wife. Not Bainbridge, though. *That* was what he wanted, he decided on the spot. That was the thing he needed in his life to make it better.

He wanted a wife.

So, he'd better go and get himself one.

Elspeth was relieved when Bainbridge made himself scarce as soon as dinner ended. She'd been afraid he might take Dare off to the library for a drink and she'd have to wait forever until he retired for the night. As it was, she asked Dare to see her to her room.

"You *are* scared of ghosts," he said, frowning at her. "Damn me. I ought never to have told you about them."

"I'm not scared when you are with me," she said, keeping her voice low and hoping he heard the invitation there. "Only when I'm alone, at night, in my bed."

There, surely that was blatant enough. Heat bloomed in her cheeks and she could not look at him.

"Have... Have you not been sleeping?" he asked, concern in his voice.

Elspeth sighed and wondered if she would have to throw herself at him. She would, if it came to it. "It's such a big property and... I did not expect to sleep alone once we were married. It gets rather... lonely."

They'd arrived at her door and she turned towards him. She looked up at him from under her lashes, something she had never done in her life before, but she'd seen her friends turn intelligent men into blithering idiots with such a glance, so it was worth a try.

He swallowed.

"Lonely," he repeated, that one word thick, his voice unsteady.

She nodded and dared to reach out a hand, tracing an intricate pattern of ivy leaves embroidered on his waistcoat. "I regret that we never had a wedding night, Daire. I know it was my fault, and I understand why you kept away. You were kind to do so when I know many men would have taken what they considered theirs. But you're not like that, are you?"

"I would never hurt you, Elspeth."

She regarded him and smiled. "I know that now. So I thought perhaps that we might... now. Unless—"

Elspeth didn't get to finish the sentence. He pulled her into his arms and kissed her.

Oh! Well, then.

She sighed and pressed against him, revelling in the way he held her, his arms banded tightly about her, his mouth demanding, taking what he needed. The sense that he needed this very badly was not difficult to discern. There was desperation in the way he kissed her, deepening the kiss, his hands sliding down to her bottom and pulling her hard against him. He groaned and the sound thrilled her to her bones. She had done that, she had made him want her. He pulled back then, his eyes dark with need, but some sense must have returned with the ragged breath he drew, for he straightened up, apparently only then realising they were still standing in the corridor.

"Hell," he said vehemently. "Forgive me. I… I ought not…."

"Forgive you for what?" she said before he could finish. "That was exactly what I wanted. I've been desperate for you to kiss me ever since we left the inn. Honestly, I know Bainbridge is your friend, and I admire him for his loyalty to you, but I could happily have consigned him to the devil when he came through that door."

Daire stared at her, obviously a little stunned by this forthright observation. He gave a bark of laughter.

"The feeling was mutual," he admitted.

"Excellent." Elspeth nodded, hoping she looked calm and in control for her heart was doing an agitated little dance behind her ribs.

She reached for the door handle and opened it, walking into her bedroom and holding the door wide.

"Well?" she said briskly, as he was standing gaping at her. "What are you waiting for?"

"I haven't the least idea," Daire replied, and hurried in after her.

Dare closed the bedroom door and turned to Elspeth. It occurred to him he'd never done this before. Well, obviously he'd done *this* before, only never with a woman who didn't know what was what and where it went. Never with an innocent. Never with his *wife*. He swallowed and tried not to let his nerves show.

Elspeth considered him. "Are you nervous?"

Marvellous. All going swimmingly so far.

"Er… a little, yes," he admitted.

She giggled and sat on the bed. "Isn't that my job?"

Daire scratched his head. "I promised not to hurt you," he said awkwardly. "I don't want to hurt you, but—"

"Oh, yes, of course. I understand. You mean it might hurt me because it's my first time," she said, as if this was an everyday conversation. It was unlike any conversation he'd had before. "But Mama said if my husband did his job properly it wouldn't hurt much at all."

"She did?"

Elspeth nodded.

Oh, wonderful. No pressure there, then. He cleared his throat. "She... er... told you then. What to expect?"

"Ages ago," Elspeth agreed. "Before I came out. She said she would not send me into the lion's den unprepared for the tricks men play."

She blushed, realising what she'd said.

Dare felt the colour drain from his face.

"Do stop looking so wretched. I know it was an accident, and it doesn't matter. Not now. I'm *glad*."

Dare gave her a doubtful look and let out a breath. "Heaven alone knows why."

"Because I like you," she said, holding his gaze. "I like you very much. You make me happy, though I admit I am the first person to be surprised by that. I didn't think we would suit at all, but we do, don't we?"

He didn't reply.

"Oh," she said, her expression faltering.

"No." Dare shook his head and rushed to her, kneeling on the floor in front of her, taking her hands. "That is, yes... yes, we do, or I want us to. I like you too, Elspeth, very much."

The smile returned to her eyes and he let out a breath of relief. But liking her wasn't the problem. Even loving her wasn't the problem. He was falling hard and fast and he didn't know how to stop it, couldn't stop it, but he was afraid that—if he did not hold just a little of himself back—she would have too much power over him. What if she left? What if she went back to her life and did not want him in it? What then? Was he to trail after her like a loyal hound, pining for her, begging for scraps from her table? Oh, God. The thought made him go cold. He'd spent too long wishing for his parents to notice him. On the rare occasions his father had returned from abroad, Dare had followed him about the house, always at a distance, torn between a fierce desperation to be noticed and terror that he would be. Being noticed never quite went how he wanted it to.

"Daire?"

Dare came up on his knees and pushed closer, between her legs, reaching for her, pulling her mouth to his. He couldn't speak about this, not with any honesty, but he could bring her pleasure. That was something he was good at, at least. You didn't need to complete any complicated mathematical equation or have read Balzac to be good in bed, thank the Lord.

She did not resist, sinking her fingers into his hair. Good, that was good, he would win her this way. If he satisfied her here, perhaps she would overlook the rest, perhaps he could keep her here with him for good, if he were skilled enough.

He slid his hands under her skirts, sliding them up over silken stockings as he'd done at the inn. Only this time there was no Bainbridge to disturb them, or there had better not be. Anyone interfering this time would regret it.

"Lay back," he said, relieved to hear the command in his voice after dithering and fretting like a terrified schoolboy up to this point.

Her eyes widened a fraction, but she did as he asked. Dare took off her shoes and then pushed up her skirts, undoing the garters on her stockings. He tugged them free then rolled down each stocking and tossed them aside. He pushed her skirts higher as they slid over her thighs. Dare bent his head and kissed the inside of her knee, trailing his lips up her inner thigh to press another kiss a little higher, and then higher still. He heard her breathing hitch and smiled against her skin.

"I want you very much," he said. "I have thought of nothing but touching you, of having you touch me."

She sat up on her elbows and stared down at him. "I want you to. I want you to touch me. Please."

Please. As if he needed cajoling.

He huffed out a laugh and pushed her skirts higher still, exposing the soft nest of curls between her legs.

"My pleasure entirely," he murmured and pushed her legs wider apart before ducking his head and trailing his tongue over the sensitive skin at the apex of her thighs.

"Oh!" she exclaimed, jolting beneath him.

Dare smiled and did it again the other side, before pressing a kiss to the top of the curls. He blew out a soft huff of air over her and she shivered. Her breathing was coming faster now, and he kissed her again, a little lower, and again.

"Daire." There was urgency in her voice, his name a plea, and it struck him it was the first time a woman had used his given name, rather than simply calling him Dare, like everyone else.

"Yes?" he asked, aware of the timbre of his voice, husky with desire.

"Daire," she said again, squirming beneath him. "Please."

He bit back a smile, his hands caressing her thighs. "Please what?"

Emma V Leech

"Oh, you dreadful man, are you going to punish me now?"

"I would never punish you, love."

"Then please...." She sounded sulky now, and he wished he could see her face, see if that beautiful mouth had shaped into a pout.

"Please what?" he persisted. "Say it."

There was a taut silence, then she exploded. "Do it again!"

He could not help the chuckle that broke from him. He bent his head and kissed her again, kissed the curls and the seam that hid the tiny bud that he knew was aching for his touch.

"Like this?" he asked, nonchalant now as she squirmed and huffed.

"I've changed my mind," she said. "I don't like you at all."

"Really?" he said, revelling in this, in the way they had sparred from the beginning.

Dare loved the way she challenged him, scolding him and meeting him head on. He had missed this, missed their bickering. Deciding he had better not tease her too much on this occasion— there would be others, after all—he parted the delicate folds with his thumbs and licked.

She gasped, jolting beneath him so that he was forced to hold her still.

"What about now?" he asked, his own body thrumming with desire, his head spinning with the heady taste and scent of her. "Do you like me better now?"

"Oh, yes," she murmured. "Oh, Daire."

"And what about now?"

He settled to his work with single-minded devotion, responding to every gasp and moan, guided by the sounds she made, learning what pleased her the most. She cried out as he slid a finger inside her and Daire sucked in a breath, imagining sinking into her fully, into that tight heat. *Oh, God. Concentrate, you bloody halfwit. This is for her, for her alone.* He would please her, learn every inch of her, until she needed him as desperately as he feared he needed her. Every time she came close to the peak he retreated, soothing her, gentling her until her desperation subsided, only to build it again, higher, fiercer, until there was no going back.

She came with a shout of triumph, grasping at the bedclothes as her body shook and bucked and it was all he could do to hold her in place, to ease her through, but the tremors did not cease, shock after shock of pleasure rolling over her until at last she was trembling and sated, gasping for air.

Holy hell.

Dare stared at her, more than a little stunned. Well, he'd been determined to please her, hadn't he?

He stood, his legs stiff and a bit shaky but he needed to get his clothes off. Now. This minute. Shedding them with as much speed as possible, he heard buttons skitter over the floor and didn't give a damn. He needed to be inside her before he lost his mind. Dare climbed onto the bed. Elspeth lay like one dead, her eyes closed.

"Elspeth?"

He reached out and stroked her cheek and she sighed, turning towards his touch. Her eyes flickered open, a flash of green, dazed and darkened with lust. Dare let out a breath of relief.

"Please," he said, his previous surety disappearing in direct proportion to his desire as his body took over from his brain. "I need...."

Her eyes widened as she stared at him, seeing him naked for the first time. After a moment of hesitation she reached out, a tentative finger touching his nipple. *Christ.* He was so overwrought that little touch was like a jolt of electricity straight to his cock.

"Yes," she said, reaching for him. "Yes."

Oh, thank Christ. He climbed over her, wishing he'd taken the time earlier to get her out of her dress, but he couldn't do it now. He didn't have a shred of patience left, and he wasn't going to last as it was. Next time. Next time. Now he needed, he had to….

She gasped as he thrust into her and Dare muttered an oath. *Virgin, you cretin! She's a virgin!*

"Elspeth," he said, trying to fight through the overwhelming surge of pleasure and lust fogging his brain. "Hell, I'm sorry. Did… Did I hurt…?"

"No," she said with a sigh. "It feels odd, a little… uncomfortable."

She wriggled beneath him and Dare groaned. He forced himself to breathe in and out, slowly.

"Perhaps if you kissed me again," she suggested.

The small part of his brain that was still functioning, kicked him in disgust.

"Excellent idea," he murmured and kissed her to give her time to grow used to him inside her, while his hands wrestled with the hooks on her gown. At least it was a front fastening one. The corset beneath was more than his mental state could deal with right now, so he just gave it a hard tug down and eased one breast free, then the other. Her nipples peeked over the cups of the corset and Dare sighed happily, lowering his mouth to one and sucking gently.

"Oh my! Oh my, oh my, oh my."

Dare chuckled as her hands sank into his hair. "Like that, do you, my lady?"

"Don't talk, do it again," she said, impatient and imperious.

He snorted with amusement and happily did as she asked. Her body relaxed about him, thank God, for he was beside himself with the desire to move. Lifting his head to see her reaction, he eased out of her and thrust inside again.

She gasped, her eyes flying open to stare at him.

"Oh my?" he suggested with a grin.

"Oh yes," she agreed, and then. "Oh, *yes*!"

"Again?

"Stop talking, drat you. Just don't stop. Don't ever stop."

Dare laughed, helpless, knowing he was utterly lost. She was everything he could ever have dreamed and so much more. She made the most delicious little noises, sighs and gasps and moans, and sometimes his name, whispered low like a secret. Her hands moved over him, bold, exploring, honest in the delight she took in him, holding nothing back. She was a gift, something he never expected, did not deserve, but would hold on to with everything he had. Too soon the crisis was upon him and though he wanted to wait, to make it last forever she felt too good, it was too wonderful, too perfect to resist and so he could do nothing but careen towards the pinnacle. But he wanted her with him, wanted her to reach the peak again and for them to fall together. He slid his hand between them, seeking out the hidden place and caressing, circling, and praying she would hurry.

"Elspeth," he said, hardly finding wit enough to say her name. "Elspeth, I... I can't... please...."

He shattered, his body given over to his own burst of joy, the cry startled from him wild and surprised by the force of his climax. Elspeth made a small sound beneath him, her hands grasping at him as she trembled with pleasure, pulsing around him and sending him higher still. Bliss held him suspended for a long moment, fading in slow, heady increments and leaving him utterly boneless in the aftermath. Dare was vaguely aware he must be crushing her and made a half-hearted attempt to shift his body, but she wrapped herself tighter about him, holding him to her.

"Don't go," she said, still breathless. "Not yet."

Dare gave a huff of laughter and subsided.

"Can't," he said shortly. "You've killed me."

"Oh?" he heard the question in her response, but could not find the energy to raise his head. "It's… It's not always like that?"

He snorted. "It's *never* like that. Only with you, Elspeth."

She sighed, her hands trailing up and down his back and Dare fought the urge to fall asleep, aware she was still dressed.

"I must be crushing you."

"Only a bit. I don't mind. Though this corset is dreadfully uncomfortable."

Dare forced his unwilling limbs into motion.

"That won't do," he said. He lifted himself on his arms and kissed her nose, before moving off her. He padded to the washstand, he poured some water into a basin and dampened a clean cloth before returning to clean her up, relieved to discover there was no blood. He washed himself quickly and hurried back to the bed.

"Right, let's do this properly this time," he said, pulling her to a sitting position.

She almost slumped again.

"I'm too tired," she complained, laughing.

"Just for a moment, I promise." Deftly, now the edge had been taken off his desire, he unhooked and unbuttoned and undid, moving her this way and that, until only her shift remained. "Lift your arms."

She obeyed him and he tugged the shift over her head and caught his breath. Elspeth bit her lip, colour rising on her cheeks and Dare laughed.

"*Now* you blush?" he teased her.

177

Much to his delight, Elspeth stuck out her tongue.

"God, I love you," he said, grinning, and then realised what he'd said as her eyes widened. His heart gave an erratic thud in his chest, but he couldn't take it back now. He wasn't certain he wanted to, only... only he felt exposed, like he'd handed her his heart on a platter, alongside a sharp carving knife.

"Daire," she said, her astonishment obvious. "You...you *do*? Say it again."

His stomach twisted, but he didn't want to deny the words, even if they scared him to death.

"I love you," he said, and the admission seemed stark and undefended, except then a smile broke over her face.

Such a smile it was too, illuminating the room, lighting him up inside with the force of it. She flung herself at him with such enthusiasm he toppled backwards onto the bed as she peppered his face and neck with kisses.

"I love you," she said. "I love you too."

The relief of those words was indescribable, setting him free. Oh, he still knew it might not last, she might grow bored yet, but for now... for now she loved him, and he would hold onto that, to her, for as long as he could.

Chapter 15

Dear Henry,

I am so pleased you have finally taken my advice and are coming home. May I hope that you are also doing as I suggested and looking for a wife?

—Excerpt of a letter from Lady Harriet Cadogan, Countess St Clair to her brother, Mr Henry Stanhope.

9th June 1839, Rowsley Hall, Derbyshire.

Elspeth woke reluctantly. She was pleasantly sleepy and so very snug. As her heavy eyelids attempted to lift, she noticed her surroundings. Her bedroom at Rowsley, the sun streaming through the curtains so brightly it must be late indeed. She had overslept. Then she remembered why that was. Dare was holding her tight, his chest to her back, his arms about her. She could feel the warm huff of his breathing against the back of her neck and smiled. *Oh, last night.* A smile curved over her mouth as she remembered, all of it. He'd been so nervous, so anxious to please her, not to hurt her, and then… goodness. Mama had explained the mechanics of what would happen on her wedding night, and how, if her husband took care of her pleasure too, there would be a little explosion of delight, like fireworks inside. Well, Mama had not been wrong. Fireworks indeed. She'd felt incandescent that first time, with his mouth on her.... A blush rose over her cheeks even thinking about it. How wicked, how indecent, how... marvellous. And then when he had entered her, after the initial discomfort... Elspeth sighed. She had wanted him to make love to her again, and it had been quite obvious he wished to do so, men were not difficult to read in that manner at least. Yet he had been worried it was too soon after the first time, that he might hurt her, and his care of her had been so touching, so tender, that she hadn't pressed him. They had plenty of time now.

All her previous misery and anxiety had gone. This would be a happy marriage, she was certain of it now. Daire still held himself back, she knew. Not in lovemaking, at least. In that he had been honest. He had not meant to tell her he loved her, she felt sure. The look in his eyes after he'd said it had told her he had shocked himself as much as he had her. Yet he did love her, and she loved him. She would have to be patient then, that was all. He would come to trust her in time. His reluctance was hardly to be wondered at. Who had loved him up until now? Who had stood by him through thick and thin, had made him feel secure and worthy of their love and attention? Her heart ached to think of it.

A masculine sound of contentment broke into her thoughts as Dare's hands slid to her hips, pulling her bottom against him. Elspeth gasped as proof of his intention pressed against her, hard and hot and insistent.

"Good morning, my lord," she said, her voice a little unsteady.

A low rumble of laughter was his response to this formal greeting.

"Good morning, Lady Roxborough," he murmured, nuzzling her neck. "And a very fine morning it is, too. The very finest of mornings."

This bit was added as one hand found her breast and squeezed. Elspeth giggled.

"I am beginning to realise my husband is a very bad man."

"*Beginning* to realise?" he repeated with a snort, as his other hand caressed her thigh. "And here was I believing I'd married a bluestocking. You're supposed to be clever, love."

"I am," she retorted. "Clever enough to know it's all a hum. You might be wicked and depraved in the bedroom, but as for being a vile seducer or a hell-born babe, what nonsense. You're a big softy."

"A softy?" There was something like outrage in his voice and Elspeth bit her lip to stifle a laugh. "I'll show you how soft I am, madam."

Elspeth gasped as he did just that, sliding inside her as he hooked his arm beneath her knee, giving himself better access.

"Oh. Oh good heavens. Can... Can you do it this way?"

A choked sound came from behind her, and his voice was strangled as he replied. "*I* can."

Elspeth believed him as moved deeper inside her and pleasure rolled through her. His hand slid between her legs and stroked her intimately, and she tipped her head back, sighing. He loved her slowly and thoroughly, his hands exploring her with lazy caresses as everything inside her quickened and that urgent, gathering sensation flickered to life once more. He pressed kisses to her neck, sometimes biting gently, and she'd never realised such a thing as that could feel so good. Little by little sensation built, overwhelming her until her mind was hazy with lust. The world shrank to just the two of them, to the places where he touched her. Elspeth held her breath as the peak shimmered behind her eyes, waiting for the moment she would glitter into that other place, like stars thrown against the night sky.

"Elspeth," he whispered, such reverence in the way he said her name, holding her tighter, his rhythm faltering as she felt his body tighten. "Oh, God."

It was enough, the sound of him lost in pleasure, in her, more than enough to send her flying. She gripped at his arms, still startled by the wild cries that tore from her mouth but holding nothing back, hiding nothing from him, trusting in him.

They lay together, breathing hard, skin passion-damp and the scent of their lovemaking enveloping them.

"I'm never leaving this bed again," Daire said with feeling.

Elspeth laughed and hoped she could always make him this happy.

After a short nap and some more delicious bed sport, Elspeth insisted they get up, much to Dare's regret. If she didn't leave their bed before midday, she said she'd never be able to look their new servants in the eyes again, let alone Parker and Mrs Grigson. Dare had protested that they were newlyweds, and it was expected of them. A sorry sort of bridegroom they would think him if his bride were fit to leave her bedchamber at all for at least a month. Elspeth had given him a fond look and kissed him, promising him she would need a nap this afternoon to recoup her strength. That was enough to brighten him tremendously and so after breaking their fast together, he left her to inspect a collection of material samples that she had ordered to begin her restoration of Rowsley to its former glory.

The idea of spending the entire day in bed was one Dare was more than willing to take with utter seriousness, but he did have things of his own to attend to, including writing to his new father-in-law and asking for advice on employing a steward. He might not be blessed with a vast quantity of brains, but he knew better than to choose by himself. The thought that he might unwittingly employ another villain like his father had done who would mismanage or even steal Elspeth's dowry made him feel ill. A recommendation from Elspeth's father, or even better, her uncle, was certainly a better idea. That wasn't the only thing on his mind. He wanted to do something for his wife.

No. Honesty, Dare, my lad. You want to do something for yourself, to keep her here.

Very well. He wanted to make her happy. If she was happy, she would stay. If he had money of his own, he would lavish her with jewels and carriages and all the things women always loved to be given. He could hardly feel comfortable spending the money she'd brought to their marriage on such things when she was so set on spending it on Rowsley. She would worry that he was as spendthrift as his parents had been, and he couldn't have her think that. It wasn't true, either. Dare wasn't even certain she would appreciate such gifts, even if he'd had the wherewithal to buy them himself. No, it needed some thinking about. Dare stalked up and down the library, pausing at a knock on the door.

"Enter."

Parker came in, bearing a silver salver with a letter on.

"Lord Bainbridge said not to disturb you earlier but wished for me to let you know he's gone back to town, my lord."

"Already?" Dare said in surprise. "I wonder what brought that on?"

"He said he was going to get married, sir."

Dare stared at his redoubtable butler and wondered if the fellow was working too hard. Bainbridge? *Married?* "You're roasting me."

"No, indeed, my lord. He was quite clear on the subject. Perhaps the letter—"

Dare snatched the letter up. It had to be one of Bainbridge's jokes. He couldn't possibly....

Dare,

Sorry to dash off without saying goodbye, though I doubt you'll notice I'm gone or lament me. I've never felt more 'de trop' than last night whilst you and your lady made sheep's eyes at each other. Good to see you so happy though and put me in mind that it was just what I need myself. Duty and heirs and the like. Hopefully, a wife will suit me as much as yours suits you. Best get on with it. Don't make any plans for the rest of the month, you're to be my best man.

> *See you anon,*
>
> *Bainbridge.*

"Good God." Dare stared at the letter in disbelief before looking back at Parker. "Good God, Parker."

"Indeed, my lord."

"Do you think the Grenville blood has caught up with the poor blighter at last?"

"It certainly seems a somewhat rash decision."

"Rash? *Rash*? He's gone off his rocker! Bainbridge doesn't know any marriageable females. He's hardly good *ton*, marquess or no. Everyone knows the Grenvilles are all mad as badgers."

"The duke certainly has a reputation for being somewhat... eccentric."

Dare spluttered. *Eccentric*? Well, that was one way of putting it.

He looked back at the letter, trying to find some hidden meaning, some hint that Bainbridge was pulling his leg. He shook his head, puzzled.

"I mean, if he'd decided to become respectable before he went about searching for a wife, I'd be all for it, but it sounds like he's just going to pick some woman at random and... and what? March her up the aisle? A June wedding, by gad. He's got three weeks!"

"I got the impression his lordship had a particular lady in mind."

Dare gaped. This was becoming more extraordinary by the moment. "Devil take it! Who? He never said a word to me about anyone."

"Alas, he did not confide that information to me, my lord. I assume we will discover it in due course, however."

"Well, I never did. I'm spiflicated, Parker. There's no other word for it."

"It is rather a surprising development, I agree, sir. Will there be anything else?"

"No, no." Dare waved the old man away, too stunned to speak any more on the subject. Bainbridge, *married*? Good Lord.

It took some time for the shock to wear off and for Dare to return his thoughts to how best to keep his wife contented and with him at Rowsley. Well, other than pleasuring her until she was too tired to run off anywhere, which he was more than happy to make the focus of his plans. There needed to be something else, though. With the best will in the world, an intelligent girl like Elspeth would need more than his undivided attention to keep her happy. She had a brain in her head that needed exercising. How upset and furious she'd been when he'd ruined everything and made her a scandal, and she could no longer....

Oh, that was it.

Dare stopped his pacing, staring out the window at the beautiful landscape outside the library window as a smile curved over his mouth. That was it.

The very thing.

14th June 1839, Rowsley Hall, Derbyshire.

It was quite astonishing how things had changed at the Hall in such a short space of time. The place was alive with new servants bustling about, cleaning, and lugging furniture from this place to that place. Everywhere had the odour of fresh paint, and you couldn't sit down anywhere without first having to move a bolt of fabric or a book of wallpaper samples. Builders crawled over the place like ants, fixing and replacing, and the gardens were being ruthlessly hacked back into something resembling order. Dare didn't think Rowsley had ever been such a hive of activity, though of course he had never seen his parent's lavish entertainments. That had all stopped once he'd come along and ruined their little idyll. He wondered about that, about how his father must have felt to almost lose his beloved wife in childbed. Dare grew cold as he imagined Elspeth in such danger. Yet it was bound to happen eventually. She might be in the family way already, for all he knew. Something in his gut clenched with terror. Yes, he could understand his father's hating him for that. If Elspeth bore him a child and....

He paused, thinking on it.

No. *No.* No matter what happened, it wouldn't be the child's fault. Any baby they made together would be a little of each of them, the result of their loving each other, and no child ought to suffer for that. The baby was blameless, and how could he revile a child that was a part of her, a part of himself? Anger rose inside him for the child he'd been, and he pushed it down like he always did, locking it away in some dark place reserved for all the things he did not wish to remember. Life was good. Life was better than good, it was marvellous, and it was all because of his wife. Which was why he was here, staring up at some dilapidated buildings on the south side of the Hall.

"This one looks perfect," he said to John Green, the mason in charge of much of the repair work. He was a sturdy, sensible man who spoke plainly, and Dare had decided he liked him a great deal.

"Aye, my lord. Reckon so. The other, though, it'll need tearing down afore you've got any little ones running about here. A death trap, it is. Dry rot throughout, like standing on cheese."

Dare nodded his agreement.

"Very well. I want every man you can spare from the Hall. Make sure the structure is sound and then get it painted and cleaned up, and not a word to my wife about it. I've got furniture arriving in ten days. Can you do it?"

"It'll mean delaying a few jobs at the Hall. Her ladyship won't like it, and how am I to explain, eh?"

"Never mind that. I'll handle her ladyship," Dare said with a grin. "Just get it done. What about that place?" He gestured at the decaying building.

Green shrugged. "Pull it down for now, I suppose. Oughtn't take much. I'm only surprised it's still standing. Two strong horses and some rope should do it."

"Excellent." Dare grinned, feeling extremely pleased with himself.

Chapter 16

Dear Florence,

I am so utterly blue devilled. I am hopelessly in love with the Comte de Villen, and he doesn't seem to know I exist. Or at least, if he does, it's even worse, for I'm certain he is running away from me.

Something must be done about it. I'm so tired of being ignored. So to that end I have borrowed the hat of dares from Cat. Yes, <u>that</u> hat. The Peculiar Ladies all found their way to happiness because of it. Mama was so shy she couldn't even speak to a man without stammering before she took her dare and look how that turned out. Oh, how romantic, to kiss a man in the moonlight when you don't even know who he is. I should do such a thing in a heartbeat if I might end up with a man as good as Papa.

I must do <u>something</u>, though. Either something to make that wretched man notice me, or to find me another that will take my mind off him for good, for I cannot carry on this way. Vivien says she never took a dare the last time Cat brought the hat out but promises she will this time. Say you'll do it too? I propose that the

Peculiar Ladies should ride again, but with a new name, of course.

What do you think of – The Daring Daughters?

—Excerpt of a letter from Miss Arabella Hunt (daughter of Mrs Alice and Mr Nathanial Hunt) to Miss Florence Knight (daughter of Lady Helena and Gabriel Knight).

20th June 1839, Rowsley Hall, Derbyshire.

Elspeth glowered at the north corner of Rowsley Hall, complete with several broken windows, through which ivy had poked its insistent limbs, badly damaging the mortar in the walls. This whole corner of the building was in terrible repair and she inspected the progress only to find there was none.

"What the devil has Mr Green been doing? He promised me faithfully that he'd have this side of the building well in hand by now and… and he's not even begun!"

Dare decided distraction was his best bet, not to mention the course of action he would enjoy most himself. He moved behind Elspeth and slid his arms about her, ducking his head to kiss her neck.

"I'm sure he has a reasonable explanation," he murmured soothingly. "You can ask him next time you see him."

Elspeth's breath caught as he nuzzled at the tender spot beneath her ear, but she was not yet distracted. "How can I ask him when the wretched man has disappeared?"

"Hmmm, a puzzle indeed, but I have a more interesting one."

"A more interesting what?"

"Puzzle."

"What puzzle?"

"How to debauch my wife in the garden with no one noticing."

"Daire!" she said, obviously scandalised. "We can't... in the garden!"

"Is that a dare, Lady Roxborough?"

She pulled away from him, swinging around to stare at him in alarm. "Oh, no. You... You wouldn't."

Dare quirked one eyebrow.

Elspeth hesitated for a bare moment and then gave a little shriek, picking up her skirts and running. Dare watched her go, grinning, before sauntering after her in a leisurely fashion. He had to give her a sporting chance after all, those skirts and petticoats must be devilish tricky to run in. She was covering a fair amount of ground, though, to be fair. Deciding his wife had enough of a head start, he ran after her.

Rowsley had once had magnificent gardens, many of them laid out over terraces that descended towards the river below. Each terrace was divided into different gardens, some with walls and others with hedges. There were plenty of paths that would take you around the garden in different directions, opening here and there as you explored, upon a fountain or a statue, or a magnificent view. There were also a great number of hidden corners and secret places, all of which Dare knew, having discovered all of them as a boy. Well, there had been little else for him to do as a child, with no one to play with.

Elspeth had run down the stairs to a lower terrace and turned right, which meant she had unwittingly given him the perfect place to seduce her, well out of sight of the Hall. The gardeners were concentrating on the front of the house at the moment, and so they were unlikely to be disturbed by them either. Dare decided he'd let her get quite far enough away and put on a burst of speed.

She gave a little shriek of laughter as he lunged for her, getting the other side of a large fountain. The water splashed merrily, glinting in the sunlight as Dare stalked her.

"I've got you now, my lady," he said but his wife stubbornly shook her head.

"No, you haven't, my lord. Look, I'm free still."

"Not for long. I shall get my hands on you any moment now, and then you'll be sorry."

"Why is that?" she demanded, and he wasn't certain her breathless question was due entirely to the fact he'd chased her through the gardens.

"Because I shall make you do my bidding, and I won't let you go until you've pleased me."

Her eyebrows shot up at that. "Pleased you?"

"Yes, pleased me," Dare repeated, enjoying himself enormously. With a bit of luck he could get her all riled up. "You promised to obey me, did you not? Well, I demand that you please me."

"Obey you? If you seriously think I meant that when I said it—"

"Before God and witnesses," he reminded her. "You are mine, wife, to do with as I please. And it pleases me to do wicked things to you in the garden."

The flush that bloomed over her face and neck was delicious.

"I intend to discover just where that flush extends to as well," he added, smirking at her.

"Oh, you... you are dreadful!" she exclaimed, but there was excitement glinting in her eyes and Dare was not fooled for a moment. He made to run after her again and she squealed, hurrying farther around the fountain.

"You cannot escape me, Elspeth. Best give up now and surrender to your husband."

"Never!" she exclaimed. "I shall never surrender."

"As you please, you stubborn creature," Dare said with a nonchalant shrug, and then feinted right before running left. Elspeth gasped as he reached out, grabbing at her. She span away with a little scream, running back down the path, her laughter echoing about the garden.

She didn't really stand a chance. Dare had won every race he'd ever entered and would have caught her with ease even if she wasn't hampered by skirts and petticoats. As it was, he swept her up, tossing her over his shoulder.

"Let me go!" she said, hitting his back, though not in the least bit hard. "Daire, I will make you pay if you don't let me down this minute, you odious creature."

Dare smacked her behind, which was less than satisfactory with so many layers in between but amused him all the same. "Not on your life."

He carried her away to a small stone bench under an arbour. It was hidden from view of the house, but the Derbyshire countryside spread out before them like a patchwork quilt in every imaginable shade of green. The arbour itself was thick with honeysuckle, the sweet scent heady on the warm air as bees and insects hummed around them. Dare set Elspeth gently down, sliding her down the length of his body and keeping one arm tight about her so she could not escape.

"Devil!" she said, glaring at him and trying her best to look outraged, but the corners of her mouth twitched, giving her away.

"Ah, well, you knew that the day we met, love. Don't make out like it's a surprise."

He chuckled and sat down, tugging her into his lap none too gently. She sat with a flurry of skirts and Dare lost no time in pulling her into his arms and kissing her. She surrendered at once, pliant in his arms, her hands reaching up to slide into his hair. Dare kissed her, slow and deep, enjoying how her breathing came faster and faster. He reached for her skirts and slid his hand beneath, sliding up her leg. Elspeth pulled away, her eyes wide.

"We can't," she protested. "Not... Not out here."

"Why not?" he asked, all innocence, his hand moving up over her thigh and stroking.

"Because!" Her indignation was just delicious as she lowered her voice and whispered urgently. "Someone might see. Let's go back to the house, to our room, and I'll... I'll do whatever you want," she added boldly.

"Whatever I want?" Dare quirked an eyebrow at her. "Well, that is indeed an extremely tempting offer, but I think you'll do whatever I want, right here and now."

"Oh! You're impossible," she huffed.

"Oh, no. Not at all. I'm perfectly docile really, very manageable. Especially for a clever girl like you. Putty in your hands, I'd say."

Elspeth quirked an eyebrow, wriggling against his erection in a most distracting manner.

"Putty?" she queried and then giggled.

"Perhaps not," he admitted. "Though I'd like to be in your hands all the same."

She stared at him and then gave a little snort. "Oh, my. The things you say."

"I'd worry more about the things I do," he murmured, having reached his destination and sliding his fingers through the soft curls under her skirts. She gasped and pressed her face against his neck.

"Oh," she said, and he swore he could feel the heat of her blush burning against his skin. "Oh, this… this is so…."

"Naughty?" he suggested.

She nodded as he caressed her, sliding between her legs and finding she was certainly as excited by their little race through the gardens as he was.

"So beautiful," he whispered.

She looked up then, still somewhat bashful, but she pressed her mouth to his and he responded happily, kissing her deeply. Her breathing hitched and she drew away.

"I… I thought I was supposed to be pleasing you," she said, her voice shaky.

Dare gazed at her with adoration. "Haven't you figured that out yet, love? Pleasuring you pleases me more than anything else on earth."

She gave a choked laugh and her head tipped back. Dare kissed her neck and the tops of her breasts.

"I want more," he growled.

Elspeth looked at him, and he bit the material of her gown where it covered her nipple.

"Oh." Being an intelligent girl, she understood at once, and now her initial shyness was evaporating she loosened her gown and wriggled and tugged until her breasts popped free.

"Thank you," he said fervently, staring at the bounty before him with his mouth watering. Yet she wasn't done, and his breath hitched as she cupped her breasts, offering them to him.

"Oh, I love you," he moaned. "I love you. I love you."

She laughed and his heart seemed too full in his chest, pressing against his ribs as her happiness spilled over him. So he showed his appreciation by feasting upon her like a man starved until she was gasping and moaning, her hand clutching at his hair now, holding him in place. Finally she tugged at his head and he looked up, only to find her mouth on his, her hands fumbling at the buttons on the fall of his trousers.

"Christ, oh, yes. Yes, please," he said, as her slender hand wrapped around him. She stroked, firm and sure, just as he'd shown her to do and he groaned, well aware he would not last. "Elspeth. Elspeth, please."

He tugged at her skirts, urging her to straddle him and doing his best to bundle skirts and petticoats out of the way.

"Oh, this is dreadful," she said, the delight in her eyes making him give a bark of laughter.

"Yes, awful," he agreed readily. "Depraved."

"Out in the open!" The wonder in her expression at their daring was a joyous thing and he pulled her down, thrusting into her as she cried out, her head falling back, eyes closed. "Oh, you wicked, wicked man."

"Shall I stop?" he asked, his voice husky now.

"Under no circumstances."

"We'll frighten the cows."

Elspeth turned her head to regard the herd munching grass with calm content on the far side of the garden.

"They can stampede for all I care," she said, breathlessly.

Dare laughed and laughed, happiness and pleasure rolling over him as he came with a choked gasp, holding on tight as her body shuddered about his and she muffled her cries against his shoulder.

"I'm so glad I caught you," he said, still clouded by the haze of euphoria as he held her to him.

"Me too. A good job you're so devilish quick."

She raised her head and smiled at him, pressing little kisses to his face. "You are rather wonderful, you know. I thought I'd have a wretched time of it turning you into a good husband, but look at you."

"Debauching you in the garden?" he said wryly. "Is that what makes a good husband, then? If only I'd known before."

She smacked his shoulder. "Not that, although… well, yes, that too, but you are kind and thoughtful, and you make me laugh so."

Dare looked away from her and rested his head against her breast. He knew she meant it as a compliment, and it was, it *did* please him only… only was that what he was? A clown to amuse her. Anxiety and unease slithered beneath his skin and no matter how he told himself he was being a fool, it wouldn't go away.

"Daire?"

"Hmmm?" he said, avoiding her too sharp gaze.

"Daire, what is it?"

"Nothing," he said at once, rubbing his face against her breasts. "These are very distracting."

She took his face between her hands and lifted it so she could look at him. Elspeth studied him, her gaze intent, as if she would see inside his brain if she could. Dare held still, keeping his expression neutral even as his heart pounded. He had to be more than a joke to her, more than an amusement. Jokes got old, and no amusement could please for long, he knew that.

"I love you," she said, and his heart skipped at the words, wanting to hold to this moment, wanting it to last forever.

Something inside him refused to believe it. She would leave. Everybody left. He would be alone again.

No.

No, she wouldn't leave him, she loved him. She *did.* He believed her.

"I love you too, Elspeth. So much."

She smiled at that and held him to her, hugging him tightly.

Elspeth luxuriated in the hot bath that had been drawn for her. The scent of her favourite scented oils rose about her, reminding her of the honeysuckle that had been all about them as they'd made love in the garden. She could not quite believe they'd done such a thing. It seemed far too exciting and licentious a thing for quiet little Elspeth Cadogan to have done. She did not think she would ever be able to smell honeysuckle again without blushing and thinking wicked thoughts. It had been quite the most exciting thing she'd ever experienced in her entire life. She could not help but wonder if there were other places about the gardens where they could do such things. Though there was no one to know she had thought such a thing she felt her cheeks heat and laughed quietly at herself. Dare would love it if she seduced him somewhere secluded. She could just see the delight in his eyes when he realised what she was about. Elspeth decided there and then that choosing a colour scheme for the small dining room could wait. Tomorrow, she was taking a thorough inventory of the gardens and the surrounding countryside and making careful notes of all the best, most private places. It was only then she realised she'd completely forgotten about speaking to Mr Green. Ah, well. That could wait too. Making Dare happy was far more important.

Pleased with this idea, she sighed, and then remembered Dare's reaction to her words about him being a good husband. She had troubled him, she was sure, despite his reassurances to the contrary. What had she said? Elspeth replayed those moments in her mind, trying to put her finger on what had upset him. She'd told him he was a wonderful husband, that she loved him because he was kind and thoughtful and funny and… and what in the world was there in that to upset him? Try as she might she could not figure it out, but she would. Eventually, she *would* understand him, no matter how long it took.

Chapter 17

Dearest Arabella,

Fear not, my friend. I am more than willing to be a Daring Daughter. We shall be every bit as bold and fearless as our mothers before us.

I say, bring on the hat! Our destinies await us.

—Excerpt of a letter from Miss Florence Knight (daughter of Lady Helena and Gabriel Knight) to Miss Arabella Hunt (daughter of Mrs Alice and Mr Nathanial Hunt).

21st June 1839, Rowsley Hall, Derbyshire.

"You've excelled yourself, Green," Dare said, slapping the man on the back and beaming at him. "Truly. I never expected it to be done so quick."

"Ah, well. The place wasn't in such a state as we feared once it was cleared. The structure is sound, and the roof was easy enough to repair with the other old barn to take from."

Dare nodded, turning to look at what remained of the other building. A huge pile of rubble and wood and tile.

"That must go," he said with a sigh.

"Aye. That don't need skilled labour, though. I've taken the liberty of engaging a local farmer by name of Fletcher to come with his lads and clear it. He'll do it free if he gets to keep the stone. I hope that suits your lordship."

"It does, indeed. We've enough on repairing what's here, without building anything else for now. If he clears it quick, it's his and welcome to it."

"That's what I figured. Ah, here's the fellow now."

Dare looked around to see a sturdy horse pulling a cart, driven by a broad shouldered man with his young son beside him. Another cart followed him with two much older boys, the biggest of whom was holding the reins.

"Morning, Fletcher," Mr Green called out.

Mr Fletcher and his sons were then duly presented to Lord Roxborough with a deal of cap tugging and politeness, which always made Dare feel something of an imposter. He bore it and did his best to put them at ease. When he offered to help them load the carts, however, they looked at him in blank amazement.

"I'm not entirely useless," Dare said, a touch defensively. "I know us idle aristos don't have a lot going for us, but I can lug a bit of stone about."

Mr Green and Mr Fletcher shared a glance which seemed to speak volumes about the whims and fancies of the aristocracy, but shrugged their accord. If Dare wanted to get himself all sweaty and dusty, that was up to him.

It took them an hour to load both carts, by which time everyone was hot and thirsty. Whilst Fletcher and his boys took the carts back to the farm, Dare went back to the Hall and got the attention of one of the gardeners. Giving the fellow instructions to tell the kitchens to bring a ready supply of drinks and snacks for the workers, he returned to the ruined barn. Whilst he was waiting, he took another look around the newly renovated school building. Though it was devoid of furniture for the moment, it was clean and tidy. There was nothing very fancy, but there was a large chalkboard on the far wall and wide windows with lots of light. By the front door, an elegant painted wrought iron sign leaned, ready to be put up.

Roxborough School for Boys and Girls.

Elspeth had taught previously at an all-girls school, but this school would serve the children of the local village, and it seemed unreasonable to Dare that they should exclude the boys. He felt certain Elspeth would not mind. After having done some discreet investigation Dare had discovered there were twenty-three children aged between four and twelve. Nine boys and fourteen girls. According to Parker, apart from the eldest child—a boy who had been apprenticed to the local blacksmith—all the other children could attend the school, some only on a part time basis. It was certainly better than nothing. Dare did not consider himself a terribly bright fellow, having done appallingly badly at school in everything but sport, but he could not imagine how difficult life must be if you couldn't read or write or do simple sums.

The rumble of wheels announced the return of the carriages, and Dare headed outside to meet them. On the first cart, the youngest boy, a lad of about nine, was leaning upon his father's shoulder. His face was flushed and his eyelids drooping with fatigue.

"Here, Toby," Dare said, reaching for him. "There's some nice, cold lemonade ready for you. It's dashed hot today for hauling stone, eh, my lad?"

Toby nodded weakly and tried to get up but stumbled. Dare caught the boy before he tumbled off the side of the cart.

"Toby!" his father exclaimed, running around the cart to his son.

"He doesn't look too well," Dare said, staring down at the boy in his arms with a frown of concern. He carried the boy over to a grassy bank and laid him down in the shade of a tree.

"Bring him some lemonade."

One of the older brothers ran to do so and brought a cool glass back to him.

"Here, Toby. Drink some of this, old chap." Dare said, supporting the boy and putting the glass to his lips.

"Sore throat," the boy said, his voice scratchy.

Dare paused with the lemonade in hand. Perhaps that would be too sour for a sore throat.

"Is there water?" he asked.

"Aye, my lord."

Another glass was brought, and Toby drank thirstily, wincing as the swallowing motion clearly caused him discomfort.

"Thank you, my lord," he said faintly and closed his eyes.

Dare frowned and put his hand to the boy's forehead.

"He's burning up," he said in alarm.

"I'd best get him home to his ma," Mr Fletcher said, shaking his head. "Too much sun, do you think?"

Dare looked up at the man. "It's a warm day, but not that hot."

"Get back."

Dare jolted as Mr Green took his arm and forced him to his feet, tugging him away. Green pointed to a rash of red spots over the boy's neck, disappearing beneath his collar.

"Scarlet fever," he said, his tone grim. "Have you had it, Lord Roxborough?"

"I...." Dare tried to remember. "I don't know."

"You'd know if you had." Green shook his head. "Fletcher, take the boy home and keep away from your neighbours. All of you. We don't want an epidemic sweeping the village. Do you know where it might have come from?"

Fletched shook his head. "Unless… his aunt came to visit the day before yesterday. She lives in town. Maybe…."

Dare saw fear in the man's expression and his heart went out to him.

"Did anyone else call whilst she was visiting?" Green demanded.

Fletcher shook his head, too shocked to speak.

Mr Green gave Dare a fierce look. "There's a chance we can contain it if the aunt brought it in and spoke to no one else, but we must keep the family apart from everyone else."

"I'll send for a doctor to attend him, Fletcher," Dare assured him. "He'll have the best care. Anything you need. Don't worry. Just get him home."

Mr Fletcher nodded, silent, gratitude in his eyes.

Dare watched Mr Fletcher and his sons take the carriages and Toby away, before turning to Mr Green. "Will he be all right?"

Why he asked he did not know. He knew as well as anyone what a wicked disease it was.

Green's face was taut.

"Doubtful," he said curtly. Dare sensed it was not callousness that fuelled the terse response but some deeper, more painful emotion. He looked back at Dare.

"My Lord, would it be an imposition if I were to seek lodgings here for a few nights. I'll sleep in the stables willingly and see no one, but I have five children, and I'll not risk taking that vile disease back to them."

"Of course. I'll have Mrs Grigson make arrangements. Not the stables, I assure you."

"I'll not impose any longer than needs be, only…." The man's voice trembled a little and Dare reached out, squeezing his arm.

"There's no need to explain, and no hurry. You stay until it is safe to return. It's not like I don't have the room."

"I won't forget it," Green said with a sharp nod, and strode away.

Dare walked over to the fence post where he had left his coat and slung it over his shoulder. Troubled, he began the walk back to the Hall. Scarlet fever was a dreadful disease that killed hundreds, sometimes many thousands as it swept through communities. Children were, as ever, the most at risk and the illness struck fear in the heart of every parent. It usually effected the poorest slum areas worst of all, and the idea of the dreadful disease taking a hold in the relatively bucolic surroundings about the Hall made Dare's blood run cold. Thank God they did not yet have children.

Dare had never been a religious man. With no one to care overmuch about his education, let alone his moral upbringing, he had pieced together a code of his own and had never had much time for considering God, but now he prayed for Toby, for all those in the surrounding villages, and asked for their safety. He was struck with the sudden and forceful desire to see Elspeth, to hold her and remember how very fortunate he was. Picking up his pace, he hurried towards the gardens.

Elspeth sighed. She had picked the perfect spot for her seduction and the dratted man had disappeared off the face of the earth. No one seemed to know where he was, or if they did, they were unwilling to tell her. Wandering the gardens a tad despondently, her heart leapt as she saw a figure striding purposely across the field that adjoined this side of the garden.

Daire.

Her breath caught as she watched him grow nearer. Whatever had he been doing? For his clothing was dirty and dusty, his coat slung negligently over one shoulder, his sleeves rolled up. What was it about seeing his powerful forearms, dusted with dark hair, that made something inside her turn all hot and liquid, like warm honey? She had seen him naked often enough now, yet just the sight of his strong hands and those arms... she sighed and hoped her plans had not been a waste of time after all. Then she saw his expression, the way his dark brows drew together.

Elspeth picked up her skirts and ran to meet him, certain that something was wrong. He stopped when he saw her and opened his arms, pulling her into a fierce embrace and holding on tight.

"What is it?" she asked, stroking his hair as he buried his face in her neck, breathing her in.

"Christ!" he said in alarm and thrust her away from him.

Elspeth gasped. "What—"

"Have you had scarlet fever?"

"Why?"

"Damn it, answer the question." His expression was one of pure terror and Elspeth answered calmly, knowing he would explain once he had his answer.

"Yes," she said. "Greer and I had it when we were babies. It was very mild. The doctor said we were lucky to have had it so young. Babies seem to survive it better than children."

He let out a shuddering breath. "Thank God. Damn me for a fool, I ought to have considered."

"Considered what, Daire? What's happened?"

"A lad from the village has it. Quick, come back to the house. I must summon a doctor to attend them."

Elspeth followed in his wake, her heart aching with fear for the village, for what this might mean. Scarlet fever could wipe out entire families in the space of hours. They could not afford an outbreak.

"The family must be quarantined," she said breathlessly, struggling to keep up with his huge strides in her heavy skirts.

"Yes, that's been dealt with. I need to get word to the rest of the village to stay away from them though, and to mix as little as possible with each other until we are certain the danger is passed. Parker," he said, upon seeing the butler as he burst in through one of the back doors to the Hall.

"My lord?"

"Get someone to fetch the doctor at once. Whoever can ride best may take my horse, but they must get him to the Fletchers' residence in the village with all haste. Their youngest son has scarlet fever. Ensure nobody at the Hall goes near the place."

"At once, sir," Parker said, hurrying away.

"Mrs Grigson!" Daire bellowed, hurrying down the corridor that led to the housekeeper's office. "Mrs Grigson!"

The woman bustled out of her room, staring indignantly at being called in such a fashion.

"What the devil...?"

"Mrs Grigson," Dare said, before the wretched woman could speak a word. "I want baskets made up to be sent to the Fletcher family. I don't know what is of most use to a child with scarlet fever, but I am certain you will know what best to provide. Ensure there are some simple repasts for the rest of the family too. His poor mother will be too frantic to think of cooking, I don't doubt."

"If there's sickness in the village, it's best no one goes near at all," Mrs Grigson said, folding her arms. "Suppose the footman brings it back?"

"The footman can leave the basket at the farm gate," Daire said impatiently, looking more like the nobleman that he was in that instant than Elspeth had ever seen him before. "You'll do as I say without question. I am grateful for the efforts you've made to keep the Hall in order over many years of neglect, but I've had quite enough of your damned insults and insinuations. I am not my father and never will be, a fact I should think you would accept by now. You will do as I or Lady Roxborough instructs, or you may find a position elsewhere."

Mrs Grigson stared at him, her face stark white, her posture rigid, and Elspeth held her breath, waiting for the woman to reply with some outrageous cutting remark. To her astonishment, Mrs Grigson let out a breath, and the tension left the woman's shoulders.

"Forgive me, Lord Roxborough. I forgot myself. I will see to it everything is done to your satisfaction."

There was respect in her tone and her manner, not even a suspicion of her usual supercilious, mocking manner.

Daire blinked, clearly as taken aback as Elspeth was.

"Will there be anything else, my lord?" Mrs Grigson asked.

"No, Mrs Grigson, that is all."

"Wait," Elspeth said, stalling the woman. "Has Lord Roxborough had scarlet fever?"

Mrs Grigson shook her head at once. "He was never sick a day in his life to my knowledge, my lady. Unless at school...?"

"I had measles," Daire said with a shrug. "I remember being in the school infirmary for that. I spent a good deal of time there, actually, but usually because I'd broken something. Most often my head."

Elspeth stared at him, her heart beating very hard.

"Did you have any contact with the child, Daire?"

"Only for a moment, don't fret, love. I'm not a child. It's rarely that severe for adults, I think?"

He glanced at Mrs Grigson, who pursed her lips and said nothing.

"I'm fine," he said again, taking Elspeth's hands, which felt clammy and cold.

Elspeth smiled as he squeezed her fingers.

"Yes. Yes, of course," she said, though fear lanced through her, making her feel a little sick.

"Will that be all, my lord? I must consult my medical books to see what is most appropriate to feed the child during the fever."

"Indeed, Grigson, I should be grateful. Do that with all haste," Daire said.

Mrs Grigson nodded.

"My lord, my lady," she said, bowing her head respectfully before hurrying away.

Daire watched this with obvious astonishment before turning to Elspeth. "What just happened?"

Elspeth smiled and took his arm. "I think she just realised that you are Lord Roxborough."

Chapter 18

Dare, old man,

I've done it.

I'm to be married in two weeks. I hope you will stand up with me. I confess I am a little nervous and should like to have a friend at my side.

—Excerpt of a letter from Lawrence Grenville, The Most Honourable, The Marquess of Bainbridge, to Daire Kelburn, The Right Honourable, The Viscount Roxborough.

22ⁿᵈ June 1839, Rowsley Hall, Derbyshire.

It happened so fast that it seemed to Elspeth she had been plunged into a nightmare.

Daire had been quiet that evening and had been too distracted to eat much at dinner. They had retired early to bed, and he had made love to her, slowly and with such tenderness that Elspeth could be in no doubt of his feelings for her. Her husband loved her deeply, and she wanted very much for him to know his feeling were returned. She had assured him that they were, and he had smiled and kissed her, but there was something in his eyes that told her he did not quite believe it.

The next morning he woke with a headache and a sore throat. By evening, a rash had appeared over his chest and neck, and his temperature was raging.

Elspeth looked around from where the doctor was tending Daire and was surprised to see Mrs Grigson appear with the jug of fresh water for which she had sent. Her maid, Bertha, had not had the illness and was staying in a room far from Elspeth's for the duration, but why the housekeeper had lowered herself with such a menial task Elspeth could not fathom. Her husband's sudden illness terrified her too deeply to consider it further.

"It's a bad case," the doctor said gravely as he turned back to her. "He'll need a lot of tending. Do any of your staff have nursing experience? If not, I shall send for someone to care for him."

"I shall nurse my husband," Elspeth said, knowing that she could never trust another to care for him as diligently as she would.

The doctor gave her a pitying look and guided her away from Daire's bedside, lowering his voice. "My lady, your desire to care for your husband is to be commended, but I do not think you understand what you are taking on. Scarlet fever is a vile disease. It is not something for a lady to—"

"I am well aware—"

"Have you seen a case before?" he asked gently.

Elspeth crossed her arms and shook her head.

"The worst cases of scarlet fever are those in which the disease begins with great severity, as with Lord Roxborough. It is likely you will see delirium set in, or even convulsions. Soon the rash will spread, and the tongue becomes covered with a white fur, through which appear little red papillae or points, giving the appearance described as the strawberry tongue. There is great swelling of the neck, making swallowing and breathing difficult. On about the fifth day, the skin, which has been the seat of the rash, begins to peel off. This process is called desquamation, and during this time his lordship must be especially protected from cold."

Elspeth swallowed, taken aback by this rather stark explanation, but no less determined to care for Daire.

"I understand that the following days will be unpleasant," she said, keeping her voice even and calm, though she wanted to scream and cry. "But my husband is the one suffering. I swore to care for him, in sickness and in health, did I not?"

"Indeed, my lady, and I urge you to keep him company as a good wife should, but the personal care of a such a sick man—"

"Lady Roxborough is more than capable of looking after his lordship," said a sharp, stern voice from behind them.

Both Elspeth and the doctor looked around in shock, the doctor stiffening with indignation to have been addressed so by the housekeeper, not that his obvious annoyance stopped Mrs Grigson.

"I'll be by to help her ladyship, having nursed a fair number of patients through various ailments in my time, sir. If you'll leave us precise written instructions for the use of any medicines or treatments, we shall take care to apply them just as you would wish. Shan't we, my lady?"

Elspeth stared at Mrs Grigson, feeling a surge of gratitude towards the cantankerous housekeeper. "Indeed we shall, Mrs Grigson."

"Well, there you are then, doctor," Mrs Grigson said, guiding the dumbfounded man from the room. "Shall you visit his lordship again first thing?"

"Well, yes, but—"

"Excellent, we shall expect you in the morning to see how he goes on. Now if you'll excuse us, we must give Lord Roxborough our full attention just as you have instructed. Good evening, sir, and thank you."

Elspeth watched as Mrs Grigson closed the door in the doctor's outraged face.

"Prosy old devil," she muttered. "Blasted quacks always think they're God almighty. As if we can't see to his lordship by ourselves, weak and feeble women as we are."

Elspeth gave a little bark of laughter, quite astonished by this, and then burst into tears, suddenly overwhelmed by the reality of having Daire's life in her hands.

"What if the doctor is right?" she whispered. "What if—"

"Nonsense," Mrs Grigson said sharply. "You're fit and strong and your husband needs you. Are you going to let him down?"

Drawing in a deep breath, Elspeth shook her head. "No. No, that I shall not do."

"Well, then," the housekeeper said.

"Well, then," Elspeth repeated with a nod, and went to tend her husband.

Five exhausting days and nights later, Elspeth wondered if she had made a horrible mistake. Daire was gravely ill, and knowing that he relied entirely on her care to survive overwhelming. Still, she worked diligently, following the doctor's orders to the letter as well as what seemed to her and Mrs Grigson to be plain common sense. Every morning, they changed the sheets on the bed and opened the windows wide to air the room, whilst ensuring Daire was well tucked up under the covers. Thankfully, the weather was warm even in the early morning and there was no risk of him catching a chill. As his throat swelled, his breathing became difficult and raspy and sometimes Elspeth would sit watching him with her heart in her mouth, wondering if the next laboured breath would be his last. His skin peeled as the doctor had warned, and Elspeth bathed him carefully with a sponge and a mixture of warm water, chlorate of potash, and spirits of nitre, hoping to give him some relief.

The nights were the worst and, just when she thought she saw some sign of improvement, his fever would rage again. This evening his breathing was a little easier, but he was deathly pale and yet burning hot, his skin like paper. His mind wandered, and he spoke to people who were not there, revealing parts of his life and myriad neglectful cruelties that made Elspeth weep for him. He called for her endlessly, and she held his hand, reassuring him she was there, not knowing if he heard her.

"You should get some rest, my lady," Mrs Grigson said, handing her a cup of tea.

Elspeth reluctantly let go of Daire's hand to take the cup from her and smiled her thanks.

"Not yet. He's so restless tonight. Perhaps if he settles."

"You'll be no good to anyone if you make yourself ill too," the woman scolded. "There's a long road ahead of us yet."

"I know. I shall take care," Elspeth reassured her.

She was grateful for Mrs Grigson's rather abrasive presence. If anyone had been kind to her and treated her gently, Elspeth did not think she could have withstood it, but Mrs Grigson's hard-headed attitude and cool competence was a bolster against her own uncertainty, shoring her up. She could not pretend she felt any warmth towards the woman who had treated her husband with so little care when he was a boy, when she could so easily have been kind to him. However, she had proven her worth these past days, and showed no signs of flagging. They would make the master well again, and that was all there was to it in Mrs Grigson's mind. Elspeth believed her. She had to. The terror of any alternative made her heart break.

"Well, if you're going to be stubborn, I shall take a nap. I'll be back in two hours to take over and I'll brook no argument from you then."

"Yes, Mrs Grigson. I will rest then, I promise."

Not that she would leave the room. She had ordered a cot set up in the far corner and slept there, so she might be at hand in a moment should Daire have need of her. The door closed quietly behind Mrs Grigson, and Elspeth sipped her tea, grateful for the extra sugar the housekeeper had added. She hoped it would help her stay awake as her eyelids were heavy, her eyes dry and scratchy, as if they'd been rolled in sand. She must look a fright for she'd not washed her hair since Daire fell ill, and only hid the tangled mess behind a lace cap. Nothing mattered but getting her husband well again.

"Elspeth, Elspeth…."

Daire writhed fretfully on the bed and Elspeth set her cup down at once.

"I'm here, Daire. I'm here, my darling."

She laid her hand gently against his cheek. His beard was prickly and his handsome face all but unrecognisable. Anyone else seeing him now might recoil in horror, but Elspeth could only see the man she loved, fighting for his life.

"Elspeth. Don't leave."

"I won't leave," she soothed him, reaching for the sponge and squeezing out the excess liquid before gently applying it to his face.

"You will. You will, you'll leave. I know… I know…. Must keep you here. Make you stay, want to stay."

"I do want to stay, love," Elspeth said, hearing her voice tremble. "I want to stay with you always."

"No. No. You'll go… bored with me."

"I won't!"

"Find someone else, someone clever…. Dare's a dunce. Idiot boy… why do you shame me? I… I didn't mean to, Father. You ought never… never been born. Your poor mother."

Elspeth sank to her knees beside the bed and wept, clinging to Daire's hand. She had heard too much of this to dismiss it as ramblings. His father had done nothing but make Daire feel worthless and stupid, and it was a damned good job the man was already dead, for right at this moment she felt as if she could have killed him with her bare hands.

"Daire, I love you," she said through her tears. "I love you and I need you. You're everything to me and I don't know what I shall do if you leave me. Please, my darling. Fight for me. Get well and come back to me. If you do, I shall prove to you just how worthy you are, and I shall never, *never* leave you."

9th July 1839, Rowsley Hall, Derbyshire.

Dare groaned and licked his dry, parched lips. His head ached as if he'd been on intimate terms with too many bottles of brandy. Blinking eyelids that felt like lead, he squinted about the room. Dim light from behind the thick curtains of his chamber suggested it was not long after dawn. Christ, what had happened? He'd knocked himself about enough over the years to be used to bumps and bruises and broken bones, but this…! Had he been run down by the mail coach? He lifted a trembling hand to his temple.

"Awake, are you, old man?"

With some difficulty, he turned his head to see a shadowy figure in the chair beside him.

"Bainbridge?"

"The very same."

"What—" Dare rasped.

"Here." Bainbridge got up and hooked an arm behind Dare, lifting him and placing a glass of cool water to his lips.

Dare drank gratefully, the water sweet and wonderfully cold against his throat.

"Thank you."

"It's not me you need to thank," Bainbridge said quietly. "Your wife has worked a damn miracle if you ask me. I thought you were going to breathe your last, old chap, I won't lie. Elspeth wouldn't have it, though. I think she kept you alive through sheer willpower."

"Elspeth," Dare said, his heart leaping in his chest. "Where?"

"Hush." Bainbridge put a finger to his lips and gestured to the other side of the room.

Dare turned to look. Elspeth was asleep on a little cot there, rumpled and snoring softly.

"She's exhausted," Bainbridge said. "She's not left your side for a moment, Dare. Do you realise you've been ill for almost three weeks? No one could make her leave you. She's barely slept. I came to help when I heard you were so ill. Mrs Grigson and I have done our best to help shoulder the burden, but she is one stubborn young lady. The best thing you ever did was marry that woman. You're a lucky man. Especially considering the state of you. Most women would run a mile if they saw you looking like that."

Dare was still coming to terms with the fact that Elspeth had nursed him so carefully for so long—*three weeks?* —and that Bainbridge, of all people, had come to help too, but he frowned at that. *Looked like what?*

"What do you mean?"

Bainbridge laughed. "I hate to be unkind, Dare, old man, but you look like you've been boiled in oil and dried in the sun."

Dare glanced down at his hand and almost recoiled as he saw his skin peeling off.

"Bloody awful disease," Bainbridge said, shaking his head. "I had it as a boy. Looked much as you do now. They didn't think I'd survive. Killed my sister, of course. Still, don't fret, you'll recover now and be good as new in no time. You'd better be, anyway. I need a best man. I delayed my marriage for you, I hope you realise?"

Dare gaped at him. "Married? You don't mean to say you did it? You got some poor girl to agree to marry you?"

Bainbridge shifted a little in his chair. "In a manner of speaking. Didn't you get my letter? But no, I suppose you must have fallen ill by then."

"What the devil does that mean? 'In a manner of speaking,'" Dare demanded suspiciously.

"Never mind what it means. You're not to get excited, so I shan't tell you. Besides, the gossip will reach you soon enough."

"Bainbridge," Dare's voice held a warning note. "What have you *done*?"

Bainbridge shrugged. "Found myself a wife, that's all. I shan't tell you any more until you come back to town, so for heaven's sake hurry up and get well again. I can't be waiting too long, or there will be even more talk."

"Christ." Dare groaned. He had the feeling Bainbridge had done something reprehensible, but he was too tired to force it out of the devil. He'd have to wait and see. "Can I at least know who the lucky young lady is?"

Bainbridge's face softened for a moment, such a rare event upon his harsh features that Dare wondered if he had imagined it. "No, for your wife thinks quite kindly of me for racing to your bedside the moment I heard you were so ill. I've been here over a week, I hope you realise. I believe your lady is a friend of my

217

affianced, however, so... I think I shall keep quiet for now. She has enough to contend with caring for Frankenstein's monster here without feeling the need to ring a peal over me."

Dare blanched. "Frankenstein's monster? Bloody hell, is it that bad? Give me a mirror."

Bainbridge laughed and shook his head. "No. Get some rest, you silly bastard, and stop being so vain. Your wife loves and adores you, even in this sorry state. If I were you, I should thank my lucky stars and hold on to her with everything I have."

"I will," Dare said fervently. "You may rely upon it."

Chapter 19

Dear Mama and Papa,

How I have missed you all these past weeks. I pray you will forgive me for my bland letters and evasive answers. I am sorry for making you worry so, but I did not want to risk your health by telling you the truth for I knew you would come at once. It is not at all because I am unhappy with my husband as you feared, quite the reverse.

Daire has been gravely ill. He caught scarlet fever from a boy in the village. Thank heavens the illness was contained quickly and did not spread, but Daire has been so dreadfully unwell. I was so afraid that I would lose him. I know our marriage did not have the best of beginnings, but I must reassure you that we all judged him far too harshly. He is a good, kind, and wonderful husband. I love him, and I know now that he loves me. My heart has been held in a vice for so long, I hardly know what to feel on writing this, but this morning he has no fever, and he sleeps peacefully. I think perhaps he has fought and won a most terrible battle. I pray so, for I do not know what I should do without him.

—Excerpt of a letter from Lady Elspeth Kelburn, Vicomtesse Roxborough, to her parents, Mrs Bonnie and Mr Jerome Cadogan.

9th July 1839, Rowsley Hall, Derbyshire.

"Elspeth?"

Elspeth jolted awake at the sound of her name to find Lord Bainbridge leaning over her.

"What is it?" she exclaimed, sitting up so fast she almost headbutted the marquess, who straightened quickly. "Daire?"

"He's fine," he said, putting a hand out to stay her. "And I would not have disturbed your rest for anything, but I thought perhaps this would make you feel better than sleep. There is someone who is anxious to see you."

Bainbridge moved aside so she could see the bed, and Daire sitting up, looking over at her. He looked exhausted, and very pale, but his eyes were bright and alert, and he was alive and smiling at her.

"Daire!" she cried, springing to her feet, and launching herself at the bed. "Daire, oh, thank God. Thank God!"

Suddenly the terror of the past weeks lifted from her and yet the shock of it was so great she could not contain herself. Elspeth burst into tears and sobbed into Daire's chest, great racking, noisy sobs as she cried out all the fear she had not allowed herself to give into whilst he was ill.

"Elspeth!" Daire said, clearly shocked. "Oh, love. It's all right. I'm all right."

"Here, my lady."

Elspeth looked up to see Bainbridge hand her a clean handkerchief and she took it from him, not caring what a fright she must look. Bainbridge was staring at her, though, with something rather like longing.

"I'll leave you now," he said gently before laying a hand briefly on her husband's shoulder. "Dare, I'm relieved to know you are recovered. I don't have so many friends that I can afford to lose any, especially you. I hope to see you in town as soon as you are well enough. My Lady Roxborough, it has been a privilege to serve you. Dare is a lucky man, but I think he knows that."

He left then, closing the door quietly behind him. Elspeth wiped her face on the handkerchief and turned back to her husband, who was watching her carefully.

"Aren't you going to hold me?" she asked, wondering why he wouldn't touch her.

"I want to," he said, his voice a little unsteady. "Only...."

He grimaced and raised one hand, the skin dry and peeling.

"Oh, you stupid man!" she said, angry now. "Do you think I only love you for your handsome face? Is that it?"

"Well, it isn't for my mind, love, now, is it?" he retorted, sounding so bitter her breath caught.

Elspeth opened her mouth to tell him he was being idiotic and then closed it again, remembering what he had revealed in his delirium. His father had berated him and told him he was stupid and worthless, an idea that had no doubt been reinforced at school when he did not excel at academic subjects.

"Daire," she said, reaching up and putting her hand to his cheek. He flinched, but she turned his face towards her. "You are the kindest, gentlest, most wonderful man I have ever known, and I love you. You are not stupid, and not being good at arithmetic—or whatever else it is you think you cannot do—is no reason not to believe in me, in us."

He gave her a doubtful glance.

"I will not tire of you, never grow bored of you. You surprise me every day with how full of life you are, with how you find joy in simple pleasures, with how you make me happy, Daire. I have never been so happy as I am when I am with you and I have been so very afraid these past weeks. For I do not know what I should do without you."

Her voice quavered and her eyes filled with tears. Daire stared at her.

"Elspeth," he said, and he did not sound entirely steady himself. His eyes glittered too brightly. "Oh, God, I love you so much it scares me to death."

"I know," she said, laughing as he finally put his arms about her and held her tight. "I know."

To Dare's great relief, he made a swift recovery. By the end of the week, except for having lost a bit of weight and feeling rather worn, he was almost back to his usual self.

Bainbridge had sent several letters asking him to come to town as soon as he was well enough, and he knew he could not put it off. Whatever the wicked devil had done was done, and Dare had better find out what it was. In the meantime, however, he'd had things of his own to do.

"It's perfect, Green. Thank you," he said, after having taken a thorough inspection of the school building. He stood outside now and looked up at the sign which had been proudly affixed to the red brick exterior and then around to where workmen were putting up the gates enclosing the wrought iron railings that ran all the way around the school and the play area behind it.

"I was pleased to do it, my lord," Mr Green said. "And may I say, I am very happy to know you are well. Myself and my family prayed for your recovery, and I was relieved to have had those prayers answered."

Dare stared at the fellow in shock. He did not know what to make of that. To have one of the men that worked for him pray for him, it… well. He was at a loss. "I… I don't know what to say, Green, other than thank you."

Mr Green shook his head. "You've treated me and my men well, my lord, and it is a pleasure to see the Hall brought back to what it once was. My father worked for the old lord and…well…."

A dark look crossed the man's face and he swallowed whatever he'd been about to say.

"You may speak plain, Mr Green. I am afraid I have few fond feelings for my father."

Green's face twisted. "Well, you're not the only one, my lord. A rare devil he was to work for. It is a great relief to the community to discover his son is not like him and that all those wicked rumours…."

He broke off again, his naturally ruddy face growing redder.

"Oh, I expect some of those rumours were true enough," Dare said with regret. "But I promise you those days are over."

Mr Green grinned at him with obvious relief. "Ah, well. Wild oats are all well and good, but there's nothing like finding a generous harvest at home."

Dare laughed. "I've never heard it put quite like that before, but I don't deny it. You have the right of it, Green. Indeed you do."

Dare hurried back to the house and went around to the stables to see if everything was ready. A shiny new cabriolet carriage awaited him, black paint gleaming, a matching black horse standing in the harness, eager to be away as it tossed its proud head. They had ordered the carriage before he had fallen ill and it had arrived some days ago, but Elspeth had hovered over him, fretting that he was overdoing it whenever he did more than walk about the garden. Her anxiety had been such a novelty, and her concern for his wellbeing so earnestly sincere, that he had been the most biddable and docile of patients. He had not exerted himself more than she deemed prudent—most frustrating *that* had been—and had even swallowed the vile concoctions she had created with Mrs Grigson. He wasn't entirely convinced that the blasted housekeeper wasn't making the disgusting tonics as horrid as possible just to torment him. However, Elspeth had told him how Mrs Grigson had worked all hours with her, doing everything in their power to keep him alive. Much as it was hard to believe, he knew Elspeth would not lie about such a thing, so he supposed he had to accept it as the truth. He must thank Mrs Grigson too, not so much for his own sake, as for supporting Elspeth when she needed it. For that she ought to be rewarded. For now, however, he had a different matter to attend to.

After seeing a large picnic basket stowed safely to the back of the carriage, he hurried into the Hall, impatient to be off now.

"Elspeth!" he hollered, and then saw her walking down the stairs towards him.

He paused for a moment, admiring the sight of his beautiful wife. She was dressed in yellow today, and to his mind rivalled the sun for the light she brought to him and everyone around her. She smiled when she saw him and his heart expanded in his chest. It was still like living in a dream to think she really belonged to him.

"Come along, come along," he chivvied, grabbing at her hand.

As she'd been trying to tie the ribbons on her bonnet, she tutted at him.

"Daire," she protested as he pulled her in his wake, making her run to keep up. "What is the hurry?"

"Things to do, people to see," he said briskly, grinning at her.

"What things? What people?"

"Never you mind," he said, leading her to the cabriolet.

"Oh, that looks splendid," she said with approval. "How very stylish."

"Not too shabby, indeed," Dare said, urging her up into it. "I think *perhaps* my wife is smart enough to drive out with me, too."

"Perhaps!" she exclaimed in outrage.

Dare laughed and swiped her bottom before she could sit down. "Well, look at you, with your bonnet all askew."

"Oh, you wretched man, that's your fault. You wouldn't let me fasten it."

"Excuses, excuses," he said, shaking his head sadly and then striding off again. "*Parker*! Parker, where are you, man?"

"Here, my lord," Parker said, hurrying outside and handing him a small parcel tied with a blue ribbon.

"Jolly good. Thank you, Parker. That will be all."

"Very good, sir."

Dare tossed the parcel to Elspeth, who caught it.

"What's this?"

"A present," he said, making the cabriolet bounce as he climbed up into it.

"For me?" she said, her beautiful eyes alight with excitement.

Dare grinned at her and tweaked her nose. "No. Not for you."

"Oh," she said, a little deflated.

He chuckled, almost bursting with the desire to tell her everything but holding it back, wanting to surprise her.

"Come here," he said, tsking at her and tying the ribbons on her bonnet. He tweaked the bow, this way and that and then kissed her, a swift press of lips that was not nearly enough for a man who'd not had any kind of bedroom antics for far too long. But that could wait too, for a little while anyway.

With a brisk command to the horse to walk on, they moved out of the yard and were soon trotting at a fast clip along the lane to the village.

"Where are we going?" she asked.

"To pay a call and deliver that parcel," he said, not taking his eyes off the road, but he felt the weight of her gaze and glanced at her. "What?"

Elspeth smiled and shook her head, refusing to answer. She looked happy, so he let it go.

It was a short drive to the village or, more precisely, the Fletchers' farm, which lay on the far side of the village to the Hall. Not more than ten minutes later they trotted into the yard, scattering chickens and making geese flap and honk indignantly as they cleared the way.

"Mr Fletcher," Dare said, waving at the fellow who had come hurrying out of one of the barns.

His sons appeared too, on the other side of the yard, each of them casting the other anxious glances. Dare hesitated as he saw how the colour drained from Mr Fletcher's face on seeing him but went around to help his wife down.

Elspeth let go of his hand and ran to Mr Fletcher. "Oh, Mister Fletcher, we have worried so over poor Toby. Tell me, is he well now?"

Mr Fletcher gazed at her in obvious anguish, his throat working.

"My lady," he said, his voice rough. "Toby goes on well, I thank you, but... but I can never tell you how terribly, terribly sorry we were when...."

Mr Fletcher turned to stare at him.

Elspeth turned, following his gaze and met Dare's eyes.

"Mr Fletcher," Dare said, keeping his voice gentle. "It was not your fault, nor Toby's. It was rotten luck, that's all, and I've had such a run of good fortune this year, I think perhaps the fates decided the books needed balancing."

His wife blushed at the look he gave her, and Mr Fletcher let out a breath of relief. "Nonetheless, my lord. If there is ever anything we can do for you.... We are indebted to you for all you did for us. The doctor, and the gifts of food... I do not know how I shall ever repay you, but I will."

"Nonsense," Dare said, feeling a little uncomfortable under the weight of such adulation. "All the thanks I require is to visit the patient. If he is well enough, that is?"

"Oh," Mr Fletcher said, his eyes growing bright. "Oh, he is. Though he's still weak, and the doctor thinks he might not grow as big and strong as his brothers, he's alive and happy and that is blessing enough when we thought we were sure to lose him."

"Indeed it is," Dare said, as Mr Fletcher showed them to the door of the farmhouse.

Their arrival sent Mrs Fletcher into a flurry, as she exclaimed and repeated much of what Mr Fletcher had said, except with a great deal more emotion and the shedding of a few tears. Much to Dare's consternation, she looked upon him with such worship in her eyes he hardly knew where to put himself. Perhaps sensing his unease, Elspeth gently suggested that they might visit with Toby for a few moments.

This was thankfully accomplished, and they were guided through a home that was small but neat and clean, and into a bright little bedroom where Toby was propped up in bed, staring out of the window with obvious longing. His eyes grew wide and round on seeing them enter his room.

"I beg your pardon for disturbing your rest, Master Toby," Dare said gravely. "Only my lady and I wanted to see how you went on."

"V-Very well, sir, I mean... Lord Roxborough." The boy turned scarlet. "And... And I'm ever so sorry that—"

"Nonsense, think no more of it. Wasn't to be helped and I won't keep you," Dare said, as if the boy had urgent business to attend to. "Only I wanted to give you this. I know how dull it is being stuck in bed with nothing to do, so I thought this might pass the time."

He gave the boy the parcel and Toby looked at it with such astonishment it was as if he'd been handed the crown jewels.

"Well, open it, then," Dare suggested.

At this the boy's hands flew eagerly to the ribbon and tugged at it, opening the paper to reveal a red metal box with a battle scene painted on the front.

"Cor," he said in awe.

Dare grinned, feeling almost as excited as Toby. "Look inside."

He watched as Toby carefully prised open the lid, and gasped. Inside were two dozen toy soldiers. The boy stared at them, looking as though he hardly dared blink in case he woke up. Though Dare's family could well have afforded such things when he'd been a boy, he'd never had anything like the box of soldiers. The other boys at school had, and he had been wild with jealousy until Bainbridge, who was older than him, had loftily told him he'd grown out of his and Dare was welcome to them. Watching Toby now, Dare wondered if that had been true, or if Bainbridge, who could be an utter devil, had been motivated by one of his sudden shows of unexpected kindness—like hurrying to a sick friend's bedside.

"I never... never...." Toby said, unable to take his eyes off the soldiers. They'd been expensive, imported from Germany, and Dare well knew he'd never have seen the like of them before.

"Well, you've suffered a great trial, Toby, and been a brave fellow, but sitting quietly like your mama says until you are well enough to run about again needs a different kind of courage. I thought perhaps these brave fellows might help you bear it."

Toby stared up at him, his eyes bright and happy.

"They will," he said fervently. "That they will. Thank you, Lord Roxborough."

Dare grinned at the lad and ruffled his hair. "Get well soon, Toby. If you do as your mother says you may come up to the Hall in a few weeks, and I'll show you about the horses. I've got a fine hunter I've barely had the chance to ride yet, and you may come and see him if you would like to."

Toby gaped, nodding wordlessly, and Dare and Elspeth took their leave.

Chapter 20

Dear Florence,

How I wish I had never taken that wretched dare. There is no possible way of untangling the dreadful mess I've made of everything so I shall just have to make the best of it. I am determined to manage this ridiculous situation. After all, there is no one to blame but myself.

Have a care before you act on your own dare, my friend, or you too may end up with more than you bargained for.

—Excerpt of a letter from Miss Arabella Hunt (daughter of Mrs Alice and Mr Nathanial Hunt) to Miss Florence Knight (daughter of Lady Helena and Mr Gabriel Knight).

14ᵗʰ July 1839, Rowsley Hall, Derbyshire.

As the horse drew the dashing cabriolet back through the village, Dare felt Elspeth watching him again.

"What?"

She smiled, her eyes shining. "I was just thinking what a very fine man I have married."

Dare fidgeted under the warmth of her admiration. It was too strange to have everyone looking at him as if he'd done something marvellous. It had only been a box of soldiers, for heaven's sake. "Oh, well. The poor devil very nearly didn't make it, you know, and he'll be abed a while yet. I broke my ankle once at his age and I nearly went mad from boredom. Would have, if not for Bainbridge."

Elspeth leaned into him and Dare turned his head, stealing a quick kiss.

"Bainbridge is a good friend to you, I think?" she said softly.

Dare nodded. "Yes. Never understood why. I was just one of the younger boys, beneath his notice, really, but... well, he took a shine to me."

Elspeth put her hand on his arm. "Perhaps he recognised the fact you would be a good and loyal friend to him. From what I've heard, he doesn't have many of those."

Dare shook his head. "No. There was me, and August and Raphe, but they never got on so well with him as I did. He can be... unpredictable."

Once again, Dare wondered what the devil his friend had been up to but pushed the thought away as they were rounding the corner of the village and approaching the lane that led to the school. He slowed the cabriolet and suddenly felt a bit uncertain. Would she think it highhanded of him to have created this for her? Perhaps it would not be to her liking. Perhaps now she was married, she wouldn't want....

"Where are we going?"

Dare swallowed.

"Er... it's a surprise," he said, feeling increasingly anxious the closer he got.

Elspeth pursed her lips, narrowing her eyes at him.

"For me?" she asked cautiously.

He laughed at that and nodded. "Yes, love, for you, only... I... Well, it seemed a good idea at the time, but if you don't like it, or... or if I got it wrong...."

"Now I am intrigued," she said, her eyes glittering with excitement.

Dare took a breath, praying he'd done this right. There was no turning back now, though.

"Close your eyes," he instructed.

She hesitated for a moment, staring at him, and then did as he asked, and Dare took them the last little way to the school. He jumped down and ran around to the other side of the carriage, and lifted Elspeth to the ground. She gave a little squeal of surprise as he manhandled her and he chuckled, carefully moving her to stand in front of the school.

"You can open your eyes now."

She did, and Dare held his breath whilst she stared, nonplussed, at the building before her.

"Roxborough School for Boys and Girls," she said, sounding a little dazed. "I didn't know there was a school in the village, I—"

Dare held very still as she turned to study him.

"There wasn't," she said, understanding dawning. "You did this. For me."

There was an awkward silence as Dare stared at his boots and rubbed the back of his neck.

"I ruined your plans," he said, once he'd found his voice. "I know you wanted to be a teacher and because of me, because of all the scandal... and I... I know this isn't the same but... *ooof*!"

Dare staggered back, almost landing on his arse as she leapt at him and threw her arms about his neck, kissing him all over his face.

"Oh, you lovely, lovely man," she said, almost dancing on the spot with excitement. "Can we go in? Please, please!"

Dare caught his breath, taken aback by her joy in what he'd done for her.

"Yes. Yes, of course!"

Elspeth caught at his hand, dragging her after him as she ran for the front door.

"Oh," she said as she stared about the freshly painted room.

There was a desk and chair for every child, each with a slate and chalk ready for use. On the shelves that lined the walls there were books, pots of ink, quills, and a neat row of colourful abacuses. Two framed maps hung on the wall between the windows, one of Britain, the other of the world. A large slate board dominated the facing wall, and to the side of it was a handsome desk and chair, ready for the teacher.

Dare watched as Elspeth moved about the room, touching the little desks and all the items arrayed about the school, awaiting its pupils.

"There are twenty-two children in the village, eight boys and fourteen girls. Some will only be able to attend part time. I hope you don't mind that it is for boys too?"

"Of course not," she said, and Dare thought her voice sounded a bit odd.

He ploughed on. "Well, I haven't given a date for the school to open, not knowing if, well, if it was what you wanted. We can hire a teacher easily enough if you don't like it, I… I only want you to be happy, Elspeth."

She made a choked sound and hurried to him, wrapping her arms about him and holding on tight.

"You did all this for me," she said, staring up at him.

Dare shrugged. "Oh, well. It's not much, really. The building was already here, I only had it repaired and cleaned up for you, bought the furniture. I didn't build it with my bare hands, love, I just wanted to replace what you'd lost, that's all. Do you think you should like to work here?"

Elspeth studied his face, watching him intently. "You wouldn't mind if I did? It's not the done thing for a viscountess, you know."

He snorted at that. "Good Lord, you think I'm going to worry about that, after all the things I've done that a viscount ought not? No, love. You do what pleases you, and the rest of the world can go hang."

"So I could come here, every day, and you wouldn't mind?"

Dare let out a breath. He had realised that might be the case, that she might want to spend all her time at the school, and he would not see nearly so much of her, but if it made her happy, that was what mattered. His own selfish needs must be set aside. "I won't mind if you are happy."

"What if *I* mind?" she asked him.

Dare frowned, not understanding. "Mind what?"

"Being away from you," she said, reaching up and stroking his face. "I thought I would lose you, and I have only just got you back. I want to spend my days with you too, Daire. I'm afraid I am terribly spoiled."

A slow smile crept over his face as her comment sank beneath his skin, warming him.

"How would it be if I taught here two or three afternoons a week? After all, I am realising how much work there is at the Hall, and there are several projects I have been meaning to speak to you about."

"There are?" he said, a little dazed. "That's funny, I've been wanting to speak to you too, about the future of Rowsley."

"You have?"

Dare nodded. He'd had a lot of time to think about everything he'd learned recently, over the past days of enforced rest. "The Hall needs to earn its keep, love. The land has been badly neglected and will take a lot of time and investment to make profitable again, and I read an article recently about how farming the land simply isn't earning enough to support these grand houses into the future. Your money won't last forever, not when the building needs such a vast staff to maintain it. We must look at new ways to finance Rowsley."

"Yes!" Elspeth said, clutching at his arm. "Papa and my uncle have been very interested in the growth of the railways and have invested with Mr Knight, so there may be something there, or perhaps something else, but you are quite right, we must look to the future, Daire. We must make the Hall safe for our children and all those who come after us."

Dare stared at her, at the enthusiasm sparkling in her eyes for the Hall, for the future.

"How strange," he said, reaching out to stroke her cheek with the back of his hand. "I have always loathed Rowsley. I hated coming back here as a child, and the place has held nothing but unhappy memories for me, yet now, seeing it through your eyes, I believe I can love it too."

The smile that dawned over her lovely face made his breath catch. "I'm so glad, Daire. For it isn't the Hall's fault that your parents were so awful and treated you so shockingly ill, and I promise I shall make lots and lots of happy memories for you. So many that there won't be room to remember everything that came before."

"I like the sound of that." He wondered if his heart could expand far enough to contain everything he felt: his love for this woman, and all the hopes he held for them, and for their future. "Did you have anything in particular in mind?"

To his delight, she flushed and avoided his eyes. She moved away from him, trailing her hands over one of the little desks.

"Perhaps," she said, glancing back at him from under her lashes.

Intrigued now, Dare stalked her about the schoolroom as she continued to move away from him.

"Oh?"

Elspeth kept walking but darted a coquettish look at him, her eyes alight with mischief. "Was that a picnic I saw in that basket, Daire?"

"It was," he said, still following her.

"Excellent." She walked briskly to the door. "For I know just the place I want to have it."

"A perfect spot," Daire said approvingly as he set down the heavy picnic basket.

"Yes, isn't it?" Elspeth said with a contented sigh.

She stared about them at the beautiful spot beside the river, bordered by trees and enormous granite boulders, some of which studded the river itself. It was secluded, hidden on all sides by thick woodland, yet the sunlight flooded this little corner. It was a glorious day, warm with a gentle breeze that eased the heat of the afternoon, ensuring the temperature did not become uncomfortable. Wildflowers bobbed their heads lazily and the sound of the river was melodic and restful.

Elspeth turned to watch as Daire knelt and shook out the blanket, spreading it over the ground beside one of the boulders.

"I found this place some time ago," she said, anticipation making her heart beat faster. "I had such plans for it, too, but then my world shattered for you fell ill, and I couldn't breathe until you were well again."

Daire glanced up at her and smiled roguishly, making her poor heart pick up and run on faster still.

"I'm well now, love," he said, watching her with curiosity. "So... what were these plans of yours?"

Elspeth swallowed, suddenly shy, but this was Daire, and he was looking at her in such a way she could not doubt his feelings for her. So she tugged at the ribbons of her bonnet and cast it down, before tugging at her gloves, one finger at a time. She held Daire's gaze as he sat back on the rug, his concentration on her every move absolute. Elspeth tossed aside the gloves to rest with the bonnet and reached for the buttons that ran down the front of her gown, undoing one after another until it was loose enough to slip from her shoulders. She stepped out of it, aware of the way his eyes had grown dark. Her bustle and petticoats followed the gown. Slowly, she unhooked her corset, and dropped that on the mound of her petticoats.

"You will have to play lady's maid later," she said, feeling more than a little exposed, standing outside in nothing but her shift and stockings.

Daire swallowed and moved to his hands and knees, prowling towards her until he could kneel at her feet.

"I'm yours to command," he said, one hand reaching out to touch her ankle. Reverently, he slid his palm higher, up the back of her calf to her knee. He caressed the tender skin through her stocking and Elspeth's breath hitched.

"I have missed this," she said, feeling wicked now, and discovering she rather enjoyed the sensation. "I have missed you, your hands upon me."

"No more than I," Daire said, his voice rough. "But tell me, what else have you missed, my lady? I have no desire to be a bad husband. If there is something you need from me, I beg you will ask at once so I may rectify the omission."

Elspeth stared down at him, seeing a combination of amusement and sincerity in his expression, his eyes dark with wanting. The sight of him, broad shouldered and so handsome, on his knees, offering her whatever she desired, made everything feminine in her quicken with excitement. Yet the words hovered upon her lips, unspoken, as what she wanted seemed so dreadfully... scandalous.

"I dare you to tell me," he said, his eyes glittering with challenge.

Elspeth let out a breath of laughter and relief, knowing that he had understood, and that he was trying to set her free. "Oh, you know I can never resist a dare."

"I was counting on it, love." He grinned at her, and Elspeth reached out, touching a finger to his mouth. He nipped at the soft pad playfully and her heart skipped.

"This," she whispered, tracing the shape of his lips. Dare opened his mouth a little, and she slid her finger inside to touch his tongue. "And this."

His breath caught, his eyes growing impossibly dark as she withdrew her finger.

"Yes," he said, and that one word was full of masculine pride, triumphant, and Daire followed her as she moved away.

Elspeth walked to the large boulder and reclined against it, waiting as her cheeks flushed, and not only from the heat of the sun that had baked the great stone so that it warmed her back. Her breathing sped as Daire's hands slid up her thighs, pushing the thin fabric of her chemise higher and higher still as he exposed her. He pushed her legs apart and Elspeth's cheeks burned as the warm afternoon breeze slid over her skin, touching parts of her that had never been so revealed outside the safety and security of their home. A small part of her feared someone would come, that they would be discovered, though this place was on their private land and completely hidden. Yet that fear was also what made her thrum with urgency and excitement. Holding her husband's gaze, she reached for the hem of her shift and pulled it off, over her head.

Daire made a sound, deep in his throat and muttered an oath, coarse and fervent. Perhaps she ought to have been shocked but, combined with the look in his eyes, Elspeth thought it the greatest compliment he had ever paid her. He was staring up at her, his gaze travelling her naked body as she lay, supine, against the boulder. She felt like an offering to a pagan god, a gift to some ancient deity that would smite the world if not for her sacrifice.

"God, Elspeth," he said, his voice deep as he gazed at her, from the little thatch of curls, over her belly, to where her breasts rose and fell, faster and faster now.

"Please, Daire," she said, beside herself with the need to feel his touch.

"Tell me," he insisted.

There was no maidenly coyness, she was too impatient. "Put your mouth on me, please. Now."

There was a low chuckle and then he did as she had begged for him to do. Her head lolled back as the rush of heat and lust rippled through her. His mouth was the wickedest of pleasures, sinful, the sin seeming all the greater for the obvious pleasure he took in delivering it. He moaned low in his throat as his tongue sought all her most private places, licking and caressing as his clever fingers slid inside her and began a sensual torment of their own. Though she thought he could scandalise her no further, he lifted her leg, hooking it over his shoulder to open her more fully to his attentions and Elspeth was lost. She writhed beneath him, wanton and shameless, glorying in the way he feasted on her, devouring her. The sun shimmered through her closed eyelids. The world was too bright and growing brighter still as he worked diligently, sending her soaring until he closed his mouth over the tender little bud of her flesh and suckled.

Elspeth flew apart into the glittering sunlight, crying out so that the birds lifted from the trees, startled by the primitive sound that rang out as Daire loved her.

She was still dazed, lingering in some dreamlike state, when she felt desperate hands upon her body, pulling her down.

"Elspeth, Elspeth, please. Oh God...."

Giddy with the pleasure still thrumming through her, Elspeth allowed Daire to lay her down, vaguely aware of the way he fumbled with the fall of his trousers, trying to release himself as he cursed and muttered. Finally he must have succeeded for he fell atop her like a man possessed and thrust inside. Elspeth cried out again as the aching throb that had not yet subsided clenched joyfully about the fierce invasion and began building once again.

Elspeth looked up at her husband, finding him staring down at her, his expression a tortured mix of pleasure and pain. She reached up, curling her fingers in his thick hair, feeling inexpressibly immoral as she lay naked in the open air with him still fully dressed, taking her with such decadent abandon.

"Wicked, wicked girl," he managed, his mouth curving irrepressibly as his words lit something inside of her and her body climaxed, tightening around him.

She held onto him as the heavy waves crashed over her and he made a harsh sound, shuddering in her arms and spending himself in a rush of warmth.

Daire groaned, collapsing onto her for a moment until he began to laugh. Still grinning. he rolled over, taking her with him until she lay on top, braced on her arms.

"God, you're marvellous," he said, reaching up to palm her breast. "I'm a lucky dog and no mistake."

Elspeth's lips quirked.

"Yes," she said solemnly. "I rather think you are."

He was still inside her. She rolled her hips against him and he gasped.

"Oh," he said.

"Oh," she repeated, thoroughly enjoying this new-found power.

His stomach growled audibly, and he gave a rueful smile. "I got up early to check all was ready at the school. I didn't have time to eat anything."

Elspeth laughed and leaned down to kiss his chest. "Ah, well. You've lost enough weight, so I suppose you had better eat. You'll need your stamina, after all."

Daire quirked an eyebrow.

"Is that right? Damn, but I like the sound of that. A quick lunch, I think, and—" He snatched her shift out of her reach as she went to pick it up. "No. Stay as you are. I'm going to have you for dessert."

Elspeth shrugged, smiling down at him. "Well, as long as I can have you for mine, that seems entirely fair."

Chapter 21

Dear Louis,

I am so sorry I missed you when you called. I would have stayed if I'd known you were coming. Anything is better than being poked and pinned by Madame Blanchet, but Mama insists I must have some new gowns. I don't see why, as I've barely worn the last ones, and no one notices what I wear.

Anyway, I read the note you left and really, how can you be so muddle headed as to think this dreadful scandal in any way your fault? I adore Arabella and she is the sweetest, kindest girl in the world, so I cannot understand what possessed her to do such a shocking thing. Well, indeed, I do know as Florence told me. She took a dare from a hat and... well never mind what prompted her. Arabella's actions were her own and, much as my heart bleeds for her, you have nothing to reproach yourself for.

—Excerpt of a letter from Miss Evie Knight (daughter of Lady Helena and Mr Gabriel Knight) to Louis César de Montluc, Comte de Villen.

14th July 1839, Rowsley Hall, Derbyshire.

The sun was beginning its slow journey down towards the horizon by the time Elspeth and Daire returned to the house. It was a perfect evening, warm and beguiling, and Elspeth was not ready to see the last of such a wonderful day.

"Walk with me in the garden," she said, taking Daire's hand.

He gave her a slow, lingering glance, a smile tugging at his mouth as she drew him away from the front of the house.

"Surely you're not thinking of having your wicked way with me *again*, love? I'm not sure I've got it in me," he murmured, once they were out of earshot of the servants.

Elspeth blushed, having already scandalised herself quite thoroughly by discovering her own insatiable nature.

"*No*," she said, trying to sound tart and disapproving, though the way her lips were twitching rather spoiled the effect. "It's just been such a lovely day, I'm not ready to go inside."

"It has been lovely," he said, pulling her closer so he could slide his arm about her waist. "*You* are lovely."

Daire ducked his head to kiss her and stilled as the sound of barking reached them.

Elspeth's eyes grew wide. "Oh! That's not—"

"Yes," Daire nodded. "That's the ghost."

"Truly?"

"Well, let's see if we can find it," he said, taking her hand and pulling her along behind him as he headed towards the source of the sound.

"No, it's this way," Elspeth said, once they were halfway across the top lawn behind the house.

Back and forth they ran, laughing as they tried and tried to catch up with the sound of barking, which always seemed just around the corner.

"Oh, I give in," Elspeth cried, breathless with laughter as Daire halted beside her, bracing his hands on his knees.

"This is terrible," he said, shaking his head. "You've ruined me, Elspeth. I've won every damned race I've ever entered and now look at me. A wreck of a man after one afternoon trying to satisfy my wife."

Elspeth gaped at him.

"Wretch," she said, smacking him playfully. "Nothing to do with the scarlet fever, then, hmmm?"

"Oh, no," he said, waving this away. "That trifling illness. No, no. it's you, love. You bad, bad girl."

She snorted at being addressed in such a way and Daire pulled her into his arms.

Elspeth stared up at him, sighing with pleasure at the sight of his handsome face looking at her with such affection.

"I love you," he said, serious now as he held her tight against him. "So much."

This time he did kiss her, clearly determined that no ghostly dog was going to put him off. Elspeth ignored the barking too, which faded as she wrapped her arms about his neck and kissed him back.

"Ahem."

Elspeth vaguely registered a sound, but it seemed a long way off and kissing Daire was worth every bit of her attention.

"*Ahem!*"

Slowly, Daire lifted his head and turned towards the sound. "Christ!" he muttered and leapt back as though he'd been caught doing something he ought not.

Elspeth looked in the direction of his gaze, still a bit lightheaded from the passionate embrace, to see a group of people standing at the top of the stairs that led down to the garden.

"Mama! Papa!" she cried, hurrying towards them with a cry of delight.

"Ah, noticed us, did you?" Papa said ruefully, watching her run up the stairs and holding his arms out to her. "Ah, Elspeth, my darling girl. We've missed you."

"Oh, my sweet girl, come here and hug your mama."

Elspeth laughed, hugging both of her parents, and discovering she had missed her twin far more than she'd realised as Greer pulled her into a fierce embrace.

"You'd better tell me everything," Greer whispered urgently in her ear. "*Everything.*"

"What about me?" her little sister piped up indignantly.

Elspeth hugged her too, kissing the girl's cheek.

"My, you've grown," she said, staring at the fourteen-year-old Alana in surprise.

"A full inch," Mama said, shaking her head. "We've had to let all her hems down."

Elspeth laughed, delighted to see her family again, and then she turned, realising Daire was hanging back, not part of the convivial scene. Before she could do anything about it, her mama hurried down the stairs and took Daire's hands in hers.

"Let me look at you," she said, giving him a critical glance. "You've lost weight. Didn't I say, Jerry? You need feeding up. Come along inside, I'm sure this damp evening air can't be good for you after being so very ill, you poor dear. Don't you fret, though, Elspeth and I shall have a word with your cook and make sure there's plenty to tempt you. Lots of red meat, I should think, build your stamina back up, eh?"

To Elspeth's combined mortification and delight, Mama gave him a naughty wink and Daire blushed furiously.

"Tell me, dear," Mama went on, lowering her voice somewhat conspiratorially. "Is it true that you and Bainbridge smuggled a greased pig into Mrs Smith's Orchid House?"

If possible, Daire turned a deeper shade of red and looked as close to embarrassment as Elspeth had ever seen him. Well he might, she thought wryly, for even she knew Mrs Smith's Orchid House was a notoriously exclusive brothel.

Daire opened and closed his mouth, clearly at a loss.

"For God's sake tell her," her father said. "She's dying to know if it's true."

Her husband cleared his throat and rubbed the back of his neck.

"Er... yes," he said, giving Elspeth an apologetic glance.

Elspeth could do nothing but giggle as her irrepressible mother bore Daire up the stairs from the garden.

"I knew it!" Mama said in triumphant delight. "Tell me everything."

"I'd like to say you get used to her," her father said to him with obvious sympathy as Mama herded Daire into the house, "but you won't. She's the most shocking creature in the world. Can't think why I married her."

"Can't you, indeed?" Mama said over her shoulder. "Then I shall have to remind you."

"Oh, my God," Greer murmured, burying her face in her hands. "Do you think they'll ever get too old to be so... so—"

"No," Elspeth said simply, taking her sister's arm. "At least I sincerely hope not, and I hope I never do either."

Greer laughed, looking at her with interest. "You've changed," she said shrewdly.

Elspeth nodded. "I have," she agreed, hanging back with Greer as Alana followed her parents and Daire inside.

"I have so much to tell you," Greer said, her eyes alight with excitement. "You'll never guess what's being going on. We all took a dare from the hat, though I've not done mine yet. Oh, I wish you'd been there so you could take one too. I suppose you can't now you are married and respectable."

Elspeth couldn't help but fall into peals of laughter.

Her twin looked at her, perplexed as Elspeth tried to calm herself.

"Whatever is funny?" Greer demanded.

"Oh, oh, nothing," Elspeth said breathlessly, wiping her eyes. "Only that I did take a dare, didn't I?"

"Did you?" Greer said in astonishment. "When?"

"When I married him," Elspeth said, still laughing as she escorted her sister back into the house.

Epilogue

Father,

I wish to inform you that I was married this morning to Miss Arabella Hunt. We will be returning to Royle House directly. I see no value in lulling the poor girl into a false sense of security, she may as well know the worst of it — of us — and get it over and done, lest she harbour any forlorn hope of finding friends among you. I would ask that you and the rest of our benighted family make her welcome, but I have no illusions on that score. I can only pray I have judged correctly that she is kind enough to take pity rather than run away screaming.

You, however, may gnash your teeth and rage all you want. The deed is done, and nothing on this earth will undo it, not even you.

—Excerpt of a letter from Lawrence Grenville, The Most Honourable, The Marquess of Bainbridge to his father, His Grace, The Duke of Axton.

19th July 1839, Half Moon Street, Mayfair, London.

Dare paused and looked back at the house, frowning.

248

"What is it?" Elspeth asked.

"I hope he knows what he's doing, that's all."

Elspeth snorted, giving an angry shake of her head.

"I shall never forgive him," she said, her heart bleeding for poor Arabella.

"He didn't do it all by himself, love," Dare reminded her gently as he handed her up into their carriage, but Elspeth was not feeling very generous towards Lord Bainbridge.

He might have been a good and loyal friend to her husband, but he had tricked poor Arabella into being his wife, and that was surely unforgiveable.

"Nonetheless, he planned the whole affair with the sole intention of trapping her."

"I nearly did the very same thing."

Elspeth looked up at her husband as he sat beside her in the carriage. "You didn't go through with it, and whose idea was it to trap me in the first place, hmmm?"

Dare considered this and said nothing, which was answer enough.

"She was going to trap Louis."

Elspeth huffed. "I don't pretend that Arabella acted well. It was ill judged, I grant you. I cannot think what got into her, but she at least was motivated by love and real desire to make Louis happy."

"And you think Bainbridge could not give the same excuse?"

Elspeth turned to look at him, frowning. "Can he?"

Dare shrugged. "I think Bainbridge is looking for someone to save him, love."

He reached out and caressed her cheek. Elspeth shivered under his touch.

"He saw how you cared for me, how you stood by me, and I think he wants that too, very badly. Everybody always remarks how kind and gentle and sweet-natured Arabella is. I think he longs for a little of that kindness for himself."

"So he took it, instead of waiting for it to be given," Elspeth said softly. "That is not how one goes about winning a woman's trust, nor her heart. And he was not alone all his life, as you were. He has a family."

Dare laughed at that and shook his head. "Honestly, love, I think the fates dealt me a better hand than Bainbridge. All those rumours of madness in the Grenville blood are not unfounded. It's a wonder he's as sane as he is."

Elspeth felt a jolt of anxiety for Arabella at his words as she remembered the rumours about the marquess's father, the Duke of Axton, and Bainbridge himself. "Is... Is *he* mad? He wouldn't... hurt her?"

She watched as Dare curled his fingers about hers. "He is a difficult and complicated man. He can be an utter devil when his temper frays, but he is never angry for long, and no, he would *never* hurt her. Bainbridge doesn't care for many people, but for those few he does, he would do anything for them, no matter what. I believe he truly cares for Arabella. I only hope she can forgive him enough to get know the man he really is."

Elspeth sighed, the knot of worry that made her shoulders tight beginning to unravel a little.

"He came to you the moment he heard you were ill," she admitted reluctantly. "And he was very kind. He even cared for you himself, to give Mrs Grigson and I some rest. I would never have believed a marquess would lower himself to do such a thing, but he insisted."

"He can be unexpectedly kind and generous," Dare agreed.

"I suppose so," she said, still uncertain but relaxing somewhat.

"Well then," he said, before reaching for Elspeth and hauling her onto his lap.

"What are you doing?" she protested, though a smile tugged at her lips. "We will be back home soon."

"I know, but I need a moment alone with my wife."

Elspeth smiled and stroked his thick hair back from his forehead as he gazed up at her.

"I'm sorry, have my family been a terrible trial to you? I'm afraid they are rather... excitable. We could have stayed at a hotel, I suppose, but Mama would have been so disappointed. She rather loves you, I think."

Dare shook his head. "Not at all. The feeling is mutual, I assure you. I've enjoyed every moment. It is wonderful to be a part of your family, to see how you all love each other, and your mama makes me laugh. She's got a very naughty sense of humour, which aligns rather perfectly with my own."

Elspeth rolled her eyes.

"You have no idea," she muttered, smiling as he laughed and kissed her fingers.

"I just never expected to be welcomed as I have been. I thought they'd hate me forever."

"No one could possibly hate you above five minutes. No matter how badly you behave," Elspeth said with a huff of laughter. "You are far too charming, and you know it."

He gave her a dubious glance. "I'm sure you hated me for longer than five minutes."

"I did not," she said indignantly.

"You compared me to mould," he reminded her, giving her a mournful glance that made her want to giggle.

"No," she said sternly, trying hard to keep her countenance. "You were the one who suggested you were growing on me—*like* mould."

"Perhaps," he said with a heavy sigh. "But you definitely compared me to the nasty black kind that grows in unpleasant places."

Elspeth bit her lip. It took a considerable effort to rearrange her face.

"But I didn't tell you to go away," she reminded him, her voice trembling with the effort of not laughing.

"No, but you threatened to hit me with a blunt object and keep my tiny brain in a jar, like a pickled walnut," he reminded her.

"Oh, Daire," she said, suddenly horrified by how she'd spoken to him that day. "I didn't know you then or I would never… never—"

He silenced her by pulling her head down and kissing her very thoroughly. By the time he released her, Elspeth was flushed and breathing hard.

"Peawit," Daire said affectionately. "I deserved everything I got, and well you know it. Besides, I adored sparring with you. I fell in love with you so hard and fast I hardly knew what was happening until it was far too late."

Elspeth sighed, laying her head on his shoulder. Daire's hand slid over her hip, a possessive gesture that made her smile.

"You know," he said, a teasing note to his words. "You also said we wouldn't have any children."

"Ah, yes." Elspeth nodded, remembering that conversation. He had made her quite exasperated. "So I did."

"Have you changed your mind about that?" Daire turned a little sideways, regarding her solemnly.

"You know very well I was not taking that conversation any more seriously than you were. You were only trying to provoke me, and you succeeded very nicely."

"I was trying to provoke you," he admitted, grinning ruefully. "But the thing is, Elspeth, I was serious too. I think that's when I knew for sure. I had this image of us together as I said the words and of a little girl, with blonde ringlets just like her mother and... and I fell."

Elspeth stared at him and blinked very hard as her vision blurred and her throat grew tight. "Oh, Daire. You wretched man. Trust you to make it impossible for me. I didn't want to tell you yet, for I'm not the least bit certain, but... Oh, come here."

She took his hand and slid it over the gentle curve of her belly.

His breath caught as he stared at his large hand, splayed over her stomach. She smiled as his gaze flew to hers.

"A child?" he whispered, his eyes wide with disbelief. "But—"

"I think so, and really I don't know why you look so astonished. It's not like we've not taken every opportunity to... well." Elspeth broke off and giggled.

Daire wasn't laughing. He was staring at her with wonder, and... and he looked rather terrified, actually.

"Elspeth," he said, panic in his voice. "I was only teasing you! I... I c-can't. *Me*, a... a father? I don't know... I don't know how!"

Elspeth reached up and took his face between her hands, forcing him to look at her.

"You didn't know how to be a husband either," she said gently, stroking his cheeks with her thumbs. "But you've made a wonderful job of that, because you are kind and generous and patient. So, you will make a wonderful job of being a father too, for you will never neglect your children, never make them feel unwanted or unloved, or anything less than perfect just the way they are. Will you?"

She held his gaze as his breathing steadied.

"No," he said, his voice firm. "No, I will never let them believe they are anything other than just what I wanted, for it wouldn't be true. Any child of yours will be just what I always dreamed of, Elspeth, and I will do my best to be a good father. I will. I promise."

Elspeth nodded, smiling at him as a tear tracked down her cheek.

"I believe you," she said. "I believe you."

She kissed him. Daire slid arms around her and held her close until the movement of the carriage stopped. He raised his head. Pulling the window curtain aside a little, he peered out and frowned.

"Why have we stopped? This isn't your parents' house."

Elspeth smiled at him, trying to tamp down her excitement. "I know, but I have a surprise for you."

"Another one!" he exclaimed. "Good Lord, Elspeth, I'm not sure my heart can take another today."

She huffed at him and shook her head. "Well, you weren't supposed to have *that* surprise today, you dreadful creature. Honestly, though, if you will go about saying such romantic things to me, it's the least you can expect you know."

"I'm sorry," he said gravely. "I shall try to be beastly to you for the rest of the day."

"Good."

They were both being absurd, but that was one of the reasons she loved him so. Unlike Greer, she had never been comfortable being so carefree and frivolous, but Daire brought out her sense of the ridiculous and made her laugh as no one else did.

She climbed off his lap just in time, as the footman opened the door. Daire jumped out and reached back to hand her down, frowning as he saw they'd arrived in the midst of a very grand stables.

"Lady Roxborough," said a large burly man who strode across the yard to greet them.

"Mr Smithton?"

"Aye, my lady, a pleasure to meet you at last."

Elspeth beamed at the man and ignored Daire's curious glance as he was clearly wondering what she'd been up to. "My Lord Roxborough, allow me to introduce Mr Smithton. Mr Smithton, my husband."

Daire greeted the man politely, at a loss to understand why they were here, but willing to go along with whatever it was Elspeth had planned for him.

"If you would like to come this way, my lord, my lady. He'll be ready to make the journey back to Derbyshire next week as arranged."

"He?" Dare asked, turning to Elspeth, but she only grinned and refused to say any more.

So, they followed the man towards the stables, where he opened one of the stalls and gestured for them to go in. Dare entered the stall, perplexed, and then stopped in his tracks as his eyes adjusted to the darkness and he heard a quiet whimpering and squeaking.

In the straw lay a large bloodhound bitch who gave a heavy sigh as her brood of squirming puppies tugged at her teats, suckling greedily.

Dare turned to stare at Elspeth.

"These are very fine dogs, I am told. Much in demand," she said, watching his face intently.

"Oh, that they are, my lady," Mr Smithton said with enthusiasm. "His lordship is keeping four, and two of them are reserved for the Duke of Bedwin. Another two are for Viscount Cavendish."

Dare looked back at the puppies, his throat suddenly tight. "There's nine."

Elspeth nodded and took his hand, her slender fingers curling about his. "You said you always wanted a dog. I thought it about time you had the real thing, and not just the ghostly variety."

As the pups had finished feeding, Mr Smithton bent and inspected them, choosing one from among the wriggling pile. "This fine fellow is yours, my lord."

Dare swallowed hard as the pup was put in his hands. It bit playfully at his fingers and Dare laughed, a choked sound as he caressed the impossibly soft long ears.

"Elspeth," he said helplessly, relieved when Mr Smithton retired from the stables, leaving them alone, for he feared he might weep like a girl.

"There might also be a little West Highland terrier waiting for you at home," she admitted, smiling at him. "Like in Landseer's painting, you see? You liked it so much and I so wanted to make you happy."

It was no good. Try as he might to behave like a grown man, his wife had completely destroyed his composure. He gave a helpless sob and Elspeth pulled him into her arms, careful not to squash the little pup between them.

Elspeth held him tight, stroking his hair as he struggled to get himself under control. Once he felt he could speak again, he pulled back a little to stare at the dog, before raising his eyes to hers.

"Thank you," he said. "Thank you so much. I never dreamed I could have this, all of this. You've given me everything, Elspeth. More than I ever dared believe possible, not in my wildest dreams."

"Well, it's only fair," Elspeth said, reaching up and curling her hand about his neck. "For you *are* my wildest dream."

Dare laughed and made not the slightest protest when she pulled his head down to hers for a kiss.

"Love me forever, Elspeth," he whispered against her lips. "I dare you."

Keep turning the page for a sneak peek of the next book in the
Daring Daughters series...

Dare to Cause a Scandal
Daring Daughters Book four

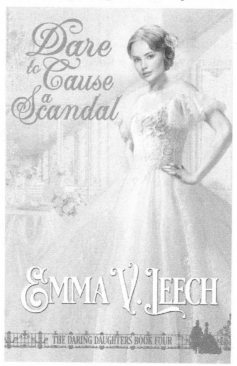

Their mothers dared all for love.
Just imagine what their daughters will do...

A one track mind...

Miss Arabella Hunt is a vivacious redhead with a kind heart
and decisive nature. The daughter of the man who owns the
notorious gambling den known as "Hunters" has set her sights on
the beautiful Louis César de Montluc, the Comte de Villain.
The trouble is, the devil doesn't know she exists.

Mad, bad and dangerous to know...

Lawrence Grenville, the Marquess of Bainbridge, is a man with a damaged reputation and an uncertain temperament. His family is renowned for every kind of vice, and madness is said to run in his blood. Having recently seen his best friend find happiness and contentment with his new bride, Bainbridge wonders if he cannot follow the same path and put an end to the dissatisfaction and unhappiness that plagues his life.

A tricky situation...

When Arabella accepts Bainbridge's help in securing the attention of Louis César, she has no idea what she is getting herself into. And when she finds herself trapped in her own net, she has no one to blame but herself.

Mad as a box of frogs...

Married to a man she does not know and is a little afraid of, Arabella hopes to find a welcome among her new husband's family. What she discovers is a household filled with chaos and calamity, and drama enough for a dozen Greek tragedies. Her husband's father, The Duke of Axton, loathes her on sight, and makes it his mission to chase her out of his son's life for good.

But for the first time in his life, Bainbridge has an ally... and the old duke has finally met his match.

Prologue

I don't give a damn for your whoring or if you drink yourself to death, so long as you marry and produce your heir before you're too poxed or insensible to do to your duty. Surprisingly, there are many women willing to overlook your shortcomings for the lure of your money and title. Even your father managed that much, if nothing else. Choose one, marry her and get a babe in her. It's not as if I expect any more from you. I assume you are capable of impregnating a wife and producing a legitimate heir? The mangiest cur seems to manage reproduction without difficulty. Do you think you could rise to the challenge for once instead of scattering your seed into every worthless, if willing, womb in the country?

—Excerpt of a letter from Her Grace, Augusta The Dowager Duchess of Axton, to her grandson, The Most Hon'ble, Lawrence Grenville, The Marquess of Bainbridge.

Two months earlier…

29th April 1839, The Countess St Clair's spring garden party, St James's, London.

It was the noise that drew him. Having grown up in a family where arguments usually resulted in damage to property and person, Bainbridge recognised the sound of a fight brewing. He didn't really know why he was here at this blasted event anyway, except that Dare was hunting down Miss Cadogan and had needed a bit of hand holding to gather courage enough to gate crash. Well the Earl of St Clair might consider telling a viscount to sling his hook, especially one as disreputable as Dare, but a marquess? Oh, that was another matter. A marquess like Bainbridge… good lord, no. Heaven alone knew what he might do if he was pissed off enough to react badly. He might cause a scene, or worse. After all, the family were all barking mad. Everyone knew that.

So they'd been let in, though the earl had made it very plain that the first sign of unacceptable behaviour would see them both strung up by their bollocks in his wife's favourite Magnolia tree. Fair enough. Besides, he was only here for Dare, who for some reason was still his best friend, no – *only* friend – despite all the aggravation that position entailed. Best behaviour then, which meant he'd better not talk to anyone. He'd resigned himself to a couple of hours of boredom and keeping out of trouble, and had retreated to a quiet corner of the gardens, out of sight. At least then he didn't have to put up with people gawking at him as if he might sprout a tail and horns at the least sign of provocation.

The quiet corner wasn't so quiet though, and Bainbridge had moved closer to see what the trouble was. A group of children, all aged roughly between ten and fourteen, were gathered around two boys.

"Take it back," one boy said, giving the other a hard shove. It was a brave thing to do, considering his foe was at least three years older and a great deal bigger too.

"I won't. She is a common little guttersnipe; everyone knows it and she ought not talk to her betters like that."

The first boy, who Bainbridge recognised now as one of the Duke of Bedwin's sons – Lord Frederick – went purple in the face at that. "And you think you're her better, do you, Scrivener?" he sneered in disgust.

"You're just a big bully!" This came from a new source, and Bainbridge watched in amusement as a small girl detached from the group and launched herself at Scrivener in a flurry of white lace and blonde ringlets.

"Argh! Gerroff, get her off me," Scrivener cried. The fellow might or might not be a bully, but even he knew better than to hit a girl, especially not one who belonged to Montagu.

"Cat! Cat! Devil take it you mad creature, leave this to me," Lord Frederick said in exasperation as he tried to prise her off Scrivener whose back she was attached to like a frilly barnacle, her small fists pounding him.

"Aggie isn't a guttersnipe," she said in fury, punctuating her words with another blow from her fist. "She's—" *thwack* "my—" *thwack* "friend!"

Thwack, thwack, thwack.

Somehow, Lord Frederick removed the struggling girl and set her behind him.

"Find Aggie and make sure she's all right," he said sternly. "I don't want her upset. Victoria, you go too, please."

Bainbridge had to smile as he heard the echo of the boy's father – the duke, in his commanding tone. The girl scowled at him but did as he asked, whirling with a swish of petticoats, and stomping off again. The older girl, who Bainbridge suspected might be the boy's sister, sighed and trailed after her.

Lord Frederick turned back to Scrivener.

"Bit pathetic getting your sweetheart to fight your battles for you," Scrivener taunted.

Bainbridge had to admit he was impressed by the speed of the fist that struck out at Scrivener and connected with his chin. There was a howl of rage and the two boys fell upon each other, fists flying.

Bainbridge sighed and was about to intervene when there was a rustle of silken skirts and a... a *goddess* entered the scene. His breath caught. She was petite and slender, with curves in all the right places, and her hair was a tumble of coppery curls that seemed to be escaping the confines of her pins on all sides.

"Fred! *Fred!* Stop this at once. Stop it now. Oh, what on earth..."

Bainbridge watched, delighted, as the young beauty took each boy by the ear until they winced and squawked, separating and pleading for her to let them go.

"Are you going to behave?" she demanded.

The boys agreed with alacrity and so she released them.

"Now," she said, looking from one boy to the other. "What were you fighting about?"

Lord Frederick rubbed his ear and glowered at Scrivener. "He was rude to Miss Smith and said she ought not have been invited, then he told me he thought she was a common little guttersnipe."

The goddess turned her cornflower blue gaze on Scrivener, whose colour deepened from a slight flush from the excitement of their scuffle to a startling shade of scarlet.

"Mr Scrivener?" she said, her voice gentle, and Bainbridge suddenly knew how the boy felt at seeing the disappointment in her eyes. A man would do anything not to have that look cast upon him, anything at all. The idea of disappointing this heavenly creature would crush anyone, let alone a mere mortal of the male variety.

"I... I..." Scrivener stammered helplessly.

"I think you know a gentleman would never speak, or even think such an unkind thought about a young lady, don't you Mr

263

Scrivener? Indeed, a *better* man would make it his duty to see they made her welcome, and that she did not feel the least bit out of place. A *better* man – a true gentleman, would ensure that he guided her through any awkwardness she might feel at an event which she has little experience of and few friends to call her own. After all, Miss Smith is a lovely girl, so kind and vivacious, and funny too. Isn't she?" She directed this last at the other children, who immediately agreed with the goddess's every word. Christ, Bainbridge didn't know who the hell she was talking about, but he would have sworn it too.

Stunned, he watched as Scrivener stammered an apology to Lord Frederick and promised he would find Miss Smith and apologise to her too.

"I'll fetch her an ice," he offered, gazing up at the young woman who smiled at him with approval. The poor boy looked dazed by the impact of that smile, his colour rising again as she smoothed down his hair and straightened his lapels.

"That, is the action of a gentleman, Mr Scrivener. We all make mistakes, but it takes a big man with a generous heart to own them. Well done."

Scrivener strode off, head held high, as he went in search of Miss Smith.

All the other children crowded around the girl, talking at once, and she laughed and sat down on the grass, there and then, heedless of her beautiful skirts. Each of them got their fair share of her attention and Bainbridge watched, entranced with some strange ache growing in his chest, as she pulled a very small girl into her lap and hugged her close, listening to some long, rambling story about a fall from an apple tree.

He wondered if she would scold him and tell him how he ought to behave if given the chance, so he might know what it was he had to do to win her approval. If he'd known the child, he would have sought this Miss Smith out and plied her with ices, and bought her a puppy or a pony, or what the hell else she wanted if this woman would turn her attention his way. He would have done anything this astonishing creature asked if he could be a better man, a man she would look at with pride and approval.

The idea lanced through him, shaking him to his core. For everyone knew Lawrence Grenville, the Marquess of Bainbridge was anything but a good man. He was unreasonable, unstable, bad tempered, and quite likely as mad as the rest of his misbegotten family. His blood might be as blue as the eyes of this lovely woman, but the idea of him being the better man... oh, that was funny. Or it might be, if it didn't make him want to throw things in frustration. He wanted to crawl into her lap like that child had done, and lay his head down, and see if she could bring him the peace he craved. Surely, she could untangle the writhing mass of... of whatever crawled beneath his skin that made him drink too much and behave outrageously and drove everyone away from him. Well, everyone except for Dare, the poor bastard, who was just as alone as he was.

Bainbridge watched as the young woman got up, the children following her with the promise of ices. Bainbridge held his breath as the woman turned in his direction. He moved back, into the shadows and out of sight, uncertain of why he'd not taken the chance to speak to her. Perhaps one of the children would have introduced them, no one else in their right mind would offer him an introduction. His reputation preceded him and no one who cared for her would risk her in such a way, marquess or no. She would be too well guarded for that, and rightly so. He would never get close to her, never see that smile turn his way. Bainbridge would only ever be able to watch her from a distance, and he knew it. He knew it was for the best too, for her at least. So she walked past him, never knowing he was there, and the opportunity was lost.

Bainbridge stared after her, stared at the way the sun glinted on her fiery curls like a halo of flame. Emotion rose inside him, a longing so profound it hurt, stealing his breath, stealing what little remained of his sanity. Thoroughly shaken by the experience,

Bainbridge did the only thing he could do, and headed for the front door with one thought in his mind.

To get as far away from her as he possibly could.

Pre Order your copy here: *Dare to Cause a Scandal*

The Peculiar Ladies who started it all…

Girls Who Dare—The exciting series from Emma V Leech, the multi-award-winning, Amazon Top 10 romance writer behind the Rogues & Gentlemen series.

Inside every wallflower is the beating heart of a lioness, a passionate individual willing to risk all for their dream, if only they can find the courage to begin. When these overlooked girls make a pact to change their lives, anything can happen.

Eleven girls—Eleven dares in a hat. Twelves stories of passion. Who will dare to risk it all?

To Dare a Duke

Girls Who Dare Book 1

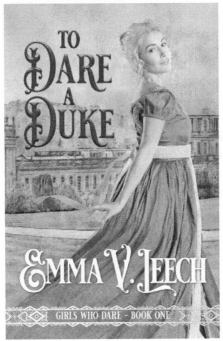

Dreams of true love and happy ever afters

Dreams of love are all well and good, but all Prunella Chuffington-Smythe wants is to publish her novel. Marriage at the price of her independence is something she will not consider. Having tasted success writing under a false name in The Lady's Weekly Review, her alter ego is attaining notoriety and fame and Prue rather likes it.

A Duty that must be endured

Robert Adolphus, The Duke of Bedwin, is in no hurry to marry, he's done it once and repeating that disaster is the last thing he desires. Yet, an heir is a necessary evil for a duke and one he cannot shirk. A dark reputation precedes him though, his first wife may have died young, but the scandals the beautiful, vivacious and spiteful creature supplied the ton have not. A wife must be found. A wife who is neither beautiful nor vivacious but sweet and dull, and certain to stay out of trouble.

Dared to do something drastic.

The sudden interest of a certain dastardly duke is as bewildering as it is unwelcome. She'll not throw her ambitions aside to marry a scoundrel just as her plans for self-sufficiency and freedom are coming to fruition. Surely showing the man she's not actually the meek little wallflower he is looking for should be enough to put paid to his intentions. When Prue is dared by her friends to do something drastic, it seems the perfect opportunity to kill two birds.

However, Prue cannot help being intrigued by the rogue who has inspired so many of her romances. Ordinarily, he plays the part of handsome rake, set on destroying her plucky heroine. But is he really the villain of the piece this time, or could he be the hero?

Finding out will be dangerous, but it just might inspire her greatest story yet.

To Dare a Duke

Also check out Emma's regency romance series, Rogues &Gentlemen Now!

The Rogue
Rogues & Gentlemen Book 1

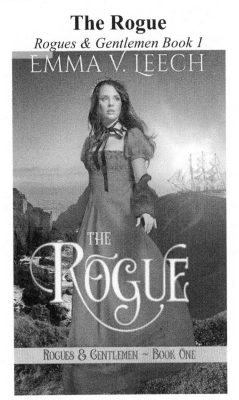

The notorious Rogue that began it all.

Set in Cornwall, 1815. Wild, untamed and isolated.

Lawlessness is the order of the day and smuggling is rife.

Henrietta always felt most at home in the wilds of the outdoors but even she had no idea how the mysterious and untamed would sweep her away in a moment.

Bewitched by his wicked blue eyes.

Henrietta Morton knows to look the other way when the free trading 'gentlemen' are at work.
Yet when a notorious pirate bursts into her local village shop, she

can avert her eyes no more. Bewitched by his wicked blue eyes, a moment of insanity follows as Henrietta hides the handsome fugitive from the Militia.

__Her reward is a kiss, lingering and unforgettable.__

In his haste to flee, the handsome pirate drops a letter, a letter that lays bare a tale of betrayal. When Henrietta's father gives her hand in marriage to a wealthy and villainous nobleman in return for the payment of his debts, she becomes desperate.

Blackmailing a pirate may be her only hope for freedom.

******Warning**: This book contains the most notorious rogue of all of Cornwall and, on occasion, is highly likely to include some mild sweating or descriptive sex scenes. ****

Free to read on *Kindle Unlimited*: The Rogue.

Interested in a Regency Romance with a twist?

A Dog in a Doublet

The Regency Romance Mysteries Book 2

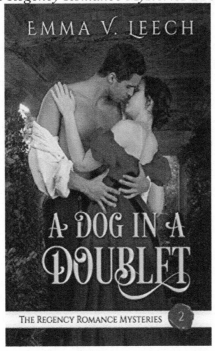

A man with a past

Harry Browning was a motherless guttersnipe, and the morning he came across the elderly Alexander Preston, The Viscount Stamford, clinging to a sheer rock face, he didn't believe in fate. But the fates have plans for Harry whether he believes it or not, and he's not entirely sure he likes them.

As a reward for his bravery, and in an unusual moment of charity, miserly Lord Stamford takes him on. He is taught to read, to manage the vast and crumbling estate, and to behave like a gentleman, but Harry knows that is something he will never truly be.

Already running from a dark past, his future is becoming increasingly complex as he finds himself caught in a tangled web of jealousy and revenge.

A feisty young maiden

Temptation, in the form of the lovely Miss Clarinda Bow, is a constant threat to his peace of mind, enticing him to be something he isn't. But when the old man dies, his will makes a surprising demand, and the fates might just give Harry the chance to have everything he ever desired, including Clara, if only he dares.

And as those close to the Preston family begin to die, Harry may not have any choice.

A Dog in a Doublet

Lose yourself in Emma's paranormal world with The French Vampire Legend series....

The Key to Erebus
The French Vampire Legend Book 1

The truth can kill you.

Taken away as a small child, from a life where vampires, the Fae, and other mythical creatures are real and treacherous, the beautiful young witch, Jéhenne Corbeaux is totally unprepared when she returns to rural France to live with her eccentric Grandmother.

Thrown headlong into a world she knows nothing about she seeks to learn the truth about herself, uncovering secrets more shocking than anything she could ever have imagined and finding that she is by no means powerless to protect the ones she loves.

Despite her Gran's dire warnings, she is inexorably drawn to the dark and terrifying figure of Corvus, an ancient vampire and master of the vast Albinus family.

Jéhenne is about to find her answers and discover that, not only is Corvus far more dangerous than she could ever imagine, but that he holds much more than the key to her heart...

Available at your favourite retailer

The Key to Erebus

Check out Emma's exciting fantasy series with hailed by
Kirkus Reviews as "An enchanting fantasy with a likable heroine,
romantic intrigue, and clever narrative flourishes."

The Dark Prince

The French Fae Legend Book 1

Two Fae Princes
One Human Woman
And a world ready to tear them all apart.

Laen Braed is Prince of the Dark fae, with a temper and
reputation to match his black eyes, and a heart that despises the
human race. When he is sent back through the forbidden gates
between realms to retrieve an ancient fae artifact, he returns home
with far more than he bargained for.

Corin Albrecht, the most powerful Elven Prince ever born. His golden eyes are rumoured to be a gift from the gods, and destiny is calling him. With a love for the human world that runs deep, his friendship with Laen is being torn apart by his prejudices.

Océane DeBeauvoir is an artist and bookbinder who has always relied on her lively imagination to get her through an unhappy and uneventful life. A jewelled dagger put on display at a nearby museum hits the headlines with speculation of another race, the Fae. But the discovery also inspires Océane to create an extraordinary piece of art that cannot be confined to the pages of a book.

With two powerful men vying for her attention and their friendship stretched to the breaking point, the only question that remains... who is truly The Dark Prince?

The man of your dreams is coming... or is it your nightmares he visits? Find out in Book One of The French Fae Legend.

Available at your favorite retailer The Dark Prince

Want more Emma?

If you enjoyed this book, please support this indie author and take a moment to leave a few words in a review. *Thank you!*

To be kept informed of special offers and free deals (which I do regularly) follow me on *https://www.bookbub.com/authors/emma-v-leech*

To find out more and to get news and sneak peeks of the first chapter of upcoming works, go to my website and sign up for the newsletter.
http://www.emmavleech.com/

Come and join the fans in my Facebook group for news, info and exciting discussion...

Emma's Book Club

Or Follow me here......

http://viewauthor.at/EmmaVLeechAmazon
Emma's Twitter page

Made in the USA
Monee, IL
16 June 2021